MARCELO in the **REAL** the **WORLD**

was published to huge critical acclaim in America:

Booklist Editor's Choice

Kirkus Best Young Adult Book

New York Times Notable Book

Publishers Weekly Best Book

Amazon Top Ten Books for Teens

"**Marcelo** is the **bravest**, most
original hero I've met in years...
Brisk, **brilliant**, unsentimental"
New York Times

"**Not to be missed**"
Publishers Weekly

"**Wholly compelling**"
Washington Post

Praise for

THE LAST SUMMER of the DEATH WARRIORS

"Exceptional"
Sunday Telegraph

"Honest, **powerful**, utterly convincing**"**
Marcus Sedgwick, *Guardian*

"Life-affirming, superb"
Bookfest

"Honest and **true**. Full of tenderness.
Powerful, **unusual**, very moving**"**
Books for Keeps

"Exceptionally moving"
Lovereading.co.uk

MARCELO in the REAL WORLD

Francisco X. Stork

SCHOLASTIC

Scholastic Children's Books
A division of Scholastic Ltd.
Euston House, 24 Eversholt Street
London, NW1 1DB, UK
Registered office: Westfield Road, Southam, Warwickshire, CV47 0RA
SCHOLASTIC and associated logos are trademarks and/or
registered trademarks of Scholastic Inc.

First published in the US by Arthur A. Levine Books,
an imprint of Scholastic Inc., 2009
First published in paperback in the UK by Scholastic Ltd., 2011
This edition published in the UK by Scholastic Ltd., 2012

Text copyright © Francisco X. Stork, 2009
The right of Francisco X. Stork to be identified as the author of this work
has been asserted by him.

ISBN 978 1407 12101 7

A CIP catalogue record for this book is available
from the British Library.

Printed in the UK by CPI Group (UK) Ltd, Croydon, CR0 4YY
Papers used by Scholastic Children's Books are made from wood grown in
sustainable forests.

1 3 5 7 9 10 8 6 4 2

www.scholastic.co.uk/zone

For Ruth, my mother

Chapter 1

"Marcelo, are you ready?"

I lift up my thumb. It means that I am ready.

"OK, I'm going to wheel you in."

Then he slides me inside the tunnel of the machine. I like the feeling of being closed in. The lights are not bright enough to hurt my eyes but I close them anyway.

"Don't forget to lift your finger when you first hear the mental music." The tunnel has a speaker. Dr Malone's voice comes out from there.

I wait for the music. It always comes. The hard part is remembering to lift my finger. There's a tiny camera that allows Dr Malone and Toby to see me from up in the control booth.

"Marcelo, Marcelo." I hear Toby in the distance. I like Toby. He's a medical doctor just like Dr Malone but he doesn't let me call him doctor. Once I called him doctor and he corrected me and said, "Toby, please." His face is covered with freckles.

"Ready for the so-called real stuff?" he asks when he slides me out.

"Yes," I say to him. The "real stuff" is what he calls the music that is piped in through the speaker in the machine. The music that comes from inside my head is not considered real.

Toby is holding a piece of paper that lists different kinds of real music. "How about choosing from this side, this time?"

"OK," I say. The music on the back of the page contains rock songs. That's Toby's favourite kind of music. I don't recognize any of the songs or composers. I finally pick a piece by a composer named Santana because the name looks like Sandoval, my own name. I also like the title of the song, "The Calling".

"Sweet," says Toby. The smile on his face means I made a good choice. "Santana and Clapton together. Sweet."

Sweet, I say to myself. I make a mental note to use that word the next time I like something.

A few minutes later Toby is back with the list. He is frowning. "You have to pick from this side. The old man thinks that rock will overstimulate your grey matter." Toby rolls his eyes while looking in the direction of Dr Malone, who is up in the booth fiddling with some controls. I do not understand the precise meaning of Toby's facial expression.

I quickly pick Beethoven's "Largo" from Piano Concerto No. 3. I like the music's simple melody. Also, I know it only lasts about ten minutes.

Toby slides me back inside the tunnel.

"What's the mental music like?" Dr Malone asks when I'm out of the tunnel. I stop tying my sneakers so that I can think about his question. But it is impossible to put into words what the internal music is like. (I prefer the word "internal" to the word "mental"

2

when referring to the music. The fact that the IM, as I call it for short, is inside my mind does not necessarily mean that it is *produced* by my mind.) What is the IM like? How many times has Dr Malone asked me that question and how many times have I not been able to answer it?

"Sweet," I say. "It is sweet." I look for Toby but he is up in the control room.

"You mean it sounds pleasant? The sounds are pleasing to the ear?"

"The music is not heard with the ears." Then I realize that "sweet" wasn't the right word. The music is pleasant all right, but it is much more than that.

"If it's not heard, then what?"

How do I describe it? It is like listening to very loud music with headphones. Only the music seems to be coming from inside the brain. It is actually a very neat sensation. "It is just there," I say to Dr Malone. Then an image comes to my mind. "It is a big watermelon."

"Excuse me?" One of the reasons I like working with Dr Malone is that his facial expressions are so clear and easy to understand. That one he just made, for example, is a textbook example of "baffled".

I expand on the image that came to me. It is the first time I have made this connection so I am not sure exactly where it will lead me. "When the internal music is there, Marcelo is one of the *seeds*. The music is the rest of the watermelon."

Dr Malone frowns. Actually, it is a half-frown, half-smile, like he is trying to remain serious. "Do you know that you just put emphasis on exactly the right word right then? That's good. A year ago you couldn't do that. Paterson has been good for you."

Paterson. I look at my watch. Aurora is driving me to Paterson after the session with Dr Malone to see the baby colt that was born last night. Harry (that is what we call Mr Killhearn, the stable master at Paterson) called this morning and told Aurora that the colt had been born at 2:35 a.m. I pleaded with Aurora to take me today even though she worked all day at the hospital. I could have waited two days until Monday, when I start my summer job taking care of the ponies, but it is too hard to wait. I had hoped to be there when he was being born, and the hours of this day have seemed as long as a week.

I have half an hour left with Dr Malone, I remind myself. This time, I must make sure that the session does not go over the allotted time, as it sometimes does.

Dr Malone is speaking again. "But let's get back to the music. What is the *content* of the mental music? Does it sound like regular music? Does it have a melody?"

"Yes and no," I say. I hate sounding so imprecise. Imprecision in this case is as close (and as fast) as I can get to accuracy.

"Okaaay." Dr Malone grins. "What part is like regular music?"

I close my eyes and imagine a cello as big as the earth and a bow as long as the Milky Way and the bow moving sometimes slow and sometimes fast across the cello strings.

I hear Dr Malone in the distance. "Music has a melody, rhythm, beat. Does the mental music have any of these components?"

Now I am thinking about my summer job and how I can be with the ponies all day long. I return to Dr Malone and his questions. I am getting paid for this, I tell myself. I have to give this process as much as I can. Besides, I like Dr Malone and I like Toby. "Not exactly."

"Can you hum it?"

"No."

"Then it's not music."

"It is the feelings of music without the sound." There. That is as precise as I can get in the kind of language that Dr Malone is seeking.

"What kinds of feelings?"

I have no idea what to call these feelings. Sometimes the music is lively and fast so I call it "happy". Sometimes it is slower and lower in pitch, so I call it "sad". Mostly the music is just incredibly peaceful. Sweet. I like that word.

"Marcelo! Come back. We're almost done here. Are they always there, these feelings of music without sound?"

"Yes. When I look for them. When Marcelo looks for them, they are always there."

"When Marcelo looks where?"

"Here." I touch the back of my head, just above my neck.

"Do these sounds ever come when you don't want them to come or stay when you don't want them to stay?"

I think about it. The truth is that the pull of the music is always there. Like just a little while ago when I was trying to describe it to Dr Malone, I wanted to slide into the music again. And it is also hard to pull out when I am there. But this is not what I tell Dr Malone. I don't know if I could find the right words to describe these thoughts. Instead, I say to him: "If that happened, then Marcelo would be crazy, would he not?"

Dr Malone laughs and nods at the same time. He is always testing, doing his research but keeping an eye on my mental health as well. Despite his unanswerable questions and his silly sense of humour, I don't mind coming to see Dr Malone. I've been doing it every six months since I was five, which means, since I'm seventeen, that I've seen Dr Malone twenty-five times. The visits last two hours and serve three functions. First, he makes sure that my brain is physically OK. Second, the data he gathers helps other people who truly need help. Third, as of last year, I get paid three hundred dollars per visit in accordance with regulations from a grant that Dr Malone received.

He starts walking towards the control room and I follow him. "This is amazing!" he says after he studies two computer screens. "Come here. I want to show you something."

I walk over to where Dr Malone and Toby are standing. Dr Malone says: "This is an image of your brain when you listened to the real music, and this one shows you listening, or remembering as you put it, to the mental music. See?"

I see two pictures of my brain. Each image has red and blue patches in different places. "When you listen to the real music, both sides of the temporal lobe are activated." Dr Malone points to a bright red splash in the front part of my brain on one picture. "But over here, when you listen to the mental music, there's something going on in the hypothalamus, the oldest part of the human brain. You know, the part that made our cave ancestors fight or flight."

"The whole limbic system's lit up like fireworks over here," Toby says, pointing at the image of my brain listening to the IM.

Dr Malone stares at me. "You're definitely absorbed with something, but you're not thinking." Then he turns to Toby and says, "Toby, look up those tests they did with the cats, you know, the ones where they scanned them while someone dangled a string in front of them. I think the hypothalamus was affected there too."

I can't help smiling to myself. I like knowing that my brain is like a cat's. It reminds me of something my uncle Hector told me once when he was teaching me to lift the weights. He told me to focus on the muscles I was using like a lion watching an intruder approach its den.

Aurora is waiting for me in the reception area. I walk past her, hoping that she won't spend time asking Dr Malone about the session the way she usually does. I want to get to Paterson as soon as possible. Harry is not a patient man. He promised me the summer job as stable man when he saw how well I did with the ponies, working with them after school. But there were other kids at Paterson who wanted the job because it is a great, great summer job, and I am nervous about not showing up on time.

But my walking past her does not work. Aurora waits for Dr Malone, who is close behind me. "Well," she says, looking at Dr Malone, "did you find anything in there?"

"Empty, totally empty." Dr Malone reaches out to touch the top of my head but draws back, as if suddenly discovering that I am now taller than he is.

"His father wants to send him to a regular high school next year," Aurora tells him.

I walk back to where Dr Malone and Aurora are speaking.

"No," I say immediately.

"I know how you feel, mister," Aurora tells me. "I'd like the doctor's opinion."

I can see Dr Malone hesitating. He knows how I feel about leaving Paterson and going to a regular school. "Of course he's ready. He could have gone to a regular school starting from kindergarten. Of course he can do it." Then he looks at me and says, "I'm sorry, buddy."

I fix my eyes on a spot on the floor while I struggle to find the words to explain why going to a regular high school would not be right for me. Then I hear Aurora say, trying to console me, "It doesn't mean you're necessarily going. Just because you're ready doesn't mean we'll do it. We'll discuss it."

"I'm seventeen," I blurt out.

"Meaning?" Aurora enquires.

"It should be Marcelo's decision." I gather up all my strength and lift my eyes to look first at Aurora and then at Dr Malone. "I should be allowed to finish the last year of high school at Paterson, where I've always been."

"Ahh, I think I'm going to stay out of this one," Dr Malone says.

"Is Marcelo's developmental age the same as other seventeen-year-olds'?" I'm looking at Dr Malone.

Dr Malone nods. That means he understands the nature of my question. "Developmental age? What does that mean? Everyone is different. In some respects you're about fifty years ahead of other kids your age."

Aurora smiles.

Dr Malone never likes to give easy answers to complicated

questions just to make people more comfortable. What I want him to say is that given who I am, I'm better off at a place like Paterson.

"Maybe it will be good to have a different experience," Aurora says.

"You know how I feel about that," Dr Malone says to Aurora. "I don't believe in suffering. If a kid is happy, understood and appreciated, he will bloom in his or her own time. Paterson has been good to Marcelo. Look at the results."

Yesss! Thank you, Dr Malone, I say to myself.

"Mmm." The sound is coming from Aurora.

"What does 'Mmm' mean?" I ask first Aurora and then Dr Malone.

Dr Malone decides to answer the question. "You definitely asked the right person about that. We in the medical profession know all about 'Mmm's. I think that in this case, your mother's 'Mmm' means that she thinks there are still some things you need to learn and that maybe, if it were up to you, you would not choose to learn those things. Does that make sense?"

"Yes," Aurora answers.

"Mmm." The sound comes from me this time. I do not mean to be funny.

Chapter 2

On the drive to Paterson I think about the nine Haflinger ponies that I will be taking care of during the summer. I know every one of their names, their ages, and the birth dates of some of them. I know how hard to work them, how much to feed them, when to water them. I especially know where they like to be brushed. As stable man, I will be in charge of their upkeep, which includes keeping the stable clean, the way Harry likes it to be kept, which is to say spotless. Prospective students and their parents are always coming in to see the ponies, and Harry wants to make sure the stables and the ponies are perfect. I am that way naturally, so I am perfect for the job.

But it is not just physical upkeep that I will be doing. As the stable man, I will be in charge of the ponies' well-being. I will determine when a pony should be fed and watered and rested. I will be consulted by the instructors and therapists on which pony is best suited for a kid with a particular disability. The truth is that all the ponies are trained to be comfortable around kids with all kinds of disabilities. Visually or hearing impaired, kids with autism, kids with cerebral palsy, multiple sclerosis, spina bifida, Down's syndrome, attention deficit disorder — it doesn't matter, the ponies are always peaceful and even-tempered. The trick, as Harry pointed out to me, is not in picking out which pony will be the most comfortable with a kid but in picking out the pony that *the kid* will like the most. Harry thinks I have a knack for this.

"You are really looking forward to your job as stable man, aren't you?" I hear Aurora ask me. It is not like Aurora to ask me unnecessary questions. Of course I am looking forward to this summer job, just like I am looking forward to my last year at Paterson. The job of stable man will continue into next year, only next year I will be involved not just with the upkeep of the ponies and the stable, but with the actual training of the ponies. Fritzy will be ready to be trained in early fall. It is an unbelievable process, to take these ponies and get them accustomed to anything and everything a disabled kid can do. No amount of noise or discomfort or even pain will cause them to hurt a child if they are well-trained.

That is why the possibility of attending Oak Ridge High is so troublesome. It cannot be allowed to happen. Arturo needs to be convinced that the best way for me to be like everyone else is to continue at Paterson, where I can learn at my own pace, where I am learning to make decisions and becoming responsible and independent, all the things he wants me to be.

"Aurora knows the answer to that question. Why does she ask?" It is possible that my words sound rude, but with Aurora I am at ease and can speak in a natural way.

"It is just that. . ." She pauses. A pause in the middle of a sentence, I have learned in my Social Interactions class at Paterson, can mean that the person speaking is about to say something that might hurt the feelings of the listener. In my chest, I feel a twang — a discordant note, like when the string on a guitar breaks in the middle of a song.

"Arturo." I mean to form this as a question but am unable to do so.

Aurora does not answer. I do not pursue it. We are entering the Paterson grounds and I always make it a point not to talk as we enter Paterson. I have been coming here since first grade, and I still get a sense that here at last is a place where I will not be hurried.

To the left as you enter the long driveway is a set of one-storey brick buildings that touch each other like a crossword puzzle that has only been partially completed. Sidewalks connect the buildings and you can tell even from afar that it would be easy for someone in a wheelchair or someone who cannot see to navigate from one building to another.

To the right as you drive in are playing fields of various sizes and shapes. Large oaks and elms line the edge of these fields so that in the summer you can walk around the edge and never leave the shade. In back of the playing fields are the stables and the riding tracks.

Aurora parks the car in the parking lot closest to the stables and we get out. Jane, one of the therapists, is leading Gambolino and a little girl I don't recognize around the oval track.

The larger circular track is empty. When summer session starts in a few days, the tracks will be bustling with instructors, therapists, kids and volunteers. The day will start at eight and go until six in the evening. I see Harry in front of the barn, waving at us.

"Come, I want to show you something!" he yells. I begin to run. Aurora speeds up. I already know what he wants to show me so I run past him into the barn. Inside one of the stalls is a newly born pony sucking from the teat of his mother, Frieda.

"He was born yesterday in the middle of the night. Didn't even have to call the vet. Out he came, easy as the morning sun."

"He is sooo beautiful," Aurora says.

I am stunned. I have seen newly born Haflinger ponies before but this one is . . . sweet. Sweeter than sweet.

"I wanted to call you last night so you could be here, but he came so sudden. When I checked at eleven all was fine. Frieda was breathing a little heavy, but I thought for sure the pony was a week or so away like the vet said. Then at midnight, I hear some barking and it's Romulus telling me something's up, and there's the little fellow halfway out, head first and all."

Romulus is the German shepherd that my uncle Hector gave to Paterson. He is sitting down next to Frieda's stall, guarding the little fellow. Romulus and I look at each other until he winks at me with both eyes.

"Have you named him yet?" Aurora asks.

"Oh gosh. The kids named him ever since we mated Fred and Frieda. Following with the general Prussian theme, it will be Fritzy. It would have been Fredricka had he been a she."

"Fritzy," I say out loud.

"I would have preferred something more like Shanny, short for Shannon."

"Good Irish name," Aurora said.

"But Haflingers are originally from Prussia. The Amish use them in America," I point out.

"And as good a working horse as any and better than most. They'll plough your field all day long and into the night. Perfect for these kids, with their backs broad enough for easy balancing and their centres low to the ground."

"May I sit with Frieda a while?" I ask.

"You may," Harry answers quickly. "She is still a little under the weather. It will do her good to have you next to her."

I open the door to the stall and go in softly and I sit near where Frieda is lying down, her knees folded. Fritzy is looking for another teat to suck. I sit close enough to her head to touch her but I don't touch her. There's no need to touch animals unless they ask you to do so by the various ways that they communicate: by coming to you, or by lifting their heads towards you, or by the way they look at you. I close my eyes and fold my arms and breathe the smell of hay and of Fritzy. In the distance I hear Aurora ask Harry if she can talk to him for a few minutes.

On the drive home, I sense that something unhappy is about to happen and my mind is trying to find the source of this foreboding. Aurora asks if I'm OK and she's waiting for a response but I ignore her question and remain silent. Aurora doesn't ask again. She knows that if I want to, I will speak in my own time.

We are halfway home and now I have identified what this strange feeling feels like. It is like when you are going down a staircase in the dark and you don't know where the last step is. I have also managed to pinpoint the origins of the feeling. I remember Aurora telling Dr Malone that Arturo wants me to attend Oak Ridge High for my senior year. I remember her pause in the middle of a sentence when we were talking about working at the stables. I remember Aurora asking Harry if she could talk to him for a few minutes. I notice so many details of what is happening and remember just about all that I notice, even though sometimes it seems as if I am not paying attention. What is hard is interpreting all the details that hit my brain at once. But sometimes I can do that. Like right now. What I gather from all that I have noticed is that my plans for next year are about to change.

When we are almost home, Aurora says, "Are you remembering?"

"Remembering" is the word that Aurora and I use to refer to those moments when I am listening to the IM or reciting in my mind a passage from one of the many holy books I like to read. When I was a child and prone to tantrums, Aurora would ask me to go someplace quiet and remember. Listening to the IM or reciting Scripture helped to calm me down. Now I choose on my own to "remember", whether I am upset or not. The fact that she asked me if I was remembering must mean that she knows something is bothering me.

After a while I tell Aurora, "Father is wrong."

"I haven't heard you refer to your father as 'Father' in a long time. What is Father wrong about?"

"About going to Oak Ridge High next year. I know that's what you are reluctant to tell me. Paterson is where Marcelo belongs. There I will learn to be independent like Arturo wants me to be. There is where I am learning to function just like he wants Marcelo to function."

"He wants to talk to you when we get home. Be open to what he has to say. Perhaps he is right."

"I am open. I have thought about it more than you know. But he is not right about taking Marcelo out of Paterson."

"He was not in favour of you attending Paterson, but you have been there since first grade. He objected to your visits with Rabbi Heschel, but you have been seeing her every other week for five years now. He didn't approve of the sessions with Dr Malone. He didn't want you living in the tree house either. Yet he allowed you to do all those things despite his misgivings."

"He was wrong about the benefit to Marcelo of all of those as well."

"What I am suggesting is that maybe it is your turn to trust his way. At least be open to it. Just listen to him with trust. Do you trust your father? Do you trust that he wants what is best for you?"

"Trust" is one of those abstract words that is hard for me to understand. Here I can substitute the word "believe" for "trust" and it seems to work. Do I believe that my father wants what is best for me?

"Yes," I say. "But he is wrong nevertheless."

Chapter 3

I get out of the car and head for the back door. I see Arturo in the backyard grilling steaks. I hoped to enter the house without him seeing me. I am not ready for the discussion that I know will take place and I need more time to anticipate his questions and memorize my replies. But Aurora yells at him from the back door.

"Sorry we're late. We got stuck in traffic."

He answers her without turning around. "I didn't see any dinner cooking, so I thought I'd grill something."

"I'll make the salad," Aurora tells him, and goes in the house.

I am about to go in when Arturo speaks. "Marcelo, can I talk to you?"

I walk as slowly as I can. Arturo is stabbing the red meat with a giant fork.

"Not done yet," he says. He closes the black lid to the grill and sits on one of the white iron chairs. "Sit down for a minute." He pulls out a chair. "How was Dr Malone?"

"He was well." I'm still standing. I'm looking at the red needle of the thermometer attached to the grill. It is moving past one hundred and fifty degrees Celsius.

"Marcelo," I hear him call. He is holding a goblet half-filled with ruby-coloured wine. I know Arturo is not fond of my visits to Dr Malone's office. He believes the tests imply there is something wrong with me, which he does not think is the case. "So, what did the good doctor do to you this time?"

"The brain was scanned while Marcelo listened to music."

"Try saying that again."

"*My* brain was scanned while *I* listened to music." I remind myself not to refer to myself in the third person. Also, I must remember not to call him Arturo.

"Thank you. Is that right? Real music or the kind you alone can hear?"

Talking about the IM, I have learned, makes Arturo nervous. I attempt to change the subject. "After Dr Malone we went to see the newborn pony at Paterson."

"That's good. But you didn't answer my question."

There is no chance of ever changing the subject with Arturo. "Real music," I answer. It is not a lie. The IM is as real as any other kind.

"How long will these visits go for?"

"They last about two hours."

"No, that's not what I meant. I mean, how much longer are these experiments or observations going to go on?" Before I can answer, he says, "I have a proposition that I want to discuss with you."

I feel my chest begin to tighten. "I am not going to Oak Ridge High." I can hear my voice tremble as I say this.

Arturo's face turns serious. I brace myself. I know how Arturo can switch from father to lawyer in an instant. The face of Arturo the father does not come out as often for me as it does for my sister, Yolanda. I get more of Arturo the lawyer: his eyes unblinking and fixed on my face, the volume of his voice modulated with complete control. He becomes a person who will lose his composure only if he wishes to.

"Here's what I would like to propose." I expect him to pause because he is speaking faster than he usually does. But he goes on speaking as fast as he speaks to Yolanda. "I want you to work at the law firm this summer."

This is a total surprise. It takes me a while to find words, any words. When I do, I say: "I have a summer job at Paterson."

"You'll help in the mailroom." He doesn't hear or chooses not to hear what I say.

"I have a job already," I repeat.

"Sit down, please." He points to the chair. I sit.

He moves forward on his chair so that our knees are almost touching. He lowers his voice. He is a father now. "Son, I want you to have a job where you interact with people, where you have to figure out new things by yourself. What do you do at Paterson that teaches you what you don't already know?"

"I will be learning to train the ponies."

"But this is the stage of your life when you need to be working with people."

"Why?"

"It is an experience you haven't had, really. At Paterson you are in a protected environment. The kids who go there are not . . . normal. Most of them will be the way they are all their lives. You, on the other hand, have the ability to grow and adapt. Even your

Dr Malone thinks this is the case. He's said so since the very first time we saw him. All these years, it wasn't really necessary for you to go to Paterson. You don't really belong there. I know you realize this yourself. There's nothing wrong with you. You just move at a different speed than other kids your age. But in order for you to grow and not get stuck, you need to be in a normal environment. It is time. Here is what I propose: if you work at the law firm this summer, then at the end of the summer, *you* decide whether you want to spend your senior year at Paterson or at Oak Ridge High."

Now he pauses. He knows I will need time to sort this out. One summer at the law firm versus a whole year at Paterson. I miss out on Fritzy's early months, but I still get to train him next year. Arturo interrupts my thoughts. "There's just one thing." I see him pick up the glass of wine and raise it to his lips. This time his words come out very slow. "You can do what you want in the fall. . ." He waits for my eyes to meet his eyes and then he continues. "But this summer you must follow all the rules of the . . . real world."

"The real world," I say out loud. It is one of Arturo's favourite phrases.

"Yes, that's right. The real world."

As vague and broad as this term is, I have a sense of what it means and of the difficulties that it entails. Following the rules of the real world means, for example, engaging in small talk with other people. It means refraining from talking about my special interest. It means looking people in the eye and shaking hands. It means doing things "on the hoof", as we say at Paterson, which means doing things that have not been scheduled in advance. It may mean walking or going to places I am not familiar with, city streets full of noise and confusion. Even though I am trying to look calm, a wave of terror comes over me as I imagine walking the streets of Boston by myself.

Arturo smiles as if he knows what is going through my mind. "Don't worry," he says soothingly, "we'll go slow at first. The real world is not going to hurt you."

There is a question floating inside of me but I can't find the words for it just yet. I open and clench my fists as I wait for the question to formulate itself. Finally, it arrives. I say to Arturo, "At the end of the summer, will Marcelo, will I decide where I want to spend my senior year . . . regardless?"

"Regardless? I don't follow you."

"You said that if I follow the rules of the real world this summer, I will get to decide where I go next year. Who will decide whether I followed the rules? I am not aware of all the rules of the real world. They are innumerable, as far as I have been able to determine."

"Ahh." It is Arturo the father who is speaking now. "Well, look. The corporate world has its rules. The law firm has its rules. The mailroom has its rules. The legal system has its rules. The real world as a whole has its rules. The rules deal with behaviours and the way to do things in order to be successful. To be successful is to accomplish the task that has been assigned to us or which we have assigned to ourselves. You will need to adapt to the environment governed by these rules as best you can. At Paterson, the environment adapts to you. If you need more time to finish a test, you get it. In the mailroom, a package will need to go out by a certain time, or else. As to who will determine what, it seems to me that for this exercise to have any meaning, there must be something at stake. If you go through the motions and just show up every day and not try, then no, you will not have the ability to decide where you spend next year because you will not have followed the rules of the real world. It seems to me that at the end of the summer, we will both know with absolute certainty whether you succeeded or not. But, if for some reason we disagree, it seems to me that the ultimate decision should be mine. I am the father and you are the son. I will be your boss and you will be the employee. Does that make sense?"

I nod that it does. I never lie. But I do now. There is something about what Arturo just said that does not make sense.

Arturo is waiting to see if there are further questions. He knows it takes me a while to process information. I do have one final question. "How will Marcelo be successful in the mailroom?" I would like to have a diagram or picture of what this means so that I can prepare for it.

"Each assignment given to you will have its built-in definition of success. You have a right to ask for instructions from anyone in the law firm who gives you an assignment. Success will be based on your ability to follow those instructions. I know this is very vague and you would like more clarity. You have to trust me. You are not going to be asked to perform tasks that are beyond your abilities. Do you trust me? I have always been fair, haven't I?"

This time I don't know how the word "trust" is being used. But "fair" I understand. "Yes," I say. It is true. Arturo has always been fair.

"Good," he says. "I will be honest with you. I am hoping that after this summer, you will choose to go to Oak Ridge High. There is a life out there that is healthy and normal that you need to be a part of. So, is it a deal?"

"There are some things I cannot do even if I wanted to," I say.

"Like what?"

"There are so many things I still have difficulties with. I cannot walk by myself in a strange place without a map. I get flustered when I am asked to do more than one thing at once. People say words I do not understand or their facial expressions are incomprehensible. They expect responses from me I cannot give."

"Maybe the reason you can't do those things is not because you are not able to, but because you have not been in an environment that challenges you to do them. Jasmine, the girl who runs the mailroom, will show you the ropes. I've talked to her about you. She'll go easy on you at first. But going slow doesn't mean you won't need to expand beyond your comfort zone."

I am thinking that next fall, I will be able to work full-time at Paterson training Fritzy and the other ponies. I can visit the ponies on the weekends this summer. Arturo is basically asking me to pretend that I am normal, according to his definition, for three months. This is an impossible task, as far as I can tell, especially since it is very difficult for me to feel that I am *not* normal. Why can't others think and see the world the way I see it? But after three months, it will be over, and I can be who I am.

"Think about it. Let me know first thing in the morning."

"All right," I say. "I will think about it." I start to walk towards my tree house. Namu, who has been lying at my feet all the time, walks by my side.

"You are getting too old to live in a tree house," I hear Arturo say behind me.

I pretend his words do not reach me.

Chapter 4

The tree house was Yolanda's idea. When I was ten, we were in the basement watching a movie called *Swiss Family Robinson*, and that's when it came to her that I should have a tree house. She thought it would be good for me to have a place of my own where I could confront my fear of sleeping in a place other than my room. A tree house would allow me to be more self-sufficient, according to Yolanda.

Yolanda went to work immediately. She found a website dedicated to tree houses and downloaded plans for one of them. The next morning she took the plans to school and convinced her high school shop teacher to make the construction of the tree house a class project.

The construction was easy. Yolanda's class even built a dog house for Namu under the tree house. The hard part was convincing Arturo to let us build it. He thought that the tree house would make me even more isolated. It took a lot of convincing but Aurora and Yolanda finally got him to agree. I still don't know how. Arturo's only condition was that electrical and cable wires be installed by a licensed electrician.

The entrance to the tree house is through a trapdoor on the floor. To enter, you have to climb a ten-foot rope ladder, lift open the door, and then swing yourself up by the force of your arms. I climb up now and lie down on the cot. My fists open and close the way they do when I am angry. I don't know what to do. I'm too restless to lie in the cot. I get up and sit on the desk chair. On the desk I have a CD player, headphones and my laptop. I stand up and open the two windows. I sit down again and am about to grab the headphones when I hear Aurora's voice.

"Open up, I'm going to fall."

I open the trapdoor and see her barely holding on. One of her hands holds a plastic bag with a sandwich and the other hand is holding on to the rope. I take the plastic bag from her and help her up.

"Whew," she sighs when she's in. "You don't make it very easy for people to visit you, do you?"

It occurs to me that she has only been in the tree house one other time. The afternoon that Abba died, she came up to let me know.

"Are you all right?" she asks.

"No."

"Your father told me that he talked to you about working at the law firm this summer."

"You already knew he was going to talk to me about that. That is the reason why you asked Harry if you could talk to him for a few minutes. You wanted to tell him Marcelo was not going to be working there this summer."

She lowers her eyes and then raises them again. "It was

important that your father be the first to tell you. He has looked forward to this for a long time now. I told Harry we would call him tomorrow and let him know. It is still your decision. Your dad said he gave you a choice."

"Working at Paterson is what I want."

"Do you see his point of view, though?"

"I see his point of view. But he is wrong."

"Tell me why you think he wants you to work at the law firm."

"It is the real world."

She laughs. "You're getting pretty good at making funny faces."

"It was not my intention to be funny."

"Your father wants you to try this type of work."

"Mailing letters in the mailroom."

"But it's not just that. He wants to you to experience going to work and walking from the train station to the law firm by yourself and interacting with people who are . . . regular people. I've met Jasmine, the girl you'd be working with in the mailroom. She's only a couple years older than you. You'll like her."

"The children who ride the ponies at Paterson are regular people. Harry is extremely regular people."

She lifts herself from the floor where she is sitting and walks over to the desk chair. When she is sitting down again, she says, "Remember when I first took you to the hospital with me? You were about nine, ten?"

"Marcelo was eight years old the first time."

"That little? I went to see Carmen. Remember Carmen? I went on a Saturday, even though I had the day off, because I knew she was in bad shape. I took you with me and left you in the play-room. When I came out, there you were, building a Lego castle with two other little boys. You weren't talking to them or even playing with them really. Each of you was quietly building the castle, side by side. You know? Then after that you did all you could to go with me to work. You felt comfortable with those little children."

"Carmen, Joseph, they all died."

"Yes. I thought it was good for you to be around the children. And it was good for them. They liked you even though you hardly talked to them. You calmed them down just by being with them."

"Marcelo listened to them." For some reason, I slip into the third person with Aurora.

"But then you were always asking me to take you. I thought it was great for you and for the children. But now I have doubts."

"Doubts."

"About whether it was all right to let you be around so much suffering, so much death."

"Suffering and death do not affect me the way they seem to affect others."

"No?"

"They are part of God's universal order."

"It's just that kids your age don't generally think thoughts like that. They're interested in other things, in being with their friends, in having fun. Your father would like you to experience a little of the world most people live in."

"What world do most people live in?"

"Paterson and even St Elizabeth's, for all the suffering that you see there, are protected environments. What you do at Paterson with the ponies and the children does not take you beyond your 'comfort zone', as your father says. It doesn't challenge you or help you grow in the areas you need to develop in order to be self-sufficient. Do you understand?"

It takes me few moments to absorb what she is saying. Then I say, "You think a seventeen-year-old should be more self-sufficient than I am."

"At Paterson you contribute by just being yourself. It is easy for you to be around the ponies and the kids who go there and to interact with them as much as you are able. The job at the law firm will require new skills from you, and you'll be around people who are not always nice."

"You think I interact well with ponies and children because I am still a child," I say.

"You are childlike. And that makes you who you are."

"But?"

"You need to learn how to survive." She seems sad when she says this.

"Marcelo is afraid."

"I know. That's the point. You're not afraid at Paterson, are you?"

"No."

"So it will be good to take on this challenge and overcome it, like you've overcome so many other challenges already."

I open and close my hands rapidly. "I do not want to work there."

Aurora is quiet. She closes her eyes and I think that maybe her efforts to convince me have made her very tired. When she opens her eyes, she asks: "Did I ever tell you about Mr Quintana?"

"No."

"When I was your age, I had a summer job as a nurse's aide

at the Thomas Jefferson Hospital in El Paso. Mr Quintana was an old gentleman with pancreatic cancer. He was recuperating from a bout of chemotherapy and was waiting to see whether the treatment had done any good. No one really believed that it had because pancreatic cancer is so deadly. But he knew there were a few good weeks after the treatment where he would feel more or less well. After that, there would probably come a final decline. Anyway, one day while I was cleaning his room, he asked me if I had my driver's licence and I told him that I did. Then he asked me if there was any way that I could take a trip with him to this amusement park that was supposed to have the scariest roller coaster in the country. He said that all his life he had never been on a roller coaster. He was terrified. But he didn't want to die without taking a ride on one. While he was in the hospital he had met a couple of kids who also had cancer, and he wanted to take them on the trip as well. All he needed was someone who could drive." Aurora stops to see if I am listening. But she knows that I am and she knows what I will ask next.

"What happened?"

"A little miracle, I guess. I said that I would go with him if my mother agreed, knowing full well that Abba would never agree. But then when I mentioned it to Abba she did not say no right away as I expected, but instead said that she would like to meet Mr Quintana first. I never, never in my wildest dreams thought she would even consider it."

"And then?" Part of me wants to figure out why Aurora is telling me the story but another part just wants to know what happened.

"She met him and afterwards she said it was OK. It was an incredible response — from Abba. But I took the fact that she agreed so easily as a sign that the trip was meant to be. So off we went on this crazy, scary, exciting, painful, joyful adventure. A dying old man, two kids in temporary remission from cancer only a year younger than me, and a seventeen-year-old girl who had never been outside of Texas. The four of us in search of the ultimate roller coaster ride."

"And everyone rode the roller coaster."

"The scariest one. A big, rattling, wooden-frame roller coaster in Tennessee called 'The Big Woodie'. It had a five-second drop with a force of six Gs. But before that, I had to convince Mr Quintana to try a couple of smaller ones. I was afraid that he would have a heart attack if he did not get used to some smaller coasters first. He was still terrified when he rode The Big Woodie, but he did it. When he got out, I asked if he was OK. You know what he said?"

"No."

"He said, 'I'll tell you when my *bolas* drop back in their sack.' Then he smiled this huge smile and said, 'Now I can die happy.'" Aurora laughs to herself. I laugh also. I like it when Aurora occasionally uses bad words. *Bolas*, I know, is a Spanish slang word for testicles. (They also teach us these kinds of things at Paterson.) But as soon as I finish laughing, I try to figure out why Aurora chose to tell me this memory of hers at this particular point. I can tell that she is hoping that I will get to the moral of the story on my own. But the story has various messages and I don't know which one to pick. Is Aurora trying to tell me that the law firm is like a scary roller coaster ride where my own testicles will travel up to my throat, figuratively speaking? I have no idea what this feels like, but I sincerely hope this is not the case.

When she sees that I am having problems responding, she says, "It's just for the summer. Your father means it when he says that at the end of the summer you will decide where to go for your senior year."

"Aurora."

"Yes?"

"Do others see me as a child?"

"You look like any other young man. Better. You're better-looking than most. You're tall and handsome and strong."

"Like Arturo."

"Yes."

"But sometimes I think like a child."

"You are who you are."

"If I am who I am, why is it not possible for me to work at a place where I can be who I am?"

She laughs and shakes her head. "You'll learn new skills and ways to deal and cope with life at the law firm."

"Different from what I can learn at Paterson?"

"Yes."

"What?"

She pauses. She takes a deep breath before she speaks. "A couple of months after our trip, Mr Queen — that's what we called Mr Quintana — died. That's when I decided that I wanted to work with children who had cancer. I always wanted to be a nurse, but it was after that trip, during his funeral, that I decided what kind of nurse I wanted to be. Of all the types of nursing, this was the one that scared me the most, but also the one where I was most likely to say at the end of my days, 'Now I can die happy.'

"But I realized that in order to work with children I needed to be gentle *and* strong. Gentle and caring with the children, but strong and tough with all that threatens to increase their suffering or diminish their chances to be healed. At St Elizabeth's sometimes I have to protect the children from arrogant or even negligent doctors. Sometimes I have to protect them from the so-called 'healthy'. I protect them from hospital bureaucrats, from insurance companies. Sometimes I have to protect them from their own parents. I protect them even from their own negative thoughts at times. I wouldn't be able to do that, to protect them, unless I was an adult, unless I was strong, unless I was willing to fight for them. Do you see?"

"Yes." It is true. I see how Aurora is gentle and strong. Then I add, "I do not want to go to Oak Ridge next year. A regular high school is not for Marcelo. I do not fit in. Aurora just said that Marcelo does not think about the same things that most other kids think about. At Paterson, the kind of things I'm interested in or the way I think do not matter. I can learn better there where there is no concern about how Marcelo is different. Aurora was able to choose on her own what she wanted to do. Abba didn't tell her that she couldn't be a nurse. No one prevented her from working with children. After Paterson I want to be a nurse like Aurora and work with Haflinger ponies and disabled kids. I do not see the difference."

She grins. "Just then you sounded very much like your father the lawyer." Then she stops grinning and nods that she understands. "You won't have to go to a regular high school in the fall if that's what you decide. And after that, well, no one will prevent you from choosing your own path. If you want to do what your mother does, heaven help you, no one will stop you."

"Arturo said that I will get to decide only if I succeed in following the rules of the real world for three months."

"Work in the law firm and do your best to be helpful. That's all you need to do. You will decide." She stands up and holds her hand over my head and then she tousles my hair. "Now help me down," she says.

When she has reached the ground, I stick my head through the trapdoor and call to her, "Aurora."

"Yes?" She is looking up at me.

"Marcelo will work at the law firm."

"Good," she says, "good. Your father wants you to start on Monday."

"Monday is only two days away."

"It's better to just dive in and not think about it too much. I'll call Harry and let him know. Unless you prefer to call him yourself."

"Call him tonight. He will need time to find a new stable man for the summer."

"Or stable woman," Aurora says.

"Whoever it is must be told that it is only a summer job."

"You will decide," she says as she waves goodbye. "Oh. I still have to register you for Oak Ridge next week. But it doesn't mean you'll go there. I promised your father. I want you to know."

"You can register Marcelo, but it is a futile act. He will not be going there in September."

Chapter 5

I turn off the alarm clock after the first beep. There are only a few nights in my life when I have not slept through the night, but the night that just ended is one of them. I lay awake, immobile inside my sleeping bag, listening to the strange sounds in my head. The IM was different. It was disjointed, jagged, with unexpected flashes, like the streaks of lightning that light up the night during an electric storm.

I was not able to complete a full day's schedule like I usually do because I wasn't sure when Arturo and I would return home from the law firm. Tonight, when I know the train schedule coming home, I'll be able to do a full one. Without a schedule to guide me through the day, I feel disoriented. This is the schedule for this morning I prepared last night:

5:00 a.m.	WAKE UP
5:05 a.m.	REMEMBERING
5:35 a.m.	FEED NAMU
5:40 a.m.	DUMB-BELLS

6:00 a.m.	CONTINUE WITH READING OF PSALMS
6:30 a.m.	BREAKFAST (INSTANT CREAM OF WHEAT, BROWN SUGAR, BANANA, ORANGE JUICE)
6:45 a.m.	SHOWER AND DRESS
7:00 a.m.	WAIT FOR ARTURO TO GO TO TRAIN STATION

Arturo informed me that we would catch the seven forty-five train out of West Orchard, which is about twenty minutes away driving at the speed limit. Arturo says he can do it in ten minutes, no problem.

I carry out each task on the schedule as planned, and at seven I'm sitting in the rocking chair in the den, the backpack with the things I plan to take to the law firm by my feet.

I hear Aurora's footsteps on the stairs.

"Good morning," she says when she sees me. "You look very elegant today."

Aurora says that every single morning despite the fact that I usually wear the same thing: white button-down shirt (short sleeves in the summer, long sleeves in the winter), blue cotton trousers (summer) or blue corduroy trousers (winter), black socks, and black sneakers.

"Aurora looks very elegant," I say. Aurora has on white nurse's trousers, a mint-green blouse with yellow smiley faces, white stockings, and white shoes with thick, white rubber soles.

"I made you lunch." She takes a paper bag from the refrigerator and brings it to me. I open up my red backpack and place the paper bag inside. "Thank you, Mother, for making me lunch," she says, to remind me.

"Thank you, Mother, for making me lunch," I say, mimicking her.

She sits on the sofa facing me. "Are you nervous?"

"Yes," I answer without any hesitation whatsoever.

"It's normal to be nervous. You don't know what to expect. But tomorrow you will be less nervous and soon going to the law firm will be a routine."

Routine. Whenever I hear that word I think of a route that is not a full route, only a tiny route. I wonder if it's the change to all my tiny routes that is making me nervous, or is it just that I am still resentful at being forced to do something I don't like?

"Tell me what you are thinking," Aurora urges me. "It's OK to say whatever it is you feel."

I turn my head away from her. I'm thinking that it isn't just Arturo and Aurora who are conspiring against my peace of mind. After the night I just had and the noises that rumbled through my head, it seems that God Himself has it in for me.

"No," I say to Aurora. I regularly say no when people ask me to tell them what I'm thinking.

"OK. I'm going to be a mother and tell you motherly things for a few seconds. You need to be alert when you are walking downtown. Cross the streets only when the white walk sign is on, the way we practised." She takes a cell phone out of her pocket. "I want you to keep this with you at all times. I programmed the phone to speed dial my phone, your dad's, Rabbi Heschel's, and Yolanda's. On the back of the phone I taped the speed-dial numbers. Keep the phone on at all times. Let's try it to make sure it works." She pushes a number and puts the phone to her ear. "Hello. Yoli? It's me. Marcelo's ready to go work with Dad. You want to say hi to him?" She hands me the phone. "It's Yolanda."

"Hello!" I yell into the phone.

"Hey, Mars. You ready for work?" I hear Yolanda's voice.

"No," I answer.

"Listen, Mars. Don't let the jerks at the law firm get to you. You're tons smarter than they are. Put the phone close to your ear 'cause I don't want Mom to hear." I press the phone hard against my right ear. "Mars, listen to me carefully. Dad made me work at the law firm one summer too. There's nothing wrong with you feeling apprehensive right now. The place sucks big-time. Most of the lawyers there are a-holes. You know, you met most of them at the summer barbecue Dad has every year at the house. Remember Stephen Holmes and his son, what's his name, Wendell? Remember when we played tennis with them one time? Assholes, both of them, father and son. Mars, are you still there?"

"Yes."

"Can Mom hear me?"

"No."

"Good. Listen, Mars. You'll get through it. I did. Do what those monks you like to read so much about do when they enter the monastery: surrender any and all hope of ever liking it. One summer, that's all. It'll be over before you know it. Just don't let anyone give you any shit. You understand?"

"Yes."

"What did I just say?"

"Do not let the a-holes give me shit."

"What? Give me that!" Aurora shouts. She grabs the phone from my hand. "What are you telling your brother? Big help you are. No, it does not. No, they are not. Not all of them anyway. OK, I'm going to hang up now. Bye!"

Aurora is laughing as Arturo enters the room. "Let's go, buddy," he says to me.

"You guys are going to miss the train," Aurora says.

"Nonsense!" Arturo is pouring coffee into a cup.

"It is seven twenty-five," I point out, looking at my watch.

"Don't forget your lunch," Aurora says.

"Goodbye, Aurora," I say.

As soon as we are outside, Arturo stops and turns me towards him. He unbuttons the very top button of my shirt. "There," he says. "You don't need to button the top one unless you're wearing a tie."

Namu starts to walk next to me. "No, Namu. Namu has to stay home," I tell him.

I wish Namu could come with me. I wouldn't have any trouble crossing streets then. I still remember the answer Arturo gave me once when I asked if I could take Namu with me to the mall: "You're not disabled," he said.

I sink down into the front seat of Arturo's sports car. The first explosion of the engine jolts me. Arturo takes a quick look at his wristwatch and then guns the car down the driveway.

We are barely parked when the train pulls in. We're the last ones to get on, and that's only because the conductor sees us running and decides to wait for us. My white shirt is hanging out of my trousers and I try to tuck it in and walk down the aisle at the same time, but the train lurches and I grab on to a woman's shoulder to keep from falling.

"Sorry," Arturo apologizes on my behalf.

She looks up and the look on her face is one of annoyance.

At the very end of the train, we find an empty seat. "I told you we'd make it." Arturo is out of breath.

"It is more relaxing to be early," I say.

"This is work, buddy. No more relaxing for you."

After the conductor takes our money, Arturo takes a newspaper from his briefcase and unfolds it on his lap. I make a mental note to bring a book tomorrow. Maybe I can read without getting dizzy like I do when I try to read in the car. It occurs to me that it is a good opportunity to say the Rosary. I take out the multi-coloured rosary beads that Abba gave me before she died and I begin to mouth the words of the Hail Mary wordlessly with my lips. I always say the Rosary in Spanish. Abba and I used to say it together that way and that's the way it stayed with me.

Arturo folds the paper carefully. "We should go over a few things," he says.

I finish a Hail Mary and stop.

"How shall I say it? You are going to be part of the business world. You know, I have nothing against your interest in religion. I want you to be religious. We've been to Mass every Sunday since your First Communion — before then even. I let you see Rabbi Heschel even though you're not Jewish, you're Catholic. I'm one hundred per cent in favour of your religious interests, your religious books, your praying or remembering as you call it, your saying the Rosary in Spanish, all of it. So I don't want you to misunderstand what I'm about to say. I want you to be religious but, at the same time, I want you to participate in the day-to-day workaday world, my world, and your world too now. And to do so, you have to abide by some established customs. People in the workaday world are discreet about their religion. They pray in private. They don't quote Scripture unless it's a figure of speech like, I don't know, 'an eye for an eye, a tooth for a tooth', 'the blind leading the blind'. Things like that. Phrases that have common usage."

"Can a blind man lead a blind man?" I say.

"Beg your pardon?"

"Jesus's exact words were, 'Can a blind man lead a blind man? Will they not both fall into a pit?' Luke, chapter six, verse thirty-nine."

"That's exactly what I mean. It's not customary to quote Scripture to someone, much less quote him chapter and verse. I think that if you're going to benefit from this experience, it's important that you try to act as is customary."

I take out the yellow notebook that I always keep in my shirt pocket. I write: *Do not pray so that others see M. pray. Do not quote Scripture. Note: listen for religious phrases that have become figures of speech. Those are allowed even if not accurate. Do not provide correct version or cite where it appears in the Bible.*

Arturo waits for me to finish writing and then speaks. "There's a chapel close to the train station. I'll show you where it is. You can stop by there before you get to work and say the Rosary if you wish."

We are silent for the next five minutes. Arturo does not open his newspaper, so I'm thinking that he wants to fill me in on some more workaday customs. If only customs were logical. If only the rules were as simple as "Don't do anything that will hurt others". If that were the only rule, I'd have at least a fifty per cent chance of getting it right. I would, for example, ask myself whether saying the Rosary silently on the train would hurt others. The answer would be no and so I would say it. As it is, the reasons as to why something is right and something is not seem arbitrary.

"While we're at it, maybe this is a good time to go over a few things about the law firm."

I was right. Arturo wants to point out to me some more dos and don'ts.

"A law firm is not like Paterson. In a law firm the environment is competitive. I compete against Stephen Holmes, for example. I try to bring in more business than he does and he tries to bring in more business than I do. The associates compete against each other by each trying to work harder and better. That's not to say that people are not friendly with each other. You can be friends with someone and still compete against them. Competition is good for all involved. The harder Stephen works, the harder and better I work. The more the associates work, the better the whole firm does. When Yolanda applied to Yale, she had to compete against hundreds of other kids who wanted to go there. She worked hard and got in while others didn't. The same will be true for you when you apply to college. You'll have to compete. But you need to be *willing* to compete. You can't be afraid of competing. That's one of the things I hope you learn this summer."

I take out my yellow notebook again and am about to write, when I think of asking, "Who will Mar . . . who will *I* compete against at the law firm?"

"Everyone. People will be testing you. They'll want to see if you can do the job or if you're just there because you're my son and I'm the boss."

I'm starting to get dizzy. Who am I supposed to work harder

than or be smarter than?

Arturo goes on. "Competition is an attitude. It's a way of understanding that the motive behind someone's action may be self-interest, and reacting to that accordingly."

"A person's motives are impossible to know with certainty," I say.

"Precisely. That's why it's helpful to assume that most people are looking out for number one."

At that moment, I picture a group of people standing on a corner waiting for a big number one to appear. Arturo must have seen the blankness in my eyes, for he says, "It's a figure of speech: *looking out for number one*. It means to consider one's own interests first."

"The first will be last," I say, forgetting that I'm not supposed to quote Scripture.

"In the world of work, the first are first and will be first and the last are last and will be last."

"I do not follow. Do you have an example?"

"I'll give you a real-life, current example. A couple of weeks ago, I mentioned to Stephen Holmes that you were working at the law firm for the summer. So last Friday, he says to me, 'Oh, by the way, Wendell will be helping us with some legal research this summer.' Remember Wendell?"

"Yes. Yolanda says he's an a-hole." Immediately I regret saying this. I hope I didn't get Yolanda into trouble.

Arturo laughs. "She may be right. But the point I'm trying to make is that after Stephen told me Wendell was working at the law firm, I asked myself what Stephen's motives were. Why is he making his kid spend the summer doing legal work? Wendell will be a senior at Harvard next year. He can get any job in the city he wants. And why did Holmes make it a point to tell me that the way he did? 'Maybe he can take your kid to lunch someday,' he said to me. And the answer is that he wanted me and everyone else to know that my son is—"

I wait for him to finish the sentence. I know that when people stop in the middle of what they're saying, it means that they suddenly realize they shouldn't say what they were planning on saying in the first place. What happens is that the person has started talking before realizing the impact the words will have on the listener. That's why I think many more thoughts than I actually express and why sometimes I come across as slow. I think too much about what I'm hearing and what I'm going to say, and that's a problem when trying to carry on a conversation. Of course, sometimes things slip out. Like a little while ago, when I told Arturo what Yolanda had said about Wendell. *He wanted me and everyone else to know that my son is* – I make a mental note to attempt to complete Arturo's sentence later, when I have more time to reflect.

The train slows down and I hear the screeching sound of metal rubbing against metal. I instinctively put my hands over my ears. Harsh noises are painful to me. "We're here," Arturo says as he peels my hands from my ears. "What I'm trying to say is that you need to develop what I call 'street smarts'. One of the reasons why I wanted you to work at the law firm is so you can get a better understanding of people's motives. It's the way it is, son. Every day I come to work, I tell myself, I'm a warrior and this is a battle. I put on my war face. That's another figure of speech. It's a way of saying that I understand I will need to watch out for people's motives and I will need to be competitive — like in a war, where some will win and some will lose. It's important that you see that side of life."

The real world. That's what I say to myself.

Chapter 6

At the law firm, I follow Arturo to the mailroom. A woman is standing in front of a huge copying machine. I know it's a copying machine because I can see a line of light move back and forth, just like the machine they have at Paterson. Arturo says "Good morning" three times before she turns around. Immediately, I feel her gaze scan me from head to feet and back again just like the light of the copying machine. When I force myself to look into her eyes, I am struck by their deep blue colour. "Azure" is the word that comes to mind. A strand of soft black hair falls over her face. I am ready to shake her hand but she doesn't walk up to where we are.

"This is Marcelo," Arturo says. Then he pats me on the back and says to me, "This is Jasmine. Jasmine will be your boss this summer. Do whatever she tells you. But watch out for her, she eats little boys for breakfast."

That must be another figure of speech, I say to myself. But I do not know what it signifies.

As soon as Arturo leaves, Jasmine turns around and continues staring at the copying machine. *Maybe she's been hypnotized by the moving light,* I think. I stand there looking at the place Arturo calls the mailroom. It is a large room separated from the rest of the law firm by a wall with a counter like the one they have in post offices. The copying machine that Jasmine is staring at is located on the wall opposite the door where we came in. There are two desks, each facing a wall so that when people sit at them, they will have their backs to each other. I decide I like that arrangement, assuming that I will sit at one of the desks. It would be very uncomfortable to have another person sitting in front of me.

The desk next to the copying machine is made of grey metal and is smaller than the larger wooden desk that is adjacent to the door. The larger desk has a white CD player with headphones connected to it, and on the wall in front of it there is a picture of a snow-capped mountain peak. The rest of the mailroom is filled with metal shelves that go from the floor to the ceiling. These metal shelves are packed with large brown folders. I notice that the metal shelves have steel wheels and that under the wheels there are tracks that allow the shelves to move sideways in order to access the shelves behind.

"You can put your backpack there," Jasmine says, turning her head briefly in my direction. With her left hand, she points to the smaller metal desk next to the copying machine.

I remove the backpack from my shoulders and place it on top of the desk. Then I stand there mesmerized by the pieces of paper spewing out of the copying machine into a series of slots. Jasmine is not doing anything but watching the line of light move back and forth, back and forth. I think that copying is something that

I will probably enjoy doing.

When the machine stops, Jasmine grabs the stacks of paper that have accumulated in the slots. "You can sit down if you want. That's your desk."

"Thank you," I say. I pull out the black chair that is tucked under the desk. Like the shelves, the chair also has steel wheels. I sit down and immediately the chair slides backwards with me in it.

"We'll get a rubber mat so the chair doesn't slide," Jasmine says.

"Thank you." I picture the rubber mat that we have in the bathtub at home and wonder how that will work. Then I notice that there are pieces of Scotch tape stuck to the wall in front of me. Maybe the last person that worked here taped up some pictures. I think that maybe I can bring a picture of Namu and tape it there. In the indentations that separate the cinder blocks of the wall someone has written something in tiny letters. I peer closer and read the following words: "Fuck this place and all the people in it." I know from Paterson that "fuck" is an inappropriate word that means sexual intercourse, but is more often than not used to convey anger and even hatred.

I turn around briefly. Jasmine has finished collecting the stacks of paper and is now putting them inside plastic binders. She's doing this at the big wooden desk that's behind me. That must be her desk. I turn around again. There is more stuff written on the wall, but I decide not to read it. I wonder if the last person who sat at this desk was also forced to work at the law firm.

"Your father said you had your own laptop." It's Jasmine

speaking behind me. I try to turn around but when I do, I slide halfway across the room.

"Oh," I say.

Jasmine walks out of the mailroom without saying a word. I sit there not knowing what to do next. In a few minutes she returns with a giant plastic square that she drops in front of my desk. So that's the rubber mat she was talking about.

"Yes," I say.

"Yes what?" she asks.

"Yes. My father informed you correctly. I have my own laptop. Would you like to see it?"

"Not necessarily. There's a connection under your desk you can hook up with. I'll tie you in to the office server when we get back from the mail run."

"Thank you." A sense of relief comes over me. With my laptop, I will feel less lost. If I don't understand something someone says, I can look it up. I bend down to take the laptop out of my backpack. I place it on the desk and open it. I think that perhaps now will be a good time to show Jasmine all the special software that I have.

"I'm not happy about you being here."

It takes me a few seconds to realize that Jasmine is talking to me. I turn in her direction. "I understand," I say. I'm wondering where I should put my hands. Whenever I say something I don't mean, I become conscious of my hands.

"You understand?"

I want to explain that I understood *what* she said not *why* she had said it, but it takes me too long to figure out how to say this.

"Let's do the mail run." I follow her to a corner of the room. "This is the mail cart. You can read, right?"

I wonder why she asks me that. Perhaps it's a joke of sorts that I don't understand.

"Yes," I answer.

"When the mail comes in, you put it in the folder with the person's name. The folders are arranged in geographical order. They follow the way the offices are laid out, so when you go around the office you just move from one folder to the next."

I think to myself that that's an excellent idea.

She continues, "There'll be some mail that is not addressed to anyone specifically and you'll have to figure out where it goes. Lots of it is junk mail. If you can't figure out where it goes, put it in this box. I'll look at it later. Nothing gets thrown away without me looking at it first, do you understand?"

This time I really do understand. "Yes," I say confidently.

"This morning I sorted out the mail already. We do four scheduled runs: one first thing in the morning, which we are about to do now, then at eleven-thirty, one-thirty and at three. Of course, if something comes in by hand delivery or by overnight mail, we deliver it right away. You'll also deliver the newspapers. What time are you planning to get here in the morning?"

I do some quick calculations in my head. It took Arturo and me twenty minutes to walk from South Station to the law firm, but we went three blocks out of the way so that Arturo could show me where the chapel was. The train arrived at eight-twenty and then if I go to the chapel. . .

"Never mind," Jasmine says. "You'll do it whenever. They can wait for their newspapers. You *are* coming to work every day, right?"

"Every day," I say. I wonder if that includes Saturday and Sunday. Arturo comes to work on those days frequently. Perhaps he expects me to do the same.

"Let's go then." She pushes the cart full of green folders. When we are out of the mailroom, she hands me a piece of paper. "This is a layout of the office with all the attorneys' and secretaries' names and where they sit. You need to memorize that so you won't waste time looking for people. Like I said, besides the scheduled mail runs, you'll need to deliver hand deliveries and overnight mail as soon as they arrive. All mail, deliveries, packages, et cetera come to the mailroom first. We log them in and then deliver them." She waits for me to catch up to her and looks at me. "I guess you can log the stuff in if I'm not around. Everything these people do is urgent and everything needs to be done yesterday."

"Yesterday already happened."

"Tell that to the lawyers who work here."

We stop at the first office. A woman is sitting at a desk in front of the office. "Hello, Marcelo," the woman says. "Remember me? From the summer barbecue at your house?"

I remember her face but I don't remember her name. Does that mean that I answer yes or no to her question? I decide to say yes since it is at least partially correct. I stretch out my hand. "Nice to meet you," I tell her. As soon as I say it, I know that's not the thing to say to someone whom you've just told you remember.

"Nice to meet you . . . again," says the woman. "Wow, you're even more handsome than your father." She looks me up and down just like Jasmine did, but unlike Jasmine, her inspection of me is slower and lingers on the middle part of my body. "My goodness! First Mr Holmes brings Wendell and now this. How's a girl supposed to concentrate with all the young fellows walking around?"

"Stay away from him," Jasmine says.

"Let's not be selfish," the woman responds.

Jasmine starts to push the cart away from the woman.

"Oh, you're just jealous 'cause you're undersized," the woman says.

Jasmine stops the cart and looks at her. "For your information I'm not jealous, but I am envious. I'm envious that if we're both in a plane flying over the ocean and the plane goes down, I won't have the same natural flotation advantages that you have."

"Oh, you rat!" The woman laughs and pretends to take a swipe at Jasmine.

We move on. Flotation devices. I know the meaning of these words, but the context in which they are being used is baffling. I take the notebook out of my pocket while we're walking and write down: *What is the difference between jealous and envious?* The distinction between those two inner states is something that has always confused me.

Once I finish writing, Jasmine says, "I'd stay away from the secretaries if I were you."

"How can I deliver the mail to them if I stay away from them?"

"I mean, I wouldn't let them get too friendly with you, especially the ones that are single and desperate, like Martha back there."

"Why?"

"Martha for one would not hesitate to jump your bones."

I think of the passage in the Bible where the prophet Ezekiel jumps up and down on a pile of skulls and bones. The rapidity with which I am encountering new concepts is making me dizzy.

"What's wrong with you anyway?"

"You need to speak clearly. I don't know what the phrase 'jump your bones' means. It would be very helpful if you were more literal."

"Literal?"

"If you used words in accordance with their primary literal meaning, not their metaphorical meaning."

"I *was* being literal. Martha would literally bounce on your bones if she could."

"Oh."

"I meant what's wrong with you, with the way you think. Your father said you had some kind of cognitive disorder."

"He said that." It surprises me to hear Arturo refer to me that way. He has always insisted that there's nothing wrong with me. The term "cognitive disorder" implies that there is something wrong with the way I think or with the way I perceive reality. I perceive reality just fine. Sometimes I perceive more of reality than others.

"I'm pretty sure those are the words he used."

"'Cognitive disorder' is not an accurate description of what happens inside Marcelo's head. 'Excessive attempt at cognitive order' is closer to what actually takes place."

"Yeah? I like excessive order myself. Is that an illness?"

"If it keeps you from functioning in society the way people

think a normal person should, then our society calls that an illness."

"Well, society is not always right, is it?"

I don't answer her because I am still thinking about my father's description of my condition. He has taught me to always question the labels that others want to stick on me. I hesitate for a few seconds, and then I speak. "From a medical perspective, the closest description of my condition is Asperger's syndrome. But I don't have many of the characteristics that other people with Asperger's syndrome have, so that term is not exactly accurate."

"Like what? What characteristics?"

This is a topic of conversation that I am knowledgeable about but not particularly fond of. Explanations about my condition are based on the assumption that there is something wrong with the way I am, and at Paterson I have learned through the years that it is not helpful to view myself or the other kids there that way. I view myself as different in the way I think, talk and act, but not as someone who is abnormal or ill. But how do I explain the differences to people? It is easier to say that AS best describes my differences. It makes people more comfortable to have a scientific-sounding term. But actually, I feel dishonest when I say I have AS because the negative effects of my differences on my life are so slight compared to other kids who have AS or other forms of autism and truly suffer. I always feel like I'm doing the people who have these conditions a disservice when I use the medical term, because then people say, "Oh, that doesn't seem so bad. What's all the fuss about?"

Reluctantly, I attempt to answer Jasmine's question. "The primary characteristics of AS, which is what Asperger's syndrome is called for short, occur in the areas of communication and social interaction, and there is usually some kind of pervasive interest. The AS person is different than most people in these areas."

"Really?"

I take my hands out of my pockets and button the top button of my shirt again. We are standing in the middle of the hall and people are passing us by as they arrive in the office. A few say good morning to Jasmine, but Jasmine is too absorbed in what I am saying to respond to them. "Yes, generally speaking," I say to her.

"That pretty much sums up every guy I've ever dated."

"Yes." I take this to be an attempt at humour on Jasmine's part so I try to laugh, but the laugh comes out more like a cough.

"And what is your particular pervasive interest?"

I put my hands back in my pockets and close my fists. This is the part that is always tricky. I have seen something like a glass wall descend between me and other people as soon as I talk about this. Therefore, I hesitate and ponder how open I should be with Jasmine. After a while I say, "Some people use the word 'obsessive' rather than 'pervasive'. But obsessive interest is not the right term. It implies some kind of compulsion or inability to stop the same thoughts and behaviour from recurring. At Paterson — that's the school I attend — we prefer to use the term 'special or pervasive interest'. It's an interest that the person chooses to think about because he gets pleasure and even joy from doing it. It absorbs the attention of the AS person to the exclusion of other interests because it is more important and more fun than other interests. AS persons with special interests become experts in that field."

"Like train schedules or adding up numbers real fast in your head."

"Those particular examples come to mind for a lot of people. But memorizing train schedules and a facility with numbers are somewhat of a caricature. A lot of AS people have special interests that require complex thinking and understanding."

"So what's yours?"

I wish I had a glass of water. There is no saliva whatsoever in my mouth. I cough again. "My special interest is God."

"Excuse me?"

"Religion. What humankind has experienced and said and thought about God. I like to read and think about that."

"Is that right?"

"I don't know if it is right or not. It just is."

She starts to push the cart again but this time very slowly. I think, *Now she thinks I'm weird. I don't want to be here anyway. At Paterson no one regards me with suspicion or stays away from me because I have an interest in religion. I have to remember never to talk about anything religious while I'm here. It scares people.* Then it occurs to me to say, "That is my special interest. But I also enjoy listening to music. I have hundreds of CDs at home." For some reason this has never been considered abnormal.

She stops the cart and asks, "What kind of music?"

"It is called classical music. Bach is my favourite. My favourite instrument is the piano. The violin is second. Solo pieces by piano or violin are what I enjoy the most. The reason for that is that in solo pieces I can hear the different notes and the different combinations of notes separately. I like that very much."

"Really?" Her lips are partly opened, like she's never heard anyone speak like that before. I think I might have overdone it in the description of my second interest.

"Yes."

It makes me happy to finally see her smile.

"I also like horses, particularly Haflinger ponies."

"Really?" She widens her eyes, which means that she is surprised.

"Yes. Really. My job at Paterson this summer was going to be to take care of the fifteen ponies the school owns." I realize that by telling Jasmine about the ponies right after I told her about religion and classical music, I am saying that the ponies are also a special interest, although I myself have never put them in this category. A special interest is something that absorbs your brain with a curiosity to know all there is to know. I never felt this way about the IM or the ponies. The IM is the IM and the ponies are the ponies. They just are. I like spending as much time as I can with them, but I do not care to know all there is to know about them.

We start walking again. After we drop off the next bundle of letters, she says, "Do you want to know why I'm not happy that you're here?"

"Yes."

"Until three months ago I had an assistant. His name was Ron. To make a long story short, I had to fire Ron. But lazy as Ron was, he was still a help to me, and when we fired him, your father promised that I would be able to replace him. I found this girl Belinda who worked here one summer when she was in high school and I was delighted because she was great. Am I going too fast for you?"

"It doesn't matter." She's actually speaking faster than I would have preferred. There are words and phrases that elude me. But one of the things I learned at Paterson was to let people talk even though I don't understand every single thing I hear. As they go on the meaning becomes clear. It took years to train my brain not to question the meaning of every single word that lands there.

She continues, "So I'm ready to hire Belinda and your dad tells me to hold off because he wants you to work here this summer."

"I understand."

"Now you know."

"I am very good at concentrating. If Jasmine shows me how to do something, I will learn."

We reach the end of the hall. Behind a glass partition there is a woman sitting at a desk bigger and somehow more elegant than the desks of the other secretaries. The woman is looking into a small mirror while applying lipstick, the colour of which I have never seen before. I think that perhaps this is what the word "carmine" looks like.

"This is Juliet," Jasmine says to me. "Holmesy's secretary."

"Mr Holmes," the woman says, correcting Jasmine.

"Whatever," Jasmine says.

"So," Juliet says, smacking her lips together, "you're the new mail boy. Mr Holmes told me you would be arriving today. He wants to see you, so I'll call you when he has a free minute."

"Why?" Jasmine asks. "What does Holmesy want with him?"

"I don't believe that is any of your concern," Juliet says.

"He works for me," Jasmine tells her.

"And you work for Mr Holmes."

"Wrongo mundo, Julie baby. I report directly to the boss, his father."

"I'm sure you do." Juliet's lips twist upwards at the corners as she says this. Then, glancing in my direction, she says, "I'll call you when Mr Holmes is ready to see you. I assume he'll have the same phone number as the young criminal that used to work with you?"

Jasmine leans over Juliet's desk and points her index finger at her. "Listen to me carefully. I'm going to tell you directly what I will tell Holmesy when I see him. He is not going to do any work that his secretary or executive mucky-muck or whatever your title is, is supposed to do. He's not going to file or copy or do anything that *you* can do. And he's not going to be Wendell's errand boy either. All work requests from you or Holmesy or Wendell go through me. If Holmesy needs work done that is above your intellectual abilities, he can ask Wendell there to do it for him." Jasmine points at the office directly across from Juliet.

In the quick second that I look at Juliet, I see her nostrils flare. Then she says to Jasmine, "Oliver Wendell is helping his father with the Vidromek litigation. He's not here to do dummy work." She looks at me when she says the last two words.

Jasmine turns to me and says, "Let's go before I lose control and do something that lands me in prison."

"Delighted to meet you," Juliet says. But when I look at her, she does not have anything that resembles delight on her face.

When we are down the hall, Jasmine exhales loudly. "That woman is a bona fide bitch. And I'm being extremely literal.

Listen to me. If she or Holmes or little boy Wendell asks you to do anything, anything whatsoever, you need to tell me immediately. Do you understand?"

"Yes. I know Wendell. He is not a little boy. He is about three years older than I am."

"Yeah, well. He has the emotional maturity of an eight-year-old."

"I played tennis with him once. Not tennis exactly. He hit the ball to me and I hit it back to him." I am about to tell her what Yolanda said to me this morning but I stop myself in time. Instead, I say, "He is going to Harvard."

"Yeah, yeah! He thinks he's God's gift to womankind. The only good thing about having him around this summer is that it's fun to see him miserable. He hates having to spend the summer here while he could be out racing yachts or something, but his father is making him do it, God only knows why."

"God knows why," I tell her. I wonder if mentioning God in the workplace is also something that should not be done, along with praying or quoting Scripture. In any event, Jasmine does not seem to mind.

"Anyway," Jasmine says, "that's why I told you I wasn't happy you were working here."

It takes me a while to recollect the conversation we were having before the encounter with Juliet.

"I agreed to have you work with me, you might as well know, only because your father is giving me an extra two thousand a month and I need the money. But I would still rather have Belinda, two thousand or no two thousand. Just so you know."

"I understand," I say again.

"The early mail run is easy because there aren't too many law-yers around. They get here around nine and work till all hours of the night. That's the corporate culture here."

"I am not happy about being here either." I hear these words come out of me and I'm not certain that it is me that is saying them. "I would rather be working at Paterson taking care of the ponies."

Jasmine looks at me steadily for the longest time and then nods like she agrees. She opens the door to the mailroom and pushes the cart inside. "This door needs to be locked every time you leave the room and I'm not here. I'll give you a key. No one comes in here but you and me. If someone needs a file, they stand on that side of the counter while we get it. I'll show you how the filing works. People used to come in and get files on their own and then one got lost and the firm got sued for malpractice. Since then no one is allowed in here, not even the cleaning people. At the end of the day, we put the trash baskets right outside the door. OK?"

"Yes."

"So let's get that laptop of yours hooked up."

Chapter 7

Jasmine connects my laptop to the law firm's system so now I can get emails from all the lawyers and staff. As soon as she leaves the room, I decide to check out the term "cognitive disorder" on the Internet. The term is unlike anything I've ever heard Arturo use and I am curious to find out what he may have meant by it. It cannot be that Arturo thinks I have a cognitive disorder. There are so many serious mental illnesses that are referred to as cognitive disorders: dementia, schizophrenia, paranoia, hallucinations (auditory and visual). I decide that Arturo used a short-cut term to describe a reality difficult to explain. That is the only explanation that makes sense. Would Arturo want me to work at the law firm or attend a regular high school or go to college if he thought I was not in touch with reality? All my life he's fought against anything that separates me from the normal.

I hear the telephone on my desk ring. The ring is loud, louder than any telephone ring I've ever heard, and for some reason the ring sounds as if it is transmitting rage.

"Hello," I say.

I hear a woman's voice: "Mr Holmes will see you now."

"Now," I repeat.

"Yes. Now. As in immediately. He only has a few minutes before his eleven o'clock. If you could get here right away that would be wonderful."

"OK." I stand up. I'm not sure I can find Stephen Holmes's office on my own. Then I hear Jasmine's voice. She has been sitting at her desk all along and I didn't know she was there.

"Let me guess, Holmes is summoning you."

"Now. He wants to see me now."

"It's always now with Holmesy."

I stand there a few moments feeling embarrassed.

"What?" she asks.

"I have forgotten how to get to his office." She stands up and motions for me to follow her. "I will memorize where everyone sits as soon as I get back. I was going to do it as soon as we got back from the mail run but I got carried away looking up something."

Jasmine does not seem annoyed by the fact that she has to walk me to Stephen Holmes's office. She seems to be preoccupied with thoughts of her own. "You might as well try to stay on Holmesy's good side. He likes it when you 'ooh' and 'aah' over his office and when you appear to be in awe of every word that comes out of his mouth. OK, there it is. When you're done, or better yet, when Holmesy's done with you, just walk out of his office, turn left and then another left and you'll be in the mailroom. Left and left. OK?"

"Left and left," I repeat.

Then she turns around and leaves. I'm standing in front of Juliet, who is clicking rapidly on her keyboard. "Go in," she says without looking up.

I walk in and see Stephen Holmes behind a big glass desk. Everything in the office appears to be made of glass and extremely breakable. Stephen Holmes covers the mouthpiece of the telephone with his hand and says, "Sit down, Gump, I'll be right with you."

At first I think that someone named Gump has come into the room, but then I remember that Gump is what Stephen Holmes calls me ever since I hit the tennis balls with Wendell at the summer barbecue. "Your son is a regular Forrest Gump," Stephen Holmes said to Arturo after Wendell and I were done.

"What exactly do you mean by that?" Arturo responded. I remember how all the people sitting on the patio suddenly stopped talking.

"You know," Stephen Holmes said, "just like Forrest Gump in that movie, with the ping-pong."

I remember how Aurora yanked Arturo back down in his chair. I remember also Stephen Holmes and Arturo later that evening as they stood together underneath the tree house and they didn't know I was up there. Arturo was explaining how the tree house was fully equipped with electricity and how Yolanda's classmates had designed and built it. Then he said, "By the way, don't ever call my son names again." The tone of Arturo's voice was different than any I had ever heard before. I heard Stephen Holmes chuckle and then say: "Don't be so touchy, Art."

The next day I asked Yolanda why Stephen Holmes had called me Gump and we rented the movie *Forrest Gump*. When I saw the part of the movie where he becomes a ping-pong champion, I understood why Stephen Holmes called me Gump. What I did not understand and still don't is why Arturo got so upset. The main character in the movie is a very good human being.

Stephen Holmes hangs up and immediately places his feet on top of the glass desk. There is nothing on the desk but the telephone and a silver pen.

"Sit, Gump, sit."

"My name is not Gump," I say. "My name is Marcelo Sandoval."

"Of course it is. Sit down, Mr Marcelo Sandoval."

Stephen Holmes pronounces my name Marchelo instead of Marselo, the way it's supposed to be pronounced.

"How's the tennis game?"

"I don't actually play tennis," I say, sitting down on the edge of a black chair.

"Nonsense. You're a regular Pancho Gonzales. Hey, you know Wendell is working here this summer, helping me with some litigation. You two should go over to the club and play some squash."

"Yolanda taught me to hit the ball back to her so she could practise. I can hit the ball back if it is close to me. If the ball is not hit directly at me, I usually don't get to it."

"You'll do well in squash. You won't have to chase the ball around like in tennis."

"I am not good at competitive sports. It is hard for Marcelo to move quickly. I tend to think too much."

"That reminds me of why I wanted to see you. I'd like you to help Wendell with the litigation project he's working on. He's a bright kid but not very good at following through on the little details. You know, organizing, filing. And there's tons of photo-copying to do."

"Jasmine said to check with her before I did work for you or Wendell."

"Jasmine, Jasmine. What your father sees in her is beyond my comprehension."

Suddenly my head feels hot. Even though I don't fully under-stand, I sense that Stephen Holmes is attacking Arturo, the one thing that always makes me angry. Without thinking I say, "Jasmine must be a good worker if Arturo likes her." I don't care if what I say and how I say it sounds disrespectful.

Stephen Holmes grins. Actually, the thing that Stephen Holmes does with his lips can be better described as a smirk. "She must be good at something all right if your father likes her." He smirks again. "See if you can figure out why your father keeps Jasmine around. That would be a good project for you this summer. In any event, don't you worry about Jasmine. I'll take care of her. "

"Marcelo does not worry." I am still angry but the anger is subsiding. I take a deep, deep breath as I have been taught to do at Paterson.

"I know Marcelo doesn't." Holmes laughs. "I wish I didn't worry about things. It must be nice to have a simple, uncompli-cated brain."

"You can if you want to."

"Oh yeah?"

"It's not hard to simplify the thought processes of the brain. All you have to do is stop unwanted thoughts from rising up."

"Is that right?"

"I found the best way to do that is to memorize a passage from Scripture and then remember that passage whenever you want to stop unwanted thoughts." I wonder if that is something that I should not have said. I remember Arturo's rule not to talk about religious matters in the workplace.

Stephen Holmes takes his feet down and places both of them on the red rug under his desk at the same time. I can feel him studying me. I always feel a sense of discomfort when I am with Stephen Holmes. "Maybe we can go to lunch someday and you can tell me just how to do that. I'm afraid I have a conference call as of ten minutes ago. I'll tell Wendell to take you out to lunch sometime. He can teach you how to profligate and you can teach him how to concentrate. Hey, that's pretty good, if I say so myself."

I stay seated, searching through my mental files for the meaning of the word "profligate".

"OK, Gump. You can go back to the mailroom and the auspices of your father's protégée. By the way, how's Yolanda doing? Is she enjoying Yale?"

Yolanda constantly complains about how hard her studies are so I'm not sure how to answer the question. I finally decide to say yes, even if this is not totally accurate.

"What's she studying? Does she want to be a nurse like your mother?"

"Yolanda wants to study the human brain. She has a job as a research assistant at a hospital in New York."

"Well, well, well. Does she? That's interesting. Well, off you go. I'll tell Wendell to take you to the club for some squash."

As soon as I step out of Stephen Holmes's office, I write down the word "squash" in my yellow notebook. I gather the word refers to some kind of game similar to tennis, but I don't know why they named it after the vegetable.

"Marchelo! Hey, Marchelo!" At first I think that Stephen Holmes is calling me from his office, but then I see that the voice is coming from the office directly across. I walk to the doorway and see Wendell sitting behind a stack of cardboard boxes. He looks like a younger, messier version of Stephen Holmes.

"My name is pronounced Mar-se-lo," I say. I think of the bad word that Yolanda used to refer to Stephen Holmes and his son, Wendell.

"Of course it is. Sit down, Marcelo, sit for a second."

"I need to help Jasmine. She's going to show me how to operate the copying machine," I say, still standing.

"Just for a minute." Wendell comes from behind the cardboard boxes and removes a paper bag from the chair where he wants me to sit. "I need a mental break from this crap."

I sit down and put my hands on my legs. I want to say something to Wendell, who seems to be waiting for me to start the conversation, but I can't think of anything to say. Despite hours of practising at Paterson, initiating "small talk" is still a formidable challenge for me. "You play squash," I finally think to say. Only I'm aware that I did not enunciate the phrase in the form of a question.

"I see you've been talking to the old man."

"Your father is not old," I say.

"I'll tell him you said that. It'll make him happy."

"It is good to be happy." I think of Jasmine. Jasmine is not happy I'm working at the law firm. I'm not happy either. The effort required to converse politely is draining every drop of happiness out of me.

"Speaking of happy, I'd be happy if I were spending my days in the same room with Jasmine. She's hot, isn't she?"

"Hot." Why is it that whenever I don't understand how a word is used, I tend to repeat it?

"Do you notice things like that, Marcelo? You know, when a woman is hot to look at, pleasant to the eyes, attractive? Do you get that urge we all get when we see a good female body?"

"No." I think the answer to that question is no. I gather that Wendell is talking about sexual attraction.

"You're kidding, right?"

"No."

"That's not possible. Are you attracted to men then?"

"No."

"Maybe your testosterone hasn't kicked in yet. If it hasn't, it soon will. The male's need to sow our seed wherever, whenever, as much and as often as we can — maybe it hasn't hit you yet. You're what, eighteen?"

"I turned seventeen on March twenty-sixth."

"Then the hormones of adolescence have long started to flow. I can tell just by looking at you. Look at you. You're almost as tall as I am and I'm six feet. Your voice is deep. You shave, right?"

"Yes."

"You're built solid. Look at those biceps."

Wendell grabs my arm and squeezes it. I try to pull it away. I don't like people to touch me without warning me first. I hope that I have not offended Wendell. "I lift weights every day."

Wendell ignores my statement and goes back to his original topic of conversation. "You mean to say that looking at Jasmine and looking at me are all the same to you."

"You and Jasmine are persons."

"But have different types of bodies."

"You are both persons. You are essentially the same."

"That's deep, Marcelo. It really is. If you really feel that way and are not trying to pull my leg, or anything else for that matter, I take my hat off to you, I guess. But I'm not so sure. I don't think you're being totally honest with me."

"You don't have a hat on." It is my attempt at humour and at changing the subject but it doesn't work on either count.

"You mean to tell me that you never," Wendell lowers his voice, "never want to, you know, do it." Wendell has made a circle with his index finger and his thumb and is sticking the middle finger from his other hand repeatedly in and out of the circle.

"It."

"It." Now Wendell lifts his arm slowly up in the air like an elephant raising his trunk.

I know that Wendell's finger poking is a gesture meant to signify sexual intercourse and that the rising arm signifies an erection. The rules regarding sexuality and conversations about sexuality are hazy, confusing. I don't know whether Wendell is joking or whether he is interested in discussing the topic seriously. I decide that Wendell is most probably joking and I don't need to respond. I stand up and say, "I need to go help Jasmine."

"Hold on, hold on." Wendell pulls me down. "I didn't mean to offend you. I was just curious, from an anthropological point of view."

"I was not offended," I say. I stand up again.

"Wait a second," he says, standing up as well. "Let me fix your collar." Before I know what he's doing, he unbuttons the top button of my shirt. "If you're going to spend time with Jasmine, you might as well not look like a dork."

When I get back to the mailroom, Jasmine hands me a piece of paper and says to me, "I made a list of the tasks you need to learn. We'll start after lunch. We're going to spend the afternoon going over things and tomorrow you'll do them on your own."

I walk to my desk and read the paper that Jasmine has given me.

12:30 p.m.	COPYING, COLLATING, BINDING
1:30 p.m.	WALK OVER TO FEDERAL COURTHOUSE TO FILE DOCUMENTS
2:30 p.m.	SCANNING
3:00 p.m.	MAIL SORTING
3:30 p.m.	FILING SYSTEM AND FILE RETRIEVAL
4:30 p.m.	LAST MAIL RUN (STAY AWAY FROM MARTHA. HER CONDITION WORSENS AS EVENING APPROACHES.)
5:00 p.m.	TIME TO HEAD FOR HOME (YOU MADE IT THROUGH THE FIRST DAY OF CAMP MINI-HELL. CONSIDER SERIOUSLY NOT SUBJECTING YOURSELF TO THIS AND STAY HOME TOMORROW.)

Aurora once told me that she knew I was different within the first few months after I was born, because as a baby, I never cried. She had no way of knowing if I was hungry or if my stomach hurt until I was old enough to point and talk. Even when I fell and it was obvious that I had hurt myself, I did not cry. When I didn't get my way, I would go off by myself and sulk or have a tantrum. But I never cried. Later, when I was eleven and Abba died, I didn't cry. When Joseph, my best friend at St Elizabeth's, died, I didn't cry. Maybe I don't feel what others feel. I have no way of knowing. But I do feel. It's just that what I feel does not elicit tears. What I feel when others cry is more like a dry, empty aloneness, like I'm the only person left in the world.

So it is very strange to feel my eyes well with tears as I read Jasmine's list.

Chapter 8

Every morning this week, after the first mail run, my task has been to go to all the copying and printing machines in the office and fill them up with paper, as well as leave packages of paper next to them. Moving around the office with a cart full of mail or paper for the copying and printing machines is my least favourite task. Inevitably someone will say something to me and I have to respond.

Small talk. I know all about small talk. I studied small talk at Paterson and have a number of set responses to small talk initiated by others, as well as a number of small talk questions for those times when, for whatever reason, I feel called upon to start the small talk. In Social Interaction class, we learned to formulate four or five questions from the day's events. By reading the paper or by searching in our computers, we memorized questions about the weather, about sports, about the latest happenings. Every morning this week, I have gone to a web page that reports on local events and have written down a few questions just in case. "What do you think of the Boston Red Sox losing to the New York

Yankees?" Questions like that.

Fortunately, I haven't had to use any of my prepared questions. When I come in the morning Jasmine is already here. She hands me my daily list and we each go about what we have to do in silence. I like it that way. I think Jasmine does as well because most of the work she does at her desk, she does with headphones on. But sometimes I wonder what Belinda was like and whether Jasmine would put her headphones on if Belinda were working here instead of me.

Opening up boxes and taking out packages of paper is something that I can do without too much concentration. Many of the jobs here at the law firm are like that, which is fine with me because then I can think about other things like I'm doing now. What I'm thinking about now is whether there is ever any "large talk" in the law firm. Sometimes I overhear the lawyers talking about their work. They talk about the content of letters they received or what someone said to them over the telephone or about what happened in a meeting. I hear a lot of "Then he said" or "Then she said" and this reporting of what other people have said is retold with a lot of emotion. This I think is the law firm's equivalent of large talk, since emotion is not something that accompanies small talk.

I wonder how I would define large talk. Most of my talks with Rabbi Heschel are large talk since they involve questions about God. The conversation that Aurora and I had after Arturo told me about the summer job at the law firm was large talk. All of my conversations with my friend Joseph at the hospital were large talk, even if they were about small things. The reason for that is that both of us knew that each word counted. The one thing I don't understand is why I never made a distinction between small talk and large talk at Paterson. I know it doesn't make sense, but for some reason all the talking that I did and heard at Paterson seemed like large talk.

"Excuse me."

Someone is speaking to me. I turn around and there is the secretary who sits in space number eighteen. I search for her name. Space eighteen. Beth. The lawyer she works for is Harvey Marcus. I stand there not knowing exactly what to say to her.

"Where is Jasmine?"

I like those kinds of questions. "She went to the post office."

"Shit!"

This is an unexpected response. Then I see a small stack of documents on the counter and I understand that she needs Jasmine to do something for her. I catch her looking at the big, white clock that hangs above my desk.

"I told her I was bringing her some documents that needed to be bound before eleven."

I know about binding documents because Jasmine pointed out the machine in the back that is used for the task, but Jasmine has not yet taught me how to use it. "She will be back by ten." I turn around to look at the clock. It is nine-thirty.

"Harvey needs these for a Board of Directors meeting that we're having here at eleven."

I look at the documents that she has placed on the counter. "There are only six documents there," I say.

"I need ten copies of each, and each one of them has to be tabbed and bound." She is not looking at me. She is writing on one of the request slips on the counter. She presses so hard on the slip as she writes that the slip tears. "Shit! Tell me this is not happening to me."

I don't think she is asking me to tell her this. I don't know what "tabbed" means and I don't know how to bind, but I can make copies, so I say, "I can make the copies. I can start."

She looks at me. "Aren't you supposed to be re . . . I mean, slow or something?"

How can I answer that? I know in this case what follows after she stopped: "retarded". So Beth somehow expected me to be retarded or slow or something, and I said something or offered to do something that deviated from that expectation. But where did she get the expectation that I was retarded? Who put it there in the first place?

"Hey, are you there?" She is snapping her fingers at me. "I guess if you work here it means you can do the work, right?"

I don't respond. But I don't think that the conclusion to her assumption is necessarily correct.

"You see these yellow stickies? These are the places where the tabs are going to go. You need to take them off the documents when you make the copies, but then you need to put them back on so you can place the tabs."

"What are tabs?"

She looks at the clock on the wall. There is a grimace on her face. I have seen kids at Paterson make that grimace seconds before they break down in tears of anger and frustration. "I really don't have time for this. Here's the request slip. I got it here in time for it to get done on time. If the firm can't hire decent support . . . Harvey is going to have to deal with it. I did my part." All the time she says this, her hands are in the air moving about.

I wonder how it is possible for her to feel what she appears to be feeling over a simple task like copying and binding.

At ten Jasmine arrives. She is carrying a plastic bag, which she places on her desk. She comes over and looks at the six stacks of documents that I have made: ten copies of each of the documents that Beth left with me. I can tell she is wondering what I am doing.

"Beth," I say. I hand her the torn request slip. "They need to be tabbed and bound. There is a meeting at eleven. She was very upset that you were not here."

Jasmine nods. Unlike many of the other people who work at the firm, Jasmine is always calm. Even when she is angry, like at Juliet for example, you can tell that the anger does not affect her. The reason I can tell is that her breathing never alters. A person who is truly angry has physical reactions that last for a while, even after the event that caused the anger is gone. "You started with the copying," she says. She picks up the top copy from the first set. "There is no table of contents. How do we know where to put the tabs?"

I walk to my desk and show her the six documents that Beth brought with the yellow stickies. Jasmine picks one up. "This is the way she brought them?"

"Yes. Like that, with yellow stickies to mark where she wanted the tabs."

"So you took the stickies out to make the copies and then you stuck the stickies back on Beth's original. You stuck them on the same page they were before, right?"

I pick up a piece of paper from my desk and show her my list of page numbers where I found the stickies. I don't have to tell her what they are. I force myself to look carefully at Jasmine's face and see the smallest of smiles beginning to form. "OK, let's get this done so Beth doesn't have a nervous breakdown." She says this as if Beth has had nervous breakdowns before.

We work in silence except for when I read out a page number. Jasmine sticks the tabs in all the copies and then she brings out the binding machine. She shows me how to place the document between two plastic sheets before it is placed in an electric press that makes the holes and binds it. After Jasmine does a few, she stands to one side and waves for me to do it.

I look at the clock. It is now ten-thirty and Beth needs these at eleven. I know what to do, but I don't think I can go fast enough to finish fifty six documents in half an hour. "I am not sure," I say.

"About what?"

"Marcelo is not as fast as Jasmine."

"Marcelo is wasting time talking about it while he could be doing it."

Then she goes to her desk and puts her headphones on.

The first document I try comes out wrong. I do not align the plastic covers correctly. I decide to put that one aside and move on to the next one rather than ask Jasmine how to fix it. The second one comes out right, but it takes me three minutes to bind. There are only a few manual movements required, but somehow the knowledge that time is passing is slowing me down. Then I think that perhaps this is the assignment that will send me to Oak Ridge. Wasn't that the deal? "Each assignment will come with its own rules," Arturo said. "Your success will depend on your ability to fulfil those rules."

I stop. I take a deep breath. I close my eyes. I think, of all things, of shovelling manure at the Paterson stable. I think of the slow movement of the shovel, of filling the wheelbarrow and wheeling it outside where later a truck will come to haul it away. Harry used to say to me that I shovelled manure as if each shovelful was gold, so carefully did I do it. This is the way I need to work now, slow and steady but continuously. What else can I do? Can Marcelo be someone other than Marcelo? When I open my eyes, I see that Jasmine has turned around and is looking at me. I look in her face for worry or for anger that I am not working fast enough, but instead I see her look at me in silence without any reproach.

At ten fifty-five I see Beth at the counter. She looks first at the documents I have bound, then at me, and then at Jasmine.

"I don't believe this," I hear her say.

Jasmine removes her headphones but doesn't stand up. "Did you say something?" she asks Beth.

"Didn't I put on the request slip that Harvey had a meeting at eleven and we needed the documents bound by then? He's about halfway done and people are already here. Harvey needs these to hand out as soon as the meeting starts."

"Harvey should have given us the documents with more leeway."

"I brought them in at nine-thirty. An hour and a half ago. I don't care, I have a copy of the request slip to prove it."

"You're going to have a heart attack. Look at you." Jasmine is seeing what I see. Beth's face is so red it is beginning to turn purple. Her hands are grasping the counter so hard that her knuckles are a pale white. She is starting to shake.

"Why aren't you helping him? If you helped him this would be done by now." Now Beth is yelling at Jasmine. I go back to the binding. "What is it with you? Do you want him to fail so you can get Belinda? Is that it?"

I stop to look at Jasmine. I wonder if that is the reason she didn't help me. Jasmine slowly gets up from her chair and stands in front of Beth.

"Everyone in the firm is going to hear you yell. Is it really worth it? Harvey's going to get his documents in half an hour. That's the same time he would have gotten them if I was working on them. And it's a one-person job. I can't help him." Jasmine walks to the table where I am working and picks up one of the documents that I recently bound. "Look. The binding is perfect. They wouldn't have come out this good if I had worked on them. I would have rushed the job and there would have been mistakes."

There's a moment when Beth looks as if she suddenly discovered that an audience of people witnessed her outburst.

"You'll have to deal with Harvey," she says. "I did my part. I brought them in on time. I have a copy of the request slip." She walks away.

Now Jasmine looks at me and shakes her head. I don't know what that gesture means. Maybe it means that I shouldn't believe anything Beth says.

"Thank you," I say.

"For what?"

"You did not tell the truth to Beth. The documents would be bound by now if Jasmine had done them. It took Jasmine thirty seconds to bind a document. The fastest Marcelo could do it without making mistakes was two minutes and twenty-five seconds."

"You timed it?"

"I had to in order to determine my optimum speed."

"Your optimum speed."

"At Paterson we call it optimum speed. It means finding the best speed to accomplish a task given who you are. Everyone has one."

"Unbelievable," she says. Then, "You better turn on your optimum speed to finish those documents before Harvey comes in here huffing and puffing. You think that Beth was high drama, wait till you see Harvey act out."

"The documents will not be done in time for the meeting."

"But you knew that already. All you had to do was multiply your optimum speed by the number of documents you still had to do."

"Yes."

"But you didn't speed up."

"No."

"How come?"

"It was not possible to meet the deadline without making mistakes."

She walks over to me. "Everyone here thinks their deadlines are important. Some are and some aren't. Nothing will happen, the world will not end, there won't be any lives or, heaven forbid, money lost if the documents are not there at eleven. The worst that can happen is that Harvey will have to say that the documents will be there in a few minutes. But he won't say that because the documents will not be discussed or even opened during the meeting. Harvey wants the people at the meeting to take documents when they leave. So the eleven o'clock deadline is all about Harvey looking good. He wants the reports on a table when people come in because he thinks that will impress them."

"It is not important to impress people."

"It is extremely important!" She shakes her hands as if with fear, but I can tell the shaking is not real. "The meeting breaks up for lunch at noon. We can take the documents then and Harvey will still look good. I'll go see if I can keep him from having a cow."

"It was Marcelo's fault."

She looks down. I thought I was the only one afraid to look people in the eye, but she seems afraid as well. "Listen, there are some real deadlines where people will, maybe not lose their lives, but they'll lose money if they're not met. It takes a while to recognize them."

"Even if I recognize the deadlines, Marcelo can only work so fast."

"What we'll have to do is divide up the work. You'll work on the jobs that are not time-sensitive and I'll do the others."

"I am very good at concentrating when I can work at optimum speed." I try to say this in a way that is funny, but Jasmine does not smile. Then it occurs to me to say, "Belinda would have met the eleven o'clock deadline." I mean to phrase this as a question, but it ends up being a statement.

"Yes."

Then I see her walk out of the mailroom. She is going to stop Harvey from having a cow.

Chapter 9

I make more and more progress each day I work at the law firm —
progress as defined by Arturo, as in being able to successfully
complete the assignments given to me. I can walk the streets if I
stick to a memorized route and follow a computer-printed map
and if I don't focus on the words and sounds of the city. Words
are everywhere. Words, it seems, cover everything. There are
words on buildings and on windows, on cars and on people's
clothes. There are people sitting on the sidewalk holding signs
like sober and homeless. If I stop to take in every word I see, I
will never get to the courthouse where I go almost every day to
file documents.

It is the same with sounds. It seems that most of my brain needs
to be turned off in order to function effectively. Hundreds of
people have no problem assimilating different sounds. They walk
and talk on cell phones. They dodge cars while having conversations. At first I was surprised at the number of people who walked
the streets talking to themselves. Jasmine had to point out to

me the tiny microphones dangling in front of their faces.

Every day during my lunch hour, I walk to a small park in front of the law firm building. I sit there eating my tuna sandwich, a granola bar and an apple. I observe. Lately I've been looking at women, trying not to stare at them, seeing if I can determine whether they are attractive. I suppose that this is the result of the conversations that Wendell and I have been having. Actually, they are not conversations. Wendell lectures and I listen. Almost every day Wendell shares with me his vast learning on the ways of womanhood.

I am walking to the mailroom after lunch when Wendell grabs me.

"Just for a few minutes, Marcelo, please. I'm going crazy here reading this crap."

"Jasmine is waiting for me to go to the Registry of Deeds," I say.

"Think of it as your daily good deed," he pleads.

I sit down.

"Do you know what I spend my time doing?"

"Reading crap."

"Right. I have to go through thirty-five boxes of crap, looking for memos and letters and reports, some of them in Spanish."

"Do you speak Spanish?"

"Sort of. I've taken three years of it in school."

"I used to pray in Spanish with my grandmother when she lived with us."

"No kidding. Speaking of praying, I'm praying that Jasmine will go out with me. I can't understand why she won't. Does she ever talk about me?"

I think about his question but decide not to answer it. Instead, I ask him a question of my own. This is something I have learned from Rabbi Heschel. When you don't want or know how to answer a question, ask a question. I ask, "Is Jasmine beautiful, in your opinion?"

Wendell's face brightens. "You have come to the right person with that question, my friend."

I wonder whether anyone considered normal has ever called me "friend" before. Even Joseph never called me "friend", although we were. It makes me happy to be called "friend" by Wendell.

"Yes, you can say with absolute certainty that Jasmine is beautiful."

"Therefore," I say, "if a woman looks like Jasmine then she too is beautiful."

"It doesn't always work that way, Mr Spock." Wendell has taken to calling me that whenever I say something that is logical in nature. "Jasmine has luscious black hair, but a blonde or a red-head or even a totally bald woman can be just as beautiful. Sometimes thin is nice, and sometimes a man craves a little more substance. But yes, as an initial point of departure, if a woman looks like Jasmine, you can safely assume that she's beautiful. But don't limit yourself. Be broad-minded, so to speak, in your appreciation of beauty." Wendell laughs to himself.

"Who else is beautiful?" I ask.

"Here at the law firm just about every secretary is hot in some form or another. It's the only redeeming quality about this place. Except maybe for old Margie. But even then you can tell that she was beautiful, oh, eighty or so years ago."

Women are Wendell's special interest, I say to myself.

"You have three kinds of feminine beauty," Wendell says. He sounds like Mr Rafferty, my social studies teacher at Paterson. "Earthy, Elegant, and Elemental."

"Can you give me examples, please?" I immediately regret asking this question. I am already ten minutes behind schedule and Jasmine is waiting for me to go to the Registry of Deeds.

"Certainly. Let's take three beautiful women here at the firm. Each of them represents one of the three categories of beauty I just mentioned. First you have Earthy Martha. Earthy women are well endowed in a motherly, mammary kind of way. They are sexy in an abundant, easy, natural manner and give freely of themselves. Sex is part of their nurturing nature. The attraction of man for the Earthy Woman originates from his childlike desire to be possessed, thereby eliciting in the woman the desire to protect.

"As for the second category, Juliet there across the hall is a representative of the Elegant Woman. Elegants are usually on the thin side. Their demeanour is cold and unapproachable. They are extremely conscious of their effect on the male species and wield that knowledge to their advantage. They call forth man's competitive drive. The attraction here is based on man's need to conquer and tame, but also to hoard and deprive others of the prize. Elegants are trophies, showy possessions. Just being seen with them generates envy in others. Hence my father hired Juliet."

Wendell is suddenly quiet.

"Jasmine must be an example of Elemental beauty," I say.

Wendell snaps out of his reverie and slaps me on the knee.

"You got it. You're learning fast, my boy." Wendell sits back in his chair. His tone is different than when describing the previous categories of beauty. He sounds solemn and serious. "Elemental beauty is less dependent on physical attributes than the other kinds of beauty. Theoretically, I suppose, it is possible for a woman to be an Elemental Woman and not be physically attractive. Have you heard of the Periodic Table of Elements?"

"Yes."

"What is it?"

"It is a chart of all the elements of matter arranged according to the number of atoms in each element."

"Right on. Why did I know you would know the answer to that question?"

"I learned that at Paterson."

"Good school, that Paterson. OK, let me continue, because I'm on a roll here. All that exists in the universe is made up of a combination of the elements on the Table of Elements."

I disagree with Wendell. The elements in the Periodic Table of Elements deal with the most obvious parts of reality, the kind we can see and touch. But there are energy forces within the atom that also make up reality, and beyond that there are forces we are not yet attuned to. I decide not to interrupt because if Wendell asked me to explain, it could lead to speaking about religious matters.

"What has all this to do with beauty, I can tell you are asking yourself."

Actually, I am asking myself if conversations with friends always feel like this — two minds bound together by their focus on the same subject.

Wendell continues. "The attractive force behind Elemental

beauty is that it holds out the promise of totality, of full, complete, and never-ending satisfaction. The woman who has this kind of beauty is like the periodic table — she has all the elements that make up womanhood, but in an understated kind of way, like matter itself."

"Jasmine is like that?" This time I manage to phrase this as a question.

"She's solid. Not only is her body solid, as in firm, as in she lifts weights every day, she's also unshakable, fearless, permanent, basic, organic. If you were stranded in the desert with her, she'd find the water."

"Jasmine lifts weights," I say mostly to myself. The thought makes me happy.

"But what's so special about this rare type of woman is that despite her strength, she remains in many ways eminently lustable. Oh, my God. It's a hard-on that comes from the depths of the soul. That's why Jasmine is Elemental."

"I see." Maybe it is the strange way Wendell mentions God, but I suddenly feel uncomfortable. I stand up. Wendell stands up also but continues talking. The lesson is not over.

"The only problem with Elemental women is that they can just as soon be loved or not be loved. It's not like they're cold and calculating, like the Elegants. They just have their own road to travel. You can climb aboard and sail with them, but they'll keep heading for their destination with you or without you. Speaking of the devil."

Jasmine stands in the doorway. She looks at me. "If I don't make it to the Registry of Deeds before they close, Riese will have a cow."

"My fault," says Wendell. "We were discussing the meaning and end-all of life."

"He's not going to do your work," Jasmine tells him.

"Easy, tiger. He's all yours."

"Goodbye, my friend," I say to Wendell.

But Wendell does not hear me. "Have you thought about what I asked you?" he is saying to Jasmine.

"What part of no don't you understand?" Jasmine is already walking away as she says this.

On the way to the Registry of Deeds, Jasmine says to me, "Watch out for Wendell. He's not someone you can trust."

"What do you mean by that?" I ask. "What has he done to make you say that?"

"It's a feeling I have," she says. "He's all appearance, just like his father, and inside just as mean. I don't trust him."

I think back to a couple of weeks ago, when Arturo asked me if I trusted him and I said yes. I do. I trust Arturo. I trust him to keep his promise and allow me to decide where I want to go to school next year. But my trust in him is more knowledge than feeling. It is based on the experience that he has always done what he said he was going to do. I never thought of trust as a feeling, but now I hear Jasmine use the word as if it were a feeling. "What does lack of trust feel like?" I ask.

"It's a creepy feeling inside."

"Creepy."

"Yeah, creepy. Wendell gives me the heebie-jeebies."

"Heebie-jeebies. Can you be more specific?"

"Have you ever been greedy for something?"

"Yes."

"About what?"

"CDs. I never seem to have enough of them. I see a CD and I want to buy it even though I don't need it, even when I have one at home with the same music."

"Right. Well, when I'm around Wendell, I feel like that CD would if it could feel."

Chapter 10

This morning as I was waiting for Aurora to drive me to the train station, Arturo asked me to pack my sneakers, a T-shirt and a pair of shorts. Now I know why. We are on our way to the physical fitness club. I had no idea that Arturo "works out", as he calls it, almost every day. His preference is to work out in the morning when he gets to work. Arturo likes to drive in by himself, even though I am awake by the time he leaves, and then Aurora takes me to the train station on her way to work. Arturo thinks I learn more about the real world from commuting on the train every day. Perhaps he thinks that I interact more with people if I take the train. But usually I make the trip in silence, trying to recollect the IM, which is getting harder and harder to access.

"How are you doing at work?" Arturo asks me.

"Hunky-dory," I respond. I try to say it the way Jasmine says it, but I don't quite get the right intonation.

"Hunky-dory?" Arturo asks.

I don't know why it is harder to reach the place of the IM. It is impossible to listen to the IM at work even on the rare occasions when I sit at my desk without anything to do. It is like the IM is afraid to be heard for fear that it will be ridiculed.

"I never heard you say that before," he says.

"Jasmine says it," I say.

"I see."

Now Arturo walks in silence. I prefer that. Around this time I usually go out to the small park in front of the building and have lunch. This trip to the physical fitness club interferes with the one hour during the day when I can direct my thoughts wherever I want without any interruptions. I was annoyed when he told me what we were doing for lunch, but I did not say anything. I know by now that I have a tendency to get annoyed about being asked to do something unexpected. I have worked very hard over the years to reduce the level and duration of the annoyance. I have been working on that for as long as I can remember.

"You and Jasmine must be getting along then."

That sounds to me like a conclusion and not a question so I don't respond. We stand at the corner waiting for the miniature person on the walk sign to turn white so we can cross. Part of the momentary annoyance at working out is that I don't need to work out. I lift the dumb-bells every morning, as I have ever since my uncle Hector taught me how to do it.

"I asked you if you and Jasmine were getting along."

So it was a question then. I hesitate because Arturo is crossing the street even though the person in the sign is still red. I remain at the kerb but Arturo waves for me to follow. I look to see if there are any cars coming as I start across. A car turns from a side street and comes towards us but Arturo does not speed up. I automatically grab his arm. That is something a small child would do, I think.

"She hasn't complained about you," he says in the middle of the street.

We reach the other kerb. Arturo seems to be speaking to himself. It takes me a few seconds to realize who "she" is.

"So everything is OK with Jasmine?"

"Yes, Father."

Did that sound rude? The intonation of my words is mostly the same regardless of what I say, although lately I have been able to raise my voice at the end of a sentence when I am asking a question. Most people are not able to tell that I am nervous speaking to them or that I am anxious about what I will next say to them. Yet that is the case with almost everyone except for Aurora, Yolanda, Rabbi Heschel, the kids at the hospital and the kids at Paterson. And now that I think of it, it is true with Jasmine as well. That is very strange. I had not thought about it before. I wonder how that happened without my noticing.

It is true that Arturo sometimes makes me nervous. He is constantly asking questions, challenging me to quicken my ability to respond. I am nervous now, walking with him to the fitness club. I have never been to a fitness club. I wonder if it will be like the exercise room at Paterson.

He opens the door to the fitness club and shows a young woman behind the desk his card.

"Good morning, Mr Sandoval."

"Hello, Jane."

Everyone knows my father and my father knows everyone. No one calls him Arturo, except maybe Holmesy. Holmesy. I must have picked that up from Jasmine too.

We are walking by the exercise bicycles and a man pedalling on one waves at Arturo. He takes a towel and wipes the sweat from his face. Arturo stops. "I need to talk to you," the man says to Arturo. He lowers his voice like he doesn't want anyone else to hear him.

"I thought you would," responds Arturo.

The man laughs a kind of muffled laugh.

"Can I call you this afternoon?" Arturo asks.

"No can do," says the man. I notice that the flesh on his stomach and thighs is loose and his arms are full of brown spots. "I'm flying to LA at three. Why don't you pull a bike up next to me now and we'll grab a few minutes?"

"I am with my son," Arturo says. He turns to me. "Marcelo, this is Mr Gustafson."

"How do you do?" I say. His large hands remain on the handlebars so I don't extend my hand.

"How do you do?" he says, imitating me. Then he laughs and says to Arturo, "Good-looking boy, eh? Like father, like son. I got another twenty painful minutes on this damn thing. I already talked to Holmes, he's OK with the process. I need you to be on board. Twenty minutes, that's all."

I am looking at the row of televisions in front of the bicycles. There must be a dozen or so sets on different channels. Then I hear Arturo say: "OK, I'll be right out."

The locker room is full of men walking around without any clothes on, so I keep my eyes down. This is something that is not hard for me, since that's where I keep them as a matter of course. I don't understand how anyone can walk without clothes in front of others without feeling it to be a violation of their privacy. The only time I've taken my clothes off in front of someone else is at the doctor's office. I raise my eyes enough to look for the showers. I am relieved to see that they have plastic curtains that can be closed.

Arturo has a locker with a combination lock. He points to a locker next to his and tells me that I can put my clothes in there, except for my wallet, which he will put in his locker. At Paterson there are no lockers in the boys' changing room. There are hooks on the wall and there's no need to be concerned about your wallet.

I find a stool and begin to change. Arturo has his shorts and T-shirt on when I have barely taken my shoes off and am unbuttoning my shirt. There is a white speaker right above us blasting popular music. I am trying to understand what the woman is singing, but it is impossible. I catch a word here and there. Her voice is drowned out by the beat of drums.

"I'll be at the bicycles," Arturo tells me as I slip my T-shirt on. "Come join me after you change."

"I like to lift the weights," I say.

"I know, but I thought we could spend some time together. After I finish talking to Mr Gustafson, we can exercise and chat about how things are going."

"Chat."

"Yes, chat. You know, as in father and son spending a little time together talking about nothing in particular. I'll be waiting for you, OK?"

"OK."

When Arturo is gone, I take my trousers off and fold them

carefully. Then I put on the blue shorts with the Yale insignia that Yolanda gave me. I realize that I did not bring any white socks, so I leave my blue socks on and put my sneakers on. I am thinking about how difficult it is for me to communicate with my father. He is the one person in the world I would most like to "chat" with. We could sit in our backyard and talk small talk or large talk. It wouldn't matter. But this requires an effort, or rather, a lack of effort that seems beyond both our powers. Now we will "chat", and I think that this is good, but it will not be easy for me. I know what he is really interested in when he asks "How are you doing?" He wants me to confirm that he was right, that I can function in the real world. I wish he wouldn't be so concerned about this. I wish he and I could chat about some of the things I chat about with Rabbi Heschel. I wish he would ask me about Buddha or Jesus or Jacob, the kind of things that fill my head.

I leave the locker room and find a bicycle next to my father. I start to pedal and a series of lights appears on the bike's control panel. Arturo is talking to the puffy man who greeted us when we came in. There is a set of headphones on the handlebars. I put them on, thinking that they might have a different kind of music, but the headphones transmit the sound from the television that is in front of us. I take them off. I want to block out the strident music coming from a hundred amplifiers but instead I am drawn to my father's voice. He and the other man have to speak loud enough to hear each other, and the volume of their voices is loud enough for me to hear as well.

"Look." Mr Gustafson is speaking and wiping his forehead with a white towel at the same time. "It's a win-win. We get our clients to settle for the sum we agreed and we give ourselves a little bonus. They would have paid the extra cash for legal fees anyway if we kept fighting."

I don't know why I feel that Arturo is looking at me. I turn and I see him questioning me with his eyes. Suspicion. That is what my father's face most closely resembles. I look away and close my eyes.

After a while I hear Arturo say, "It will take a lot of work to convince the Vidromek people to settle. I mean, they hate your law firm. They think you rounded up five people hurt by their windshield and pretty much told them they would be rich if they sued. Vidromek wants me to destroy you, really. They want me to drive you into the ground with discovery and delays until you regret ever taking this on."

"Don't get too righteous on me. We didn't have to try too hard to 'round people up', as you put it. My five clients came out of the woodwork pretty easily."

"You're not the only one suing us, you know. There's a bunch of ambulance chasers out there waiting in line for some payoff. We've said no to all of them, even to the ones that we could have paid a few thousand bucks to go away. Vidromek does not want to settle with anyone."

It occurs to me that I have never heard my father talk about his business. Here I am working at the law firm and I'm not sure what it is he does.

"Yeah, but that's the point. Those other saps are being represented by garbage. I'm the only one that Vidromek has to worry about. You get rid of me and my five clients and you're home free. You can squash the other ones."

Arturo lowers his voice. "Listen, this is very risky on many counts, as you know. In order for this to work I will have to convince my client that you will be the only exception and that we can do this without anyone else finding out. Then we have to do the paperwork so that it looks good. The risks outweigh the 'little bonus', as you put it."

"So what are you saying?"

"I don't want to talk about it here. Talk numbers with Stephen. Whatever he agrees to is OK with me."

"Hell, Art, don't make me talk to Holmes. He's as greedy a little pig as there ever was."

"That's why I let him handle little bonuses."

"Ha, ha. All right. I'm out of this torture chamber, and I'm not just talking about the machines."

I hear him get off the bike and walk away. My eyes have been closed throughout the conversation. I have been trying to maintain a steady rhythm with my legs but have not been successful. The conversation between Arturo and Mr Gustafson absorbed me. It reminded me of when I was learning sign language. The kids at Paterson would move their hands so quickly that I would only pick up a word here and there. But there was something else about this conversation. It was like hearing something I wasn't supposed to hear or seeing a side of my father I was not meant to see.

"Are you awake or did you fall asleep?" I realize Arturo is speaking to me.

I open my eyes. "Awake."

"Did you hear what Mr Gustafson and I were talking about?"

For a second I am tempted to say that I did not. Maybe it was the way he asked the question, like he was hoping that I hadn't.

But I say, "Yes, I heard it."

"And what did you think?"

"Think."

"About the conversation. What impression did you get? What did you gather?"

"I did not understand all the terms. What does it mean to settle a case?"

"It means that we agree to pay the people that are suing us without going to court. We make an agreement with them. We pay them and they stop suing us."

"There were words like 'hate' and 'destroy' used, but there was no anger between Mr Gustafson and you."

"That's right. That's the way it is. It's just business. Nothing personal."

"Vidromek wants you to put Mr Gustafson's law firm out of business. Vidromek hates Mr Gustafson."

"Not necessarily Mr Gustafson."

"'Hate' is a very strong term. It is a desire to hurt someone physically or emotionally by word or deed. Did you mean to use that word?"

"Yes. I guess that's right. They don't want to hurt him physically but they would like to hurt him financially and . . . maybe emotionally as well."

"They want Arturo to hurt Mr Gustafson financially and maybe emotionally."

"I am Vidromek's lawyer, so, yes, I'm the one."

"Arturo can do that? You can do that?"

"Yes. Sometimes it is necessary. You stopped pedalling. Is something wrong?"

Not too far from the bicycles that Arturo and I are on, there is a water cooler. "Excuse me," I say. I get down from the bicycle, walk over to the water cooler and pour water into a paper cup that is shaped like a cone. I can feel my heart beat in my chest and my face is hot, as if it were sunburned. It is not from the bike, I know. I don't know what has come over me. It is a strange feeling. Like the time when I touched my chest and discovered I had lost the cross Abba gave me just before she died.

"Are you all right?" I feel Arturo's hand on my shoulder and without thinking I shake myself away from it.

"Yes. I would like to lift the weights now."

I can feel Arturo looking at me, wondering what I'm thinking. I stop and say to him: "You asked some questions of me before that I did not answer."

"Which ones?"

"You asked how I was doing at work. Then you asked how I was getting along with Jasmine."

"That's right. Good memory."

"I would like to answer your questions now. I am doing OK at the law firm. I can do the tasks that are given to me, although some of them I do slower than what is expected. I still do not like working there. With regards to your second question: Jasmine and I get along in the sense that we do not disagree with each other and she is kind to me and does not reproach me for the mistakes I make. I am pretty sure that she would still rather have Belinda. It was not right to give her Marcelo when she had been promised Belinda."

"Well, that's a pretty good summary of how things stand. Don't worry about Belinda. And there is no need for you and Jasmine to be friends or even to talk to each other about anything other than the task at hand. You should make friends with Wendell. He can be helpful to you. Go ahead. Go lift your weights. I'll come get you when it's time to go back."

I move on to the section where the free weights are located. I am not sure if my father and I had the kind of chat he was hoping for, as in father and son spending a little time together talking about nothing in particular.

Chapter 11

Probably the most stressful assignment at the law firm is the filing of documents at the courthouse. The assignment is stressful because the lawyers for some reason are not able to have the documents ready until the last possible second. It takes Jasmine at least thirty minutes going full speed to get the documents over to the courthouse and get the clerk to stamp them with the date and time. It takes me double that time. That is why Jasmine handles the real, real rushes or comes with me, like today.

Once you get to the courthouse you need to go to the Clerk's Office, where there are always people in line. It seems that waiting until the last minute is a rule universal to all law firms. Jasmine and I are standing behind three other persons looking at the black hands of a white clock tick closer to five. We came together today because Juliet did not get us the documents until 4:35.

"She did it on purpose, I'm sure of it," Jasmine says. She is talking about Juliet.

"Why would she do that?" I ask. "If the documents are not

filed on time, it is Stephen Holmes and his client that are harmed."

"To get us in trouble. I wouldn't put it past her. 'I gave it to them with plenty of time to get there.'" Jasmine imitates Juliet's high-pitched voice.

I am not worried about filing the papers before five. I have been to the Clerk's Office with Jasmine before and I have seen the assistant clerk, whose name is Al, talk to Jasmine. He is always very friendly to her. The last time we were here, he accepted her documents at 5:03 but somehow managed to have the time stamped on the documents read 4:59. Now I can see him looking up at Jasmine and smiling as he stamps other people's documents.

"Is Al your boyfriend?" I ask.

Jasmine looks at me as if I had just appeared out of nowhere. "Noooo," she says.

"He likes you," I say.

"Why do you say that?"

"He is always looking at you and smiling at you, and he is nice to you in a way that he is not to other people. When I came by myself last Wednesday, I tried on purpose to see whether he was as nice to me as he is to you and he wasn't. He did not smile at me. Not even once."

We move up the line. "Really? Mmm. I always thought he was nice to everyone."

"Does Jasmine know that she is beautiful?"

"'Does Jasmine know that she is beautiful?' What kind of question is that? How is a person supposed to answer that?"

"It is just a question."

We are going to make it with plenty of time. Al is working incredibly fast. He has just time-stamped fifteen documents from the woman ahead of us in about thirty seconds. He is now nodding and smiling at Jasmine. Jasmine doesn't seem to be paying any attention to him. Maybe she is thinking about my question.

"How am I supposed to answer that? It's kind of a stupid question," she says, but she doesn't seem to be mad.

We are up next and I decide to watch Al as carefully as possible. I have this way of seeing where my head is down but my eyes move up or sideways. People think I'm not paying attention to them but I am. It is something that I need to work on because it confuses people, but sometimes it is helpful. It allows me to observe undetected.

Al seems nervous in Jasmine's presence. He holds a document with both hands while he asks how her day has been going and I see the document tremble.

"I'm sorry to get here at the last minute," Jasmine tells him. "You know how it is."

"Oh, no problem, my pleasure. No problem at all." I can actually see Al's cheeks deepen in colour from shades of pink to light red. He seems to be unable to lift his eyes and look at Jasmine directly, as if Jasmine were the sun. Then I turn my gaze towards Jasmine. She is exactly the same with Al as she is with every other person that she talks to. She rarely smiles at anyone. Her concentration is like a laser on whatever it is she is doing. She is courteous with people, says "please" and "thank you" when the occasion requires it, jokes with people or snaps at them when provoked, but she always seems to be reacting rather than initiating and her reaction is extended only to the point that it is necessary and no further. It is as if the sun did not want to shine too much.

Outside, once we are down the steps of the courthouse, she says, "If we hurry, you can still catch your train."

"I am driving home with Arturo today." It is time again for a periodic assessment of Marcelo's progress.

"Your father works late." I notice that Jasmine is not walking at her usual fast pace.

"I brought a book to read."

Jasmine nods. We walk side by side without talking. It occurs to me that at this very moment Jasmine is thinking. What is she thinking about? Does she see her thoughts go by on a screen the way I see mine?

"What are you reading?"

Her question startles me. I was expecting our trip back to the law firm to be in silence as it usually is. But also, it is not a question that I thought Jasmine would ever ask me. "It is a book that Rabbi Heschel lent to me. It is called *God in Search of Man*. It is written by a man named Abraham Joshua Heschel, but Rabbi Heschel is not related to him."

"Who's Rabbi Heschel? I thought you were Catholic. I've seen you pray the Rosary at your desk . . . when you thought no one was looking."

"Oh," I say. I feel a sensation of heat travel through my body. It is as if I have been caught doing something bad. How strange that I now feel this way about something I always thought was good.

"Don't worry, I won't tell your father," she says, smiling. She must have seen a look of worry on my face.

I nod. I am grateful that she saw me say the Rosary and did not say anything to me at the time. "My family goes to Catholic church. Not all the family, Aurora does not come with us. She is religious in her own way. She just doesn't go to church. Ever since Marcelo was a child he has liked to read about religions. Rabbi Heschel works with Aurora at St Elizabeth's. I go to see her every couple of weeks. We talk about the religious texts I read. Sometimes we concentrate on particular texts and sometimes we jump around. Now we are reading the Psalms."

"My mother loved the Psalms. She had many of them memorized," she says.

"I memorize many of them myself," I say. It is great to talk about my special interest. I warn myself not to monopolize the conversation, like I tend to do when talking about what I love the most, but to ask questions as well. I wonder if Jasmine is religious, but then I think of something else I want to ask her. "You used the past tense when you talked about your mother. You said your mother *loved* the Psalms."

"She died four years ago." Jasmine is looking at a red stoplight. When people tell you that a relative of theirs has died, you are supposed to say that you are sorry. I am about to say that when Jasmine says, "You are doing better in the mailroom."

She is changing the subject, but sometimes people need to do that, to avoid memories that are painful. I follow along with her. "Is Marcelo better than Belinda?"

"No." Jasmine's response is very quick, quicker than I expected. Then she adds, "But Marcelo's work is OK." I can see a smile trying to form on her lips, but then it disappears. "Are you liking it better? Working at the law firm, I mean?"

"No." It surprises me that my "no" is as quick as Jasmine's.

Then I think of asking, "Does Jasmine like working at the law firm?"

"Ehhh." Again her response is immediate.

"What does 'ehhh' mean?" I wrinkle my nose when I say this, the same way she did.

"It means it's OK. It means it's a job. All things considered, it's not so bad. There are worse jobs. When I started working there a couple of years ago, I was the assistant to this older woman, Rose, who had been doing the job since your father founded the firm. Then about a year after I started working there, Rose retired to be with her husband. I applied for her job. I had seen Rose do her job and I knew I could do it, but a lot of people in the firm didn't think an eighteen-year-old was old enough to handle the responsibility of paying bills on time, sending out invoices for legal work, keeping track of supplies, all those things we do. I convinced your father to let me try and he gave me a chance."

"You did not disappoint him."

"There have been moments. It was hard with Ron. He was only there six months but it was difficult. He was older than me, and it was difficult to be a boss and earn someone's respect."

Jasmine and I walk in silence for a full block. I think of the words that are written on the wall in front of my desk.

"Ron didn't like to work at the firm."

"No." I see Jasmine look at me as if she's trying to make a decision. When she speaks, she speaks in a way I've never heard her speak before. Tentative. That's what I think of when I hear her speak. "There's a park nearby that I like to go to. Do you want to go? I want to show you something. You'll be back in time to meet up with your father, but you probably won't have time to read your book. Is that all right?"

"OK." It is not scary at all to walk the city streets with Jasmine, and I think that choosing to walk with Jasmine, seeing the sights of the city, hearing its sounds, smelling its smells, is something that Abraham Joshua Heschel himself would do. I want to hold on to her arm so that I can walk and talk more comfortably, but I do not know the rules regarding touching someone like Jasmine. What is Jasmine anyway? Is she a friend or my boss? Am I to her what Ron was to her? Only there is no need for her to earn my respect.

"The park I want to show you is a few blocks from here."

We are walking on the sidewalks next to streets clogged with cars. The sidewalks themselves are difficult to walk because of the number of people rushing to catch trains and buses, I suppose, or just to get away from their jobs as fast as they can. But then, as we move from the centre of town, there is more room and I can walk next to Jasmine without having to dodge rushing people. I decide to tell her what has been stuck in a corner of my mind since we walked into the courthouse. "It was not a stupid question."

"What?"

"Marcelo was truly interested in knowing whether Jasmine knew she was beautiful."

"It *is* so a stupid question. Why do you ask that?"

"Men find Jasmine beautiful."

"What men?"

"Wendell."

"Be still my beating heart!" She places her hand over her chest and palpitates it like a heart.

"That is called sarcasm," I say. There is no need to be proud of myself for recognizing it, but I am.

"If you're asking all this because of Wendell, forget it. Wendell has a few marbles missing when it comes to women."

I like that expression very much, even though I disagree. If anything, Wendell has more marbles than he needs when it comes to women. I say to Jasmine, "Other men look at Jasmine. Al, all the lawyers at the law firm. They look at you the way one looks at the stars at night."

"And you're a poet now?" Jasmine is laughing. Her laugh is new to me. It is a little girl's laugh. I slow down. It is hard for me to talk and walk at the same time. Jasmine slows down as well. "Is that what makes a woman beautiful? That men look at her?"

"I do not know." I am suddenly at a loss as to what to say. Then something occurs to me. Assuming that Jasmine is indeed beautiful, it must be hard for her to go about always being noticed. To have people stare at her.

"You do not know?"

I sense that maybe Jasmine is making fun of me, but she begins to walk faster and I am unable to see the expression on her face. I catch up to her and try to keep up as best I can. I want to say something in response to her question. We are talking about a mystery that maybe she can help me unravel, since by all accounts she is supposed to be beautiful. But in order to articulate this I need to be still. Talking about what makes a woman beautiful and walking is something that is beyond all my powers.

"There it is," she says.

When she said we were going to a park, I imagined a large field of grass and trees and flowers and paths and benches. Her "park" is a chain-linked square of cement not much larger than our tennis court at home. It seems like every inch of space is full of children. There are tiny creatures climbing the jungle gym and sliding down a metal slide. The noise coming from the park is like the buzz inside a beehive amplified a hundred times. By the chain-link fence there is a row of benches. Jasmine opens the gate and walks over to an empty space.

I sit on the edge of the bench next to her. "This is where you come?"

"Look at the faces," she says, pointing at the kids.

I look and see dozens of faces beaming and yelling and squealing and laughing.

"They are Chinese," I say. I recognize their facial features from my geography class at Paterson.

"Mostly. The school and day care centres are just around the corner so they bring them here to play. I like it when they walk here. They either come two-by-two holding hands or else they come single file, each holding on to a rope, like little prisoners."

I think that maybe now that we are sitting down, I can continue my conversation. "I do not know what makes a woman beautiful," I tell her.

"You're still on that?"

"I need to know."

"Why?"

I swallow hard. "When I look at Jasmine I do not know whether she is beautiful or not beautiful. I do not feel that she is beautiful. I do not feel that she is not beautiful."

"Hmm. That's bad."

This time I know she is making fun of me.

"I never thought there was anything wrong with how I felt. But . . . maybe there is something wrong with me. Maybe I will never feel that someone is beautiful."

"Maybe."

A little girl with pigtails comes over to a woman sitting next to Jasmine. The little girl squeezes in between the legs of the woman and begins to suck her thumb. The woman strokes her hair and bends down to tell her something in a language I don't understand. "It is something that is on my mind," I say. Did I break a rule by talking about what is inside of me with Jasmine? Every time I glance at Jasmine she is intent on watching the different activities of the kids. Just when I decide not to pursue the topic of our conversation any more, I hear Jasmine ask: "What is it that you find beautiful?"

"Beautiful? I do not find any person beautiful."

"Not just people. Is there something you can say 'That's beautiful'?"

"Yes. I think I can. I can say it about music. There is some music I can call beautiful."

She nods. I am expecting her to ask me to describe the music, but she doesn't ask. It is as if she knows exactly what I mean.

"You know what else is beautiful?" she asks me.

"No."

"That," she says.

She waves her hand across the noisy playground.

Chapter 12

After my session with Rabbi Heschel is over, we walk outside and sit on the concrete steps that lead to the back door of Temple Emanuel. The parking lot is empty except for Rabbi Heschel's car, a red Volkswagen Beetle she calls Habbie, after the prophet Habakkuk, because, she says, the car, like the prophet, has been crying for years without anyone paying attention. "I wish I had a cigarette," she says, sitting down on the back steps.

"Smoking is bad."

"I know it. But sometimes I get so nervous I wish I had one."

The side of the building shades the steps. That's good because it is a hot afternoon. Rabbi Heschel is wearing bright orange trousers and a phosphorescent lime-green blouse. When it is cold outside she wears a hat that reminds me of the cat in Dr Seuss's books. Her black, fluffy hair has patches of white that resemble snowflakes.

"Do you know," she says without looking at me, "why Aurora brought you here — how long ago was it? Seven years ago? Gosh, you were only ten at the time."

"She didn't want Marcelo to misread the holy books."

She sighs. "Remember that little boy Joseph that loved you so much? When he died, she said she brought you because she was worried about you. But I think she was worried about *me*. His death, for some reason, hit me so hard, and you seemed so at peace with it."

"Aurora brought Marcelo to Rabbi Heschel because you are a holy man. A holy man that is a woman."

"Ha! This holy man that is a woman, as you say, is not sure she can teach you much more."

"Marcelo has a question."

"Oh no. Not about Buddhism. If you ask me what the Buddha means by 'emptiness', I'll go inside my office and start pulling out my hair."

"That is supposed to be a joke. I can tell. Emptiness is easy to understand. I have a question from Genesis, Rabbi Heschel's favourite holy book."

"I think I'm being set up. OK, let's have it." She takes a deep breath. I can tell that she enjoys my questions, especially the hard ones.

I take the yellow notebook from my shirt pocket and read: "Why did Adam and Eve feel shame that they were naked after they ate the fruit from the tree of the knowledge of good and evil?"

"Oh, that. I thought you said it was a difficult question."

"The rabbi knows the answer?" I thought it was a hard question. At least I wasn't able to answer it myself, even after reading and rereading the passage and even after thinking about it for many hours.

"I'm just kidding," she says. "They don't get much harder than that. Tell me what the Bible says first."

"Adam and Eve were naked before they ate the fruit of the tree of good and evil but they were not ashamed. Then after they ate the fruit, they realized that they were naked. They did not even know they were naked before. Adam was afraid to be seen by God. It is implied that he was ashamed. What was it about nakedness that made it evil? Why were they ashamed?"

"Mmm. Do you think nakedness is evil?" It is always annoying, the way she answers my questions with questions of her own.

"God does not see nakedness as evil because when He made man, He made him naked, and after He made man, He said that what He made was very good. Woman came from man's rib, so she's very good too."

"Excellent," she says. "Although I always have problems with that rib thing." Then she is quiet for a few moments before she says, "Before we delve into the interpretation, can I ask you a question?"

"Yes."

"Why do you ask me this now? Did something happen at the law firm to prompt this question?"

"No. Maybe. Yes. I have been thinking about the nature of attraction and about physical beauty. Wendell, someone Marcelo works with, has been talking about attraction that for him is sexual. But. . ."

"Tell me."

"There is something about the way he feels towards women that seems wrong, but I don't know why."

"I see."

"It is hard for Marcelo to look at women the way Wendell does.

When I tried to see a woman the way he does, there was something that made me think of Adam and Eve when they saw each other naked and felt ashamed. Why? If sex is good, why is there shame?"

I see her run her fingers through her hair. Then she grabs one of the patches of white and begins to twist it with her fingers. Finally, she speaks: "Remember a little later in Genesis when Cain killed Abel?"

"Yes. But why was Cain jealous? I cannot imagine what 'jealous' feels like."

"Hold on, hold on. Let's try to scratch one itch at a time, otherwise we'll end up without any skin! Do you remember what Cain used to kill Abel?"

"It does not say."

"OK, let's say he used a rock."

"We don't know for a fact that he did."

"We don't know for a fact that Cain existed at all, so humour me on this one. He used a rock."

"He used a rock. Maybe."

"Good. OK, now when Cain looked at that rock lying there on the ground, he didn't just see a rock, he *imagined* the rock as a weapon that he could use to kill Abel. You follow me so far?"

"Yes." I try to imagine a rock as a weapon.

"Cain also had the knowledge of good and evil, which means that he could imagine how good things could be put to bad use. You see where I'm going? With Adam and Eve's nakedness, I mean?"

"No. Marcelo does not see where the rabbi is going at all."

"Actually, I'm not sure *I* know where I'm going. But let's see.

After Adam and Eve ate of the fruit of the tree of good and evil, they became aware that their nakedness, which was good, could also be used in an evil way. Before, as you said, everything that God created was good, and man was more than good, he was very good. So it follows that the body, naked or not, is good also. But now man and woman were aware that the good body, theirs or somebody else's, could also be used for evil, if they were so inclined. After the fruit, Adam and Eve recognized that they had in themselves an inclination for evil alongside their inclination for good."

I close my eyes. There is a picture of Adam and Eve that I remember from the Bible that Abba kept in her room. They were naked except for fig leaves and they were looking away from each other.

"I cannot imagine how a naked body can be used for an evil purpose. Evil is a destructive act, like the murder of Abel by Cain. But I cannot see what Adam saw when he looked at Eve's naked body and imagined doing something that was evil. What was it that Adam imagined doing?"

Rabbi Heschel asks me slowly, "Have they talked to you about sex at Paterson?"

"Sexual intercourse is how humans procreate. The erect penis of the man goes into the vagina of the woman. I am not a child."

"I'm sorry. I didn't mean to be condescending. Of course you are not a child. You're a young man."

"It is just that part of me would like to feel what Wendell feels and part of me thinks there is something not right with that, but I don't know what. It is frustrating not to understand. How can sexual intercourse be wrong?"

"People call sexual intercourse, 'making love'. Have you heard that term?"

"Yes. Some terms for sexual intercourse are acceptable and some are not. 'Making love' is acceptable. 'Fuck' is not."

"Excellent. Sexual intercourse is pleasurable and it is good. God gave it to us so that two persons could come together and *make* love, that is *create* love in the world, through the children that come from the act as well as from the closeness that people feel in the act itself."

I wonder silently what that closeness is like. Is it something that I will ever experience?

She continues, "What the author of Genesis wants to tell us, I think, is that man, when united with God, is not divided. In this unity, there is no good and evil. All of our inclinations, even the sexual ones, are good when we are in Eden — that is, when we walk with God and all our actions, words and thoughts seek to follow His will. But man can choose to be separate from God, and in this separateness he creates evil by imagining ways to use what is good in ways that hurt him or others, and then acting upon what he imagines."

"Marcelo can't imagine how sex can be used for evil."

"Oh, my. That's because you are special. You walk with God in Eden. May the Holy One, blessed be He, be always with you."

"Give Marcelo an example."

Rabbi Heschel folds her hands and closes her eyes as if she were praying.

"Father, not my will but Your will," she whispers, looking up to heaven. Then she turns to face me and says, "The ways we use sex to hurt each other are innumerable and unspeakable. Anytime we treat a person as a thing for our own pleasure. When we look at another person as an object and not as a person like us. When sex consists solely of taking and not giving. When a person uses physical or psychological force to have sex against another person's will. When a person deceives another in order to have sex with them. When a person uses sex to physically or emotionally hurt another. Any time an adult has sex with a child. Those are some of the ways sex becomes evil. I can't describe it any more. It's not for me to give you images of evil. It saddens me to know that you will find out soon enough the different ways that we have devised to hurt each other."

She stops and rubs her eyes the way a person with a headache rubs her eyes. I want to tell her not to worry about me, but I remain silent, unable to find any words to comfort her.

Chapter 13

Wendell and I are having lunch on the top floor of what he calls "the club". The tall wrinkled-face man who met us at the door went into a back room and came out with a blue jacket and a red-and-blue striped tie. He handed them to me and I didn't know why until Wendell told me I had to put them on. Wendell helped me with the tie. Wendell is already wearing a jacket and tie, so the man did not have to get him anything.

We sit by a window overlooking Boston Harbour. Another older-looking waiter comes by and Wendell orders a drink called a "martini". I order a Coke.

"I recommend the salmon," Wendell says to me when he sees that I have trouble deciding what to get.

"I'll have a salmon," I say to the waiter, who has been waiting for me.

As soon as the waiter leaves, Wendell says, "I need your help with something."

"Marcelo's help? My help."

"Yes. Why do you look so surprised?"

"I didn't know there was anything I could do to help you."

"There is something you can help me quite a bit with."

The waiter comes and gives Wendell a martini and me a Coke. The martini is an extremely small drink. I look for a straw but there is none. Wendell eats the olive and drinks half of the martini in one gulp.

"I need you to help me get Jasmine." Wendell puts his glass down and looks at me with a look I don't recognize.

"What does 'get' mean?"

"What do you think 'get' means? Take a guess."

"I'm not sure," I say. "Do you want to get Jasmine to love you?"

"Mmmm. That wouldn't be necessary." He finishes his drink.

"Do you love Jasmine?" I ask.

"'Love' is a peculiar word, isn't it?" Wendell is lifting his glass at the waiter. The waiter nods. "The word stands for so many things. I love a dry martini, for example." He waves the empty glass. "I love my father's yacht. If by 'love' you mean wanting something so bad it hurts and feeling like you'll die if you don't have it, then, yes, I love Jasmine."

"Do you want to marry Jasmine?"

Wendell shakes his head. It could be that he's saying he doesn't want to marry Jasmine, or the gesture could mean something else. Sometimes people shake their heads like that when I say something that they can't believe I just said.

"People like me don't marry people like Jasmine." He is smiling when he says that, but it is not a friendly smile.

"But she is an Elemental Woman. You told me so."

"I'm going to have to explain the way it is to you, my friend."

Wendell waits for the waiter to place the plates on the table. I stare at the pink flesh of the salmon. "Let me ask you this." He puts a forkful of salmon in his mouth. After he swallows it, he asks me, "Has she ever said anything about me?"

This is a question that Wendell continually asks and it never ceases to be difficult. Jasmine has said things about Wendell. She has told me that she doesn't trust him, for example, and that he makes her feel "creepy", whatever that means. She has communicated to me in no uncertain terms that she doesn't like him. But I believe those things were said to me in confidence and I'm not sure that I should repeat them to Wendell. On the other hand, I want to be Wendell's friend. How do you stay loyal to two people when one of them doesn't like the other? Don't you have to choose one or another at some point? After a while, I say, "She doesn't trust you."

"What did she say exactly?" Wendell seems very interested in the answer to that question.

"It is a feeling she has about you." Now I'm not sure whether Jasmine said that Wendell was creepy or that he made her feel creepy.

"You see? That's where you come in. She trusts you because you're harmless. What I'm thinking, and this is how you can help me, is that one day after work, you, Jasmine and I go out on my father's yacht for an evening cruise around Boston Harbour. She won't come with me alone, I know. But if you ask her to come with us, she'll come."

It feels good to be needed by Wendell, and I want to help him as I believe friends should. But I also feel uncomfortable. There is something that is not right about Wendell's request, and I wonder whether this is what "creepy" feels like.

"What's the matter? What are you thinking? We can make it a double date if you like. We'll invite Martha. She likes coming on the yacht quite a bit. I know that for a certain fact." He winks at me.

I need to retrace what Wendell has said to me so far so that I can find the source of the discomfort. There are words in the conversation we have just had that don't fit logically with other words. Finally, I remember what was disturbing to me. "Why is it that people like you don't marry people like Jasmine?"

"You haven't taken a bite of your salmon. What's the matter?"

I lift up my fork, move the rice around and then put the fork down again. How is it that people can chew and taste and think and talk all at the same time? My head feels full, as if Wendell's words are food that my brain is unable to digest. "I always thought one could marry whomever one loves. And you say you love Jasmine, although I never heard love defined the way you defined it."

"Marcelo, Marcelo. Do you always have to think so much about things? I'll break it down for you step-by-step. Yes, you can marry whomever you 'love' as you say. But the person also has to be, how can I put it, worthy enough to be a part of your life. Can you imagine Jasmine at dinner conversing with my father and mother about world events? Jasmine barely finished high school for one, and for another Jasmine has been . . . around."

"Around."

"Let's just say that she is so unbelievably and incredibly hot that whatever she is or has done is not important for purposes of my summer objectives. Besides, there's something about someone saying no to me that burns me up. No one says no to me. Especially someone who has—" He stops suddenly, reconsidering what he wanted to say. Wendell's look at that moment scares me. I have seen it before in the eyes of some of the kids at Paterson when frustration turns to rage. "In any event, what and who she is does not matter for anything beyond this summer. Now, what I want to know is whether you are willing to help me. All you have to do is say that I asked you to go for a cruise, and ask her, as a personal favour to you, if she would come as well. Then all you have to do on the yacht is entertain yourself for a while up on deck while I take Jasmine below."

It doesn't make sense to me. Why does Wendell want to be alone with Jasmine? Jasmine does not trust him. She will not agree to anything he asks of her. "Why?" I ask.

"Why what?"

"Why do you need to take her below to talk to her? Will it make a difference to the way she feels about you?"

"Once we're below deck, it won't matter what she feels about me. I'll take care of her feelings. There are ways to create feelings or change them or make them disappear for a while."

"You want to fuck her." I hate using the word, but it is the word that most accurately describes what I think Wendell wants to do. The other alternatives like "making love" or even "sexual intercourse" do not seem precise enough.

Wendell laughs so hard people sitting at the next table turn to look at us. "Why, Mr Marchelo, you are making progress in the ways of the world indeed. Don't worry, I'm not going to hurt her. She just won't be able to say no." Then the laughter stops and he fixes his eyes on me. "Well? What do you say? Can I count on your help, my friend?"

The way Wendell is looking at me makes me feel that he will be extremely angry if I say no. If I am to continue being his friend, I need to say yes — that's what he is making me feel. I am afraid. I cannot distinguish whether I am afraid for Jasmine or for myself. Is this what lack of trust feels like, I wonder — this sense of hurt to come?

"No." I look into Wendell's face when I say this and see his pupils widen with surprise.

"Pardon?"

"No. I will not ask Jasmine to go." I am hoping that he will not ask me why. I don't remember any other time in my life when I have said something based solely on a feeling, without having figured out why I am saying it.

"I see." Wendell's face is red. It is either anger or embarrassment. He wipes his mouth with the napkin and then bunches it up and puts it on his plate. His face is looking everywhere around the room except in my direction. When the waiter comes, he tells him, "Put it on my father's bill and add twenty per cent."

"Yes sir, thank you."

He stands up and then sits down again. I can feel him staring at me for a long time. I don't know where to place my eyes while he is looking at me. I look out the window. I want to say that I am sorry for refusing to do what he has asked me to do, but I'm not sure that it is appropriate to say that. I am sorry that he is disappointed in me and I am afraid to lose him as a friend. But I am not sorry to keep Jasmine away from him. At that moment, she seems more important to me than Wendell's friendship.

The waiter brings him another martini. Maybe Wendell asked

for it while I was looking out the window. His head is swaying slightly as he speaks.

"Do you want to hear an interesting story?"

The way Wendell asks this, I think that maybe Wendell and I can still be friends. He seems his old self again.

"OK, here it goes. I'm going to go fast, so see if you can follow me. Once upon a time there were these two supersmart lawyers. Both of them went to Harvard, both graduated at the top of their class, both ended up working after law school with the most prestigious law firm in Boston. One of them went into litigation, the other became a patent attorney. One was from an old Boston family. You could trace the family's lineage all the way to the folks that arrived on the *Mayflower*. You've heard of the *Mayflower*, right?"

"Yes, I learned about it at. . ."

"Yes, I know, Paterson. Wonderful school, that Paterson. They teach everything there. Where was I?"

"One was from an old Boston family," I remind him.

"Right. The other was what you call in professional circles a 'minority hire'. Do you know what that is?"

"No."

"What? There is something you didn't actually learn at Paterson?"

Sarcasm is very difficult for me to detect except when Wendell uses it. "There are many things," I say.

"A minority hire is someone whose descendants are from another continent or country, whose skin is darker than the majority of folks, someone not born lily-white. A firm hires these people to show how broad-minded and compassionate they are."

"I do not understand."

"It doesn't matter. The concept is not really relevant to the story. Let's just say that for some reason these two lawyers did not like each other. There are various accounts floating around as to the origin of their animosity. One of them, the one I am most partial to, is that Minority Hire turned out, unexpectedly, to be an excellent lawyer. Not just in the sense of being super-proficient in his area of the law, but in his entrepreneurship. He went out and brought clients to the firm. Big, rich clients. What Minority Hire did was actually kind of brilliant. He travelled to Mexico and other countries in Central and South America on his own and found scientists who were working at universities or small laboratories, scientists who were inventing new chemicals and gadgets. Minority Hire promised them that if they became his clients, he would get their inventions patented in the United States and he would help them find companies that would pro-duce their inventions and everyone would make loads of money." Wendell raises his glass. The waiter nods. "Are you following me so far?"

"The person you call Minority Hire is my father," I say. Aurora has told me the story of how Arturo became successful, but she did not tell the story quite the way Wendell is now telling it.

"Wonderful. I don't care what anyone says — I think you are brilliant."

"Thank you," I say, even though I believe that to be sarcasm as well.

"Well, the other lawyer, let's call him the Mayflower Lawyer for ease of identification, was consumed with jealousy of Minority Hire. That's my theory anyway. It's only speculation, but I have reason to believe in its accuracy because, how shall I say it, I am privy to insider information." The waiter comes with another martini. "Any questions so far?"

"Is the Mayflower Lawyer your father?"

"Yes." I expect him to say more but he doesn't. It may be the first time that Wendell has answered one of my questions with a single word.

"Your father and my father are partners," I say. "They work together and own the law firm together."

"Yes. Fifty-fifty. Equal partners. But we are getting ahead of the story. The real interesting thing here, the conundrum that needs to be deciphered, is why these two lawyers who disliked, even hated each other — yes, I don't think hate would be too strong a word here — why these two individuals who hated each other so much nevertheless decided to be partners." Wendell stops. There is a crease in the middle of his forehead and I can tell he is thinking hard, perhaps trying to find the answer to the conundrum, as he calls it.

"They need each other," I say.

Wendell beams at me. "Marchelo, you never cease to amaze me."

"MAR-SE-LO," I say.

"Whatever. You are absolutely right. But what does it say about that need when it can overcome hate?"

"Hate is when you want to inflict harm on someone," I say. "Arturo and your father do not want to harm each other." Then I remember what Arturo said to me on that first train ride to work. "You can be friends with someone and still compete with them."

Wendell smiles. I have seen that smile before but I don't know where. It means that someone knows something that you don't and they are not telling you what it is. "Well, the story goes that after a while Minority Hire did not want to share all the money he was making from his new clients with the big law firm, so he took his clients and started his own firm. But you can't have a good patent practice without a litigation department. When others develop products that copy the ideas you patented, you have to sue them. Minority Hire needed the best litigator around. He also needed someone with powerful and prestigious connections, and that was the Mayflower Lawyer. It was a perfect match. So he offered the Mayflower Lawyer fifty per cent ownership in the new firm. And the Mayflower Lawyer, knowing that he would make much more money partnering with Minority Hire than in the prestigious firm, swallowed his pride and joined him. That's the story. Interesting, isn't it?"

"Yes," I say. There are in fact many questions to ponder in that story. I make a mental note to replay Wendell's story and reflect on the conundrum, but right now I am wondering whether the telling of the story means that Wendell and I will continue to be friends.

Wendell tips the glass so that the last drop of martini falls on his tongue. I can feel him staring at me. He is sitting on the edge of the chair and I can tell that as soon as he finishes saying what he is about to say, he will get up and leave. "I am going to let you think a little more about your decision not to help me," he says.

"Jasmine." He is talking about my refusal to help him "get" Jasmine.

"My father and your father, despite their hatred for each other, have never betrayed their bond — based on mutual need to be sure, but a bond nevertheless. What we have at the law firm is kind of a balance of power between two forces. The enterprise runs smoothly so long as the power remains equally balanced. The thing is, in a patent law firm, after a while, if there is no new patent work coming in, the litigation department can become more important. Take, for example, the litigation I am working on right now, Vidromek. Vidromek is the firm's biggest client. Your father's biggest success story. He brought Vidromek in when Vidromek was just a couple of chemical engineers working in the back of a house someplace in Mexico. But now it is my father and his team who do all the legal work related to Vidromek. What keeps my father from doing something that will make Vidromek totally his client? What prevents my father from moving beyond the fifty per cent boundary into your father's side, or wiping your father completely from the playing field? If, for example, the people at Vidromek were told about a big mistake your father made . . . they could decide that he is no longer needed."

"My father does not make mistakes." This I say with certainty. Again I feel the heat of anger rise as it does whenever someone says something bad about my father. The anger clouds my mind. I do not know how the story he just told relates to Jasmine. Moreover I am afraid. The tone of voice that Wendell uses is menacing.

Wendell is speaking in a softer voice now. "I will tell you what prevents your father and my father from stepping over the fifty per cent line: the bond. You can have bonds based on hate, you know. I'm sorry. You look like you are totally lost. Let me make things simple. The bond between our fathers extends to you and me. Keeping that bond, that balance of power, is extremely important. We keep the bond by putting each other first above anyone else. It doesn't mean you have to like me more than anyone else. You can hate me if you wish. It doesn't matter. We keep the bond by helping each other. If you asked for my help with something, I would give it to you. It's part of the bond."

Wendell stands up slowly. I start to stand but he motions for me to sit down. Then he sits down again too.

"Tell me something that *you* want."

"Want."

"Yeah, what do you want the most?"

"Like Wendell wanting Jasmine?" I have never experienced a want like that.

"Anything. It doesn't have to be 'wanting' another person, as you so crudely but not incorrectly put it."

The answer is suddenly obvious. "I want to go to Paterson next year. I want to go to Paterson and train the ponies."

Wendell narrows his eyes. He is concentrating. "Explain."

"Arturo, my father, said I could go to Paterson for my senior year of high school if I succeed at the law firm this summer."

"There you go. I can help you with that. Easy."

"Help me."

"I will."

"I mean, help Marcelo how?"

"We'll ask your father to let you help me with the Vidromek litigation that I'm working on. Your father will agree because . . . he just will. Then we tell your father how well you have done. We'll make sure he's proud of you. In fact, I can guarantee to you that if you help me get what *I* want, you will get what *you* want. I guarantee it! One hundred per cent!"

"Jasmine needs me."

"What you do in the mailroom anyone can do. We'll get Jasmine a temp or something."

I feel uneasy. I like working side by side with Jasmine, even though sometimes hours go by and we don't say a word to each other.

"I know," Wendell says. "I wouldn't want to give up working with Jasmine either." How does Wendell do that — read the thoughts inside my mind? "OK, we pull you away from Jasmine just for a couple of hours, once or twice a week, in a way that allows you to do all your work in the mailroom first. What? Tell me. What are you thinking?"

"I am confused." I have never been so confused in all my life. It is all so complicated, so much to consider. My brain is a wad of sticky bubble gum.

"Well, think about it. You help me and I help you. The Sandoval and Holmes alliance at work. The bond." He stands up quickly. "I think I'm going to take the rest of the afternoon off," he says. "Do you mind going back by yourself?"

I feel embarrassed saying it, but I say it anyway. "I do not think I can find my way back to the law firm on my own."

"Robert will give you directions." He points at the waiter. "You will consider what I said?" he asks.

"Consider."

"You will consider helping me. That is my understanding. Is it yours as well?"

"Maybe." I say this automatically, without thinking.

"Maybe will do for now. I'm thinking that later this week,

we should take the afternoon off and just go for a boat ride, you and me."

But before I can say anything, Wendell has turned around and is walking out of the room.

Chapter 14

I leave the club and start walking in what I believe is the direction of South Station. I'm not going back to the law firm. I'm going home. Once I get to South Station I will wait for the West Orchard train, and when I get there I'll sit on one of the benches by the tracks until Aurora gets home from work, and then I will call her and ask her to pick me up.

I walk with my head down, looking at my feet take one step after another. It has never been hard for me to stop my brain from thinking. My brain is like a water faucet that I can turn on or off. Only now there is no off and the water of thoughts just flows.

I want to sit down and write some of the words expressed by Wendell, but there are so many I don't know where to start. *There are ways to make feelings disappear for a while. . . Need that overcomes hatred. . . She's been around. . . balance of power. . . Bond. . . Minority Hire. . . No one says no to me. . . Fuck.* This last word is one that Wendell never used, but it is the one word that is loudest in my mind — a blaring, honking, angry word that blasts at me. It seems to be the one upon which everything else hinges.

I walk as if bedazzled by the word, trying to feel what Wendell must be feeling, to want Jasmine as he does, for fucking. Jasmine asked me once if I was greedy about something and it must be that what consumes Wendell is like the greed I feel for a CD, only more desperate and reckless. Want. Maybe this "want" for another human being is love, something that I have never felt before because of who I am.

I realize I am lost. Actually, I knew that I was lost almost as soon as I left the club. Only now it begins to matter. I don't recognize where I am, and the buildings on the street I'm walking on prevent me from seeing the tall outline of the law firm's building, which I hoped to use as a landmark to guide me. What kind of seventeen-year-old gets lost only four blocks away from his destination? In some way, the strange-looking streets are simply a reflection of my thoughts. It seems perfectly natural to be lost outside when that's the way I am inside. No landmarks anywhere.

The smell of fish reaches me and I take a deep breath. I like strong smells. A store has the fish laid out on ice, their eyes like buttons, looking cloudy and serene. They seem at peace, the fish. In front of the store with the fish there is an empty wooden crate. I sit there. It is strong enough to hold my weight. Chinese people walk by. They don't pay any attention to me.

As I sit there on the wooden crate, I suddenly begin to hear Beethoven's "Ode to Joy". The sound of the music is vibrating in my thigh. It takes me a few disconcerting seconds to realize that what I'm hearing is in the present and that the sound is emanating from the cell phone in my pocket. Aurora programmed it to play "Ode to Joy" for its ringtone. I remove the cell phone from its container, stare at it, and then decide to press the button that reads TALK.

"Marcelo, are you there?" It is Jasmine's voice.

"Yes."

"Where are you?"

"By the dead fish," I say, looking up to see where I am.

"What? Where? What are you doing?"

"I am lost."

"What? Can you see the building?"

"No."

"Can you read the name of the street?"

I stand up and walk to the corner. I think: *Now I look normal like everyone else, walking and talking on the cell phone.* I read the street sign to Jasmine. "It says 'Ping On'."

"Stay there. I know where it is. I'll be there in about ten minutes."

"OK."

"Don't move from there."

"No. I am going to sit on a crate. In front of the fish."

"Right. OK, bye."

I turn off the cell phone. I turn right and walk back towards my crate where I feel safe.

What I try to remember is the conversation that I had with Rabbi Heschel a few days ago. When is sex evil? Anytime we use another person as an object. But Wendell does not seem to be restrained by such considerations. He is unburdened. At this moment I wish I was like Wendell, and I realize that this is what envy feels like. There's a part of me that envies Wendell and his freedom. Marcelo on the other hand is stuck in a mire of questions. It is as if Marcelo ate the apple from the tree of knowledge of good and evil, but Wendell was too smart to fall for the wiles of the serpent.

"Marcelo, Marcelo." It is Jasmine standing next to me. She is breathing deeply and fast. "How did you end up here?"

"I walked."

"Nooo!"

She is trying to be funny, I can tell, but I don't smile.

"Let me catch my breath and we'll walk back. What happened? Where's Wendell?"

"He left."

"Left where? Didn't you go to lunch with him? You've been gone for two hours. I thought Wendell had taken you to one of his bars or . . . I thought maybe he was going to try to get you drunk."

"We talked and then he left."

"He left you alone?"

"I can walk alone."

"You got lost."

"It is hard to see the sun in the city. The buildings block it and cast shadows all day long." I don't want to talk about getting lost or being lost or about Wendell.

Maybe she understands that something bad happened, because after walking for about half a block she says in a quiet tone, a tone that doesn't sound like worry: "Back home in Vermont where I grew up, the only shadows are from trees and barns. The clouds look so close you feel like you can touch them sometimes. The clouds here look like they're part of the sky. Over there they look like they're part of the mountains. You ever laugh or smile or anything?" she asks.

"When I am by myself," I respond.

She giggles. "Me too. I always catch myself smiling or laughing by myself like an idiot. I guess that makes us both idiots."

"Idiots," I repeat.

"That's not a good word, is it?"

"It is not accurate. An idiot is a mentally deficient person having intelligence in the lowest possible range, unable to guard against common dangers and incapable of learning connected speech. Sometimes people think I am an idiot. It is only true in some respects."

"Trust me, people think I'm an idiot plenty of times."

"Juliet said you were an idiot once."

"She said that to you?"

"Yes. The day before yesterday she came when you weren't there and said, 'Where's the other idiot?' She was asking about you. I was the idiot that was there."

"Don't pay any attention to her. She's got an ego so big there's no room for any brain cells."

"We are not doing the three o'clock mail run."

"After I called you on your cell phone I closed the mailroom and put up a sign. I told them I had to go to the courthouse and that the three o'clock and five o'clock would be delivered together. Patty at the reception desk can handle any packages that are delivered while we're gone."

"You lied so that you could come get me."

"I thought maybe you had taken an early train, but I saw the next train was at four. Good thing you taped the train schedule to the wall in front of your desk."

"It covered up the 'Fuck you's."

I can feel her stare at me briefly. Jasmine and I are walking very slowly. I guess we are walking back to South Station and the reason we are walking slowly is because the next train to West Orchard doesn't leave for another hour and a half. Still, I wish we would walk faster. I am afraid to talk to Jasmine because I feel something sad inside of me and I'm afraid this sadness will come out.

"I don't want to work at the law firm any more."

"Why? What did you and Wendell talk about?"

"He said things that confused me."

"Like what?"

"I don't want to talk about it."

"You seem angry. What did Wendell say to make you angry?"

I recognize that along with everything else, there is also anger. I wonder how Jasmine could tell. What, of all the things Wendell said, caused me to be angry? "I don't know," I say.

"Anger can be good," she says. We stop at an intersection and wait for the white walk sign to flash. "Anger can help you to do what you need to do. You've been doing great at the mailroom. Don't let the likes of Wendell get you down."

"Anger is never good," I say. "It makes you want to say and do hurtful things to others."

The white walk sign flashes on and we cross the street. Jasmine grabs my arm and pulls me back as a car unexpectedly appears. "If you're not capable of anger, people will run over you, literally," she says.

"The picture of the mountains that you have in front of your desk. Is that Vermont?"

"That picture is what I see from the front door of my house."

"The mountains are so beautiful. Do you need anger in the mountains?"

I can feel her stop for a fraction of a second before she resumes walking. "No," she says, "you don't *need* anger in the mountains. You need something like it. My dad calls it fight. 'You gotta have fight, girl,' is what he says to me. And even in the mountains people still get angry."

"At what? Were you ever angry?"

"I was angry at a horse for the longest time," she says, laughing.

"Why?"

We are walking by the same children's playground that we saw before, only now it is empty. Jasmine walks in and sits on a swing and I sit on the swing next to her. She begins to swing slightly back and forth, her feet not leaving the ground. "My older brother and a friend of his got it into their heads that they wanted to buy a Kentucky racehorse and bring it to Vermont and make money from renting the horse to stud." She stops to look at me. "You know what that is?"

"Yes," I say, a little embarrassed. I'm embarrassed not at the meaning of the word but at the fact that Jasmine felt it necessary to ask me if I knew what that meant. "At Paterson, I worked after school with the ponies," I tell her. "I know what 'stud' means, both the noun and the verb."

She goes on, "Everyone told them not to do it. A thoroughbred racing horse doesn't belong in Vermont. They need exercise. What's the horse going to do during the long winters? But James, my brother, and his friend Cody, they don't listen to anyone. They drive down to Kentucky with a trailer and bring back a two-year-old racehorse. They call him Kickaz, like kick *ass*, you know."

"Kickaz is the horse you got angry at."

"Kickaz was always real jittery. James and Cody had to work with him to train him to be calm. One day they were in the cow pastures leading him around with a short rope. Cody was holding the rope and James was walking on the other side when suddenly Kickaz got spooked by something, probably a bee, and he reared sideways and kicked James in the stomach."

Jasmine stops swinging. I don't want to look in her direction. I wait for her to continue speaking.

"James seemed OK. We took him down to the Medical Centre in West Lebanon just to make sure. Nothing showed up on the X-rays or the MRI, but they kept him overnight anyway just for observation, and then that night he fell asleep and just kept on sleeping. When he didn't wake up a day later, they operated, thinking there must have been some internal bleeding that wasn't showing up, but they didn't find anything. He died a couple of days later.

"Everyone hated that horse. Cody wanted to kill him. I wanted to kill him. Everyone. Only Amos, that's my father, only Amos said that he wanted to keep the horse. We were all shocked because he was the one that had been the most against James getting it in the first place. 'It ain't the horse's fault,' Amos said. He put him in the barn with Morgan, our workhorse. 'Morgan will train him,' he said. But for the longest time I couldn't even stand to look at that horse. I swear that horse is probably why I decided to leave Vermont and come to Boston. I couldn't bear to look at him."

"You are still angry at Kickaz?"

"Naah. You should see him now. He's as gentle as old Morgan. Amos takes him up in the mountains hunting, Kickaz like a mule, lugging all the gear. In the winter, Amos ploughs a track around the cow pasture and walks him around a few times each day no matter how cold or snowy it gets. They're perfect for each other, those two."

"Will you return to Vermont?"

"Yes."

"I don't want to work at the law firm," I say.

"I don't like working there either. But I do it."

"Why?"

She pushes herself off the swing. "Come with me. I want to show you something."

We cross the street. Jasmine is standing in front of a glass door but she doesn't open it. It is as if she is thinking for a moment about whether opening the door is the right thing to do. Then she opens it and beckons me to come in.

We climb a winding wooden stairway. We pass dozens of wooden doors on our way up. Most of the doors have Chinese characters written on white pieces of paper. "Who works here?" I ask.

"I work here," she says, giggling.

We reach a place where the stairs end and we open the last of the wooden doors. When the door opens and I walk in, we are in a rectangular room only slightly larger than my tree house. "My home away from home," she says.

"I thought Jasmine lived in the mailroom."

"Ha, ha, very funny."

But I didn't mean it to be funny. Of course Jasmine has to live someplace. It just never occurred to me that she did.

"This used to be a dorm for medical students attending Tufts," she explains. "Now it's mostly used by immigrants from Cambodia. It is very cheap and very safe. This is the living room, dining room, den, kitchen, and bedroom. The bathroom is through there." She points at a door at the back of the room.

On one side against the wall there's a cot covered with a quilt of multicoloured patches. At the head of the cot is a zoo of stuffed animals: a brown bear, a jaguar with black spots, a dog with floppy faded-white ears, a polka-dotted horse, a grey walrus, a tan kangaroo. At the end of the bed, on the side closest to where we stand, occupying all of the space between the bed and the door, is an electric keyboard that I can tell has all eighty-eight keys of a regular piano. Resting on the keys is a pair of padded earphones still connected to the keyboard's panel. On the other side of the room, opposite the keyboard and the bed, there is a desk, a metal file cabinet, a structure made out of balsa wood that has clothes hanging inside, a window with blue curtains, a stove and a miniature refrigerator. Every available space on the walls of the room is lined with shelves filled with hundreds of CDs. The only space on the walls that has not been fitted with shelves is the space above the metal file cabinet, over which hangs a white poster. I walk up to it and study it. The poster has white edges. On the top, I read:

KEITH JARRETT
THE KÖLN CONCERT

Below these words I see the black-and-white image of a man playing a piano. His eyes are closed, his head is lowered and his chin rests on his chest. I immediately recognize the posture of someone in deep prayer. The man is playing the piano, but I am certain he is also remembering.

Jasmine stands next to me in silence. She seems willing to give me as much time as I need to see what there is to see and to understand what there is to understand. When I finish taking in every detail of the poster, I turn towards the keyboard and press the middle C key softly with my finger. The tension of the key is softer than the tension of the keys in our piano at home. Jasmine reaches over and pulls out the headphone jack from the panel of the keyboard. I touch the key again. The single sound that fills the air is crisp, sharp. It reminds me of a blast of winter air.

"You play the piano," I say.

She takes out a black-cushioned stool from underneath the keyboard, fiddles briefly with the controls on the console, closes the door to the room, and then she plays.

It is not like any type of music I have ever heard before. It starts off sounding like Bach, but then the notes follow sequences my brain does not anticipate. There are notes and chords that jar with the notes and chords that precede them, but then a few seconds later what seems dissonant turns out to be part of a basic melody, the original Bach-like melody that has been there all along, hidden but constant. What is different about the music that Jasmine is playing is the rhythm. There is more of it. As if the piano wanted to be a drum or a wild heartbeat or thunder. Jasmine's left hand strikes a steady beat that sounds like a pumping heart, and then, as if to counteract the regular sound made by the left hand, the right hand lunges into a melody too complex to fully grasp.

She stops playing and then she opens her eyes and looks at me as if she forgot that I was standing there.

"This is why I work at the law firm. So that I can come to this little room and do this."

It is clear that she has been playing for many, many years. I know because when I was small, Aurora took me down the street to Mrs Rockwell for piano lessons. But it was no use. I could not read the notes and play at the same time. Nor could I move the left hand and the right hand simultaneously. My mental wiring simply cannot handle the voltage required to play the piano.

"You invented that music. It came from your head."

I see her blush. For a moment, I'm afraid I said something that hurt her feelings.

"It is unbelievable," I say. "How do you do that?"

"You practise and practise and then one day the music is there," she says. "It's OK. The music I make is OK. It's not great. It's not even close to the kind of music he makes." She looks in the direction of the poster. She stands up and goes to one of the bookshelves and grabs one of the CDs that are stacked there. "Here, take this."

The cover of the CD is the same as the poster on the wall.

"He is remembering," I say.

"Remembering what?"

"It's a word I use for praying. Sometimes it's like waiting for music to come out of the silence."

Jasmine takes the CD from my hand and studies it as if to see what I see. Then she puts it back in my hand. She turns and stands in front of me, and when she does that I suddenly feel like laughing.

"What?" she asks. She looks like a little girl, the way she says this.

"Nothing," I mumble.

"We should go now," she tells me, still looking at me.

"Yes," I say. "Thank you."

"For what?"

"For showing me."

That's all that I can think of saying.

Chapter 15

I'm at my desk in the mailroom binding documents at optimum speed and waiting for Wendell to call me. He asked Arturo if I could help him and Arturo said yes. According to Wendell, Arturo was very happy. Jasmine is not happy. For one thing, it means that she'll have to finish binding the documents I promised Martha for this morning.

"I don't trust him. He must have something up his sleeve," she says.

"What if he's wearing a short-sleeved shirt?" I say, trying to make her laugh.

She ignores my joke. She is thinking hard. "Does he know you got lost after your lunch?"

"No."

I want to ask Jasmine why she asked that question, but the phone rings and she picks it up. I hear her speak loudly into the receiver. "One afternoon. That's it. I need him here tomorrow morning." It makes me smile to see her so grumpy over losing my help.

"That was Jerk Junior. He's waiting for you."

Wendell is wearing khaki trousers and a crimson polo shirt. I smile to myself because the shirt has short sleeves and so there is no chance for Wendell to hide something up his sleeve, as Jasmine says. He is standing over his desk, casually arranging stacks of manila folders.

"There you are," he says when I enter the office. "Am I glad you can help me. Father is too. He's having a shit-fit because today is the last day to turn over documents to another law firm and I have to be at an orientation meeting for the new squash players. Come over here. I'll show you what you need to do."

Wendell is the same friendly, joking Wendell of before we went to lunch.

"How's Jasmine? Is she upset because I pried you loose from her for a few hours?" Wendell asks me.

"She needs me in the mailroom," I say.

"This won't take you more than one afternoon at the most. She can live without you for three hours, can't she?"

"Yes," I answer.

"I *have* to be at Harvard. I'm the captain of the team. So let's get to it. What you need to do is really quite simple. This is part of the Vidromek litigation. You know about Vidromek, right? Very *importante.* If we mess this up, it is *kaput.*" Wendell draws his hand across his neck as if it were a sword. "The people suing Vidromek are folks who claim they've been hurt because the windshields don't shatter into a million harmless pieces like they're supposed to. These people are trying to find out whether Mr Acevedo, the president of the company, knew about the windshield's danger but went ahead and manufactured them anyway. You with me?"

"Yes. I think so."

"The other side submitted a list of the documents they want from us. Those documents, if we have them, are in these two boxes. I've gone through all thirty or so boxes and found what they needed, but I didn't get a chance to put the documents in order or to take out multiple copies. That will be your job. You need to look at the list they gave us and put the documents in separate piles in accordance with the list. The list is very specific. It'll say 'letter from Mr So-and-So to Mr So-and-So, dated such-and-such'. Are you with me so far?"

"Yes, I am here with you."

"Sometimes you'll find multiple copies of the same document. We only need to save one. The other copies you can put in this box marked 'Trash'. OK? If there are various documents under the same category, you'll need to put them in some kind of order, you know, chronological or by author or by recipient. Take item number twenty-five here on the list." Wendell lifts a sheaf of papers and reads from it. "'All offers made by Sandoval & Holmes to settle the litigation related to windshields.' In the boxes, you will see a small number twenty-five written in pencil on all documents that fall under this category. You need to take all those documents and organize them. You're good at that, aren't you Marcelo?"

"Yes. I like to organize things."

"That's why I asked your dad if you could help me. You should have seen him. He was bursting with joy. Vidromek is your father's biggest and oldest client, so it's only right that you have a hand in this. You're the man. This is a little more important and requires more brainpower than what you're used to doing with Jasmine. You have to make sure you look carefully at every single document in these two boxes. If we tell them that we don't have something when we do, it'll be. . ."

"*Kaput.*" I make the same sword-motion with my hand.

"That's exactly correct. Up shit creek without a paddle."

"OK," I say. I wonder if Wendell's efforts to have me work with him are his way of letting me know that he wants to be friends again.

"Just leave the boxes here when you finish. Juliet will make a copy of all that we send them tomorrow morning." Wendell stops talking but he doesn't leave. Is he waiting for me to say something?

"OK," I say again. "I understand."

He steps closer to the edge of the desk. "So, we are on our way to getting you what you want."

"Yes." But I don't really know what he is talking about.

"The bond that you and I talked about. I am fulfilling my part. I got you to work with me on an easy assignment. And there will be others like this the rest of the summer. Then we tell your father of your success. Right? That was our agreement."

"Yes." I am confused. What is it that we agreed? Wendell is going too fast for me.

"Yes? Yes as in yes, you are going to do your part. You are going to ask Jasmine to go on the boat ride. That was the agreement, right? Have you asked her yet?"

I'm trying to remember exactly what was said at our lunch. What did I agree to? I am certain I did not agree to ask Jasmine. Did I agree to consider it? Is there any way that I could have even considered it?

Wendell looks at his watch. "I gotta go. I will take that as a yes.

We'll work out the details later."

I stand there looking at the boxes. What happened? Why did I hesitate in telling Wendell I will not help do anything that may harm Jasmine? How could it be that even as I understand Wendell's views on sex, I am still pulled towards success in my father's eyes?

I start to work on the assignment. I want to get it done so that I can return to the mailroom. Aurora told me that when I was little, I would take the daily mail and sort it into different piles. The order of the piles, she said, was hard to figure out. Sometimes it was by the size of envelope, sometimes by the colour of the stamp. But there were times when no matter how hard she tried she could not discern my logic. I don't remember doing that, but I imagine that it must have been hard to find the one unifying element amongst many possible ones. My CDs come to mind. Sometimes I sort them by composer, sometimes by instrument, sometimes by the length of time I've owned them. Right now they are sorted in a way that no one in a million years could ever figure out. For the past year I have been sorting them by the music's predominant emotion: joy, sorrow, longing, loneliness, serenity, anger. The reason no one could ever figure out the categories is that I myself am often at a loss at how a particular CD ended up in the happy category, for example, when it is clear as I listen to it again that the music is anything but happy.

This is what I'm thinking about as I go about the task of organizing the documents in the list. First I find on the list all the documents that fall under the same category. Then I look for the documents in the boxes and begin to separate them into piles. I do the obvious ones first. All letters written *by* Mr

Reynaldo Acevedo, President of Vidromek, go in one pile. The documents in that list I arrange in chronological order. All letters written *to* Mr Acevedo in another pile. Then there are memos from staff of Vidromek *to* Mr Acevedo and memos *from* Mr Acevedo to staff. I make another pile of what looks like reports that contain different types of data and then another pile composed of various letters and envelopes addressed to the law firm. Altogether I come up with nine categories of piles.

About one hour has gone by and I think that in another hour I will have completed Wendell's assignment. What if Arturo asked me to work full-time with Wendell? On the one hand this sorting is more fun than the mindless copying and binding that occupy most of my time in the mailroom. On the other hand I would not like working with Wendell. I like working with Jasmine. I like the way it feels when we work in silence together or when she wordlessly drops a new jazz CD on my desk. It reminds me of the times when Joseph and I would work side by side on paint-by-number pictures.

In another hour I am done with the assignment. I decide to check the documents I have placed in the "Trash" box to make sure that I have not placed a document there by mistake. Wendell did not ask me to do this, but it only makes sense to do so. We should have one copy of every document that is in there. At the very bottom of the box I find a single brown envelope. I open it. Inside the envelope there is a picture.

I look at it for only a fraction of a second and immediately put the picture face down on the desk. I close my eyes but the image of what I saw remains. It is possible to simply put the picture back in the envelope and walk away. I know that if I look at the picture again, the image will affect me like a burn. Yet I have to look. I am drawn to it. It is like the force of the IM when it is most powerful.

I turn the picture over slowly. I focus on the eyes of the girl. She is my age, maybe a year younger, but it is hard to tell. Her eyes remind me of someone. Eyes that I have seen before. Half of her face is intact but the other side is missing. The skin on the deformed side is withered and scarred, as if the cheek and jaw had been carved away with a dull knife. There is a mouth with lips that end halfway, an ear that seems about to fall off. I take the envelope and place it over the picture so that it covers the bottom part of her face. Those eyes. Her eyes are unaware of what is happening with the rest of her face. It is as if she had yet to look in a mirror. And there is something else in her eyes: a question directed at me.

"Marcelo, how's it going?"

Arturo is behind me. I put the picture back in the envelope as fast as I can. There is not enough air for my lungs in the whole law firm, it seems.

"What's wrong?"

"Nothing."

I turn around and hide the envelope with my body. Arturo is standing in the doorway. How long has he been standing there, and did he see me put the picture away? I am overwhelmed by the sense that I need to hide the picture from him. It is as if I don't want him to take away from me what the girl made me feel.

"Well, did you get everything done that Wendell wanted you to do?"

"Yes."

"Wendell asked me if you could work full-time with him for the remainder of the summer. I think it would be great if you did. It will give you a chance to do something more challenging. And—"

"Jasmine needs me," I say. I can feel anger rising.

"And, as I was saying, I think you need to be around a young man like Wendell. You need to have the experience of working with men. You will learn more from him than from Jasmine."

"It is not fair." Even to me this sounds like what a child would say.

"What is not fair? What is it about working in the mailroom that is so important to you?"

I realize that there is no reason why it is not fair for me to be moved out of the mailroom. It simply feels unfair all of a sudden. I try to explain as best I can. "It is not fair to take away Jasmine's help. And it took Marcelo a long time to learn the mailroom work. I work well there. Jasmine and Marcelo work well together. We help each other."

"You are raising your voice. I haven't seen you do that in a very long time. That's interesting. Anyway, I will get Jasmine the help she wanted to begin with. She'll be all right." He comes closer to where I am. I step back, hiding the envelope from his view. "Wendell asked for you. He obviously thinks that you can help him. The work with him will involve more reading, more analysis. It is more intellectual work. You will learn more working with him. That's what this summer is all about, isn't it?"

I want to tell him that the only reason Wendell asked for me is that he wants to use me to get at Jasmine, but I cannot say this. I feel too spent to say anything. All the energy of anger has rushed through me and carried with it all the words. Besides, I know that on my own, without Aurora's help, there is no changing Arturo's mind once he determines what is best for me.

I grip the envelope as hard as I can, and then nod in acceptance of his new command.

Chapter 16

If the object is to make it through the summer, to simply complete the assignments given to me, why does the picture of the girl unsettle me so much? I did precisely what I was told. Had I not looked in the trash box on my own initiative, I would not have seen the picture and I would not have her eyes burning within me. Why can't I forget about what I found and move on, count the days left in this job?

Here, in the dark of my tree house, I try as best I can to understand what happened, what is happening. I saw a picture of a girl who must have been disfigured by the manufacturer of the windshields that Arturo represents. The picture was in the trash box and this could not have been a mistake. There was something about the girl that did not matter, that was not significant to the law firm, to . . . Arturo? I am reminded of the way Arturo spoke to the man at the gym — like he had secrets he could not speak openly about. What does my father do?

I have seen autistic kids at Paterson affected by things that do not affect a normal person. Like the time Alexandra refused to speak for weeks after a teacher's aide accidentally threw away the postcard that fell from Alexandra's desk. No one could understand Alexandra's sadness over the postcard except a few other autistic kids. Is that what is happening to me? An overreaction caused by my condition, whatever that is? This that I now feel for the first time — is it simply a symptom, something a normal person would not feel?

I have been around kids that suffer at Paterson, at St Elizabeth's. It's like I have walked among them without noticing the pain that must exist beneath their skin. Now I notice the girl in the picture and feel as if I were responsible for her pain.

I close my eyes and in my mind there appears the portrait of Jesus that Abba kept when she lived with us. In the middle of Jesus's chest there is a red heart and around the heart there is a crown of thorns. A flame of fire shoots up from the top of the heart. One day Abba saw me looking at the portrait and she said, "That's Jesus's heart. It shows how He feels for us." Then she took the picture down and sat beside me on her bed. "The thorns are His sorrow for all that we suffer, and the flame is His love."

Now, here in the dark, the envelope with the picture of the girl on my desk, I understand what it was about that portrait of Jesus that so captivated my attention that all I could do when I entered Abba's room was stare at it. There was something about the image that was not right, something out of place. The eyes of Jesus were soft with what I took to be the look of love, but the flame in His heart burned with a fire that would scorch you if you touched it. I replace Jesus's gaze with the eyes of the girl in the picture, and the portrait of Jesus finally makes sense, the eyes at last reflecting the intensity burning in His heart.

I hear Namu below me whimpering. He knows that I've been awake all night, even though I have not moved in my sleeping bag but have stayed still, staring at the stars that pass across the skylight of my tree house. Namu can hear the turmoil in my mind and is offering comfort.

I search for the IM but can't find it. Then I try to block out the rushing thoughts by remembering a favourite piece of Scripture, but the remembering is not focused. It has a life of its own and what it presents are lines from different parts of Scriptures, senseless and disconnected, like an inner Tower of Babel.

Now dawn is breaking. I see the blackness of the night fade slowly. I put on a T-shirt, a pair of shorts, and sneakers. I climb down and touch Namu's head. "You want to go for a walk?" I ask him.

He turns and picks up the leash that is dangling from the roof of his doghouse.

I let him lead me. He decides to take the steeper path.

Chapter 17

I am gathering my things from my desk, getting ready to move. The only good thing about getting reassigned to Wendell is that it will be easier for me to go through the Vidromek boxes and gather more information about the girl. I don't know what I will find out. I am afraid of what I may discover. But last night, or rather early this morning, I decided that I had to follow this uncomfortable need to know more about the girl regardless of where it takes me.

"Hey." I hear Jasmine's voice in the distance. Then she sees me putting my things in a box. "What's going on?" She sounds worried.

"I have been assigned to work with Wendell full-time," I say. I am afraid to look at her.

"What the. . . When? How?"

"Yesterday. After I finished helping Wendell. Arturo decided. He was going to make sure you had help. Maybe Jasmine can still get Belinda." Then I see amongst my things the list that Jasmine made for me that very first morning, and my eyes well up again.

"I cannot believe this!" I have never seen Jasmine so upset. "Wait. Stay here. Is your father in yet?"

"Yes."

She walks out of the mailroom determined. She is going to fight for me to work with her. A warm glow fills me.

Ten minutes later Jasmine is back, a look of dejection on her face. "I guess you'll be working with Wendell from now on," she says. She plops down on her chair.

"What did Arturo say?"

"You can help me part-time until I find someone else. I'll work out a schedule with Queen Juliet, don't worry. This is all very strange. Did anything unusual happen yesterday when you were working on Wendell's assignment?"

"No. Yes. Not with Arturo. Something else happened."

"What?"

I think about it for a while and then I take out the picture of the girl. "I found this in the box marked 'Trash'."

She wheels her chair so that it is directly in front of mine and takes the picture from my hand. "Oh."

I can tell it is hard for Jasmine to look at the picture.

"I don't understand. What does the picture have to do with you being assigned to Wendell?"

"I need to find out more about the girl in the picture."

"You found it in a box marked 'Trash'?"

"Yes."

"You don't know who she is?"

"No."

"Wait. We can try to figure out who the girl is later. Right now

I have to figure out why I lost my help. Did you ask to work with Wendell?"

"No. Wendell asked Arturo."

"Why?"

The boat ride. I suddenly remember it. "He wants to help me succeed at the law firm so that I can go to Paterson next year." I am not sure whether this is a lie or not.

"Yeah, sure he does."

I can barely look at Jasmine's face. I don't know if I should tell her about the boat ride — that Wendell thinks he and I have an agreement and that is why he is doing all of this. But Wendell is wrong. There is no agreement between us.

"I guess I should try to call Belinda. Maybe she's still available."

In Jasmine's face I see disappointment. How can she be disappointed about losing me and getting Belinda back?

"Will Jasmine help me find out about the girl in the picture?"

She looks long and hard at me. The unformulated question on her face is *why*. Finally, she says, "Let's talk about it. Meet me here at noon. We'll go to the cafeteria. We can strategize. I don't have the slightest idea what's going on. What a place!"

On the way out of the mailroom, my arms around the small box with my things, Jasmine stops me for a second. "Here." She drops a CD into the box. "I got this for you."

I know it is not the case, but when I walk out of the mailroom, I feel as if I am leaving on a long, long trip.

She has pea soup in a Styrofoam cup and I have the tuna sandwich that Aurora made for me. We sit at the farthest table of the cafeteria, behind a pillar, where no one can see us. The cafeteria is located only one floor above us so we can take the stairs if we want to. It is only the second time I've been here.

"So," Jasmine says after she crumbles a cracker in her soup, "about the girl in the picture."

"Tell me."

"The girl was hurt by a Vidromek windshield. You know that, right?"

"The windshield is supposed to shatter into little harmless pieces upon impact."

"Right. So the girl was hurt by a windshield and her parents are probably suing Vidromek. That's how the picture ended up in Wendell's boxes. You know all about suing and settling a case and all that?"

"Yes." I remember the conversation that Arturo had with Mr Gustafson at the fitness club. "People fight against each other like enemies."

"Yeah, that's about it. The girl's parents probably hired a lawyer and the lawyer is asking Vidromek for money because they think Vidromek is at fault."

"Vidromek made the windshield. They are at fault."

"I don't know all the legal ins and outs, but if it was that simple there'd be a lot of lawyers and mailroom clerks out of work."

"But Vidromek made the windshield and the windshield did not break into little pieces like it was supposed to."

"OK, see this soup. I can tell it's scalding. If, knowing this, I go ahead and slurp it and inflict a first-degree burn on my tongue, can I sue the makers of the soup or the cook? Suppose there was a little crack in the windshield made by a flying rock or something, and the girl's parents did not fix the crack, and the crack made the windshield lose the glue or whatever it was that makes the windshield break into tiny pieces. That would be a defence that Sandoval & Holmes would use. They would say that it was the girl's father's fault because he didn't fix the tiny crack. There are many others."

"Does Jasmine think that happened?"

"I know the lawyers in the firm are doing all they can to prove that Vidromek is not responsible. Vidromek is being sued by a lot of people over these windshields and the law firm doesn't want to settle any cases. They're afraid that settling would be like admitting they are at fault."

"They are."

"Why do they make this so scalding that it takes ten minutes before a person can eat it? Why not try to get the right temperature so that a person can just sit down and slurp without thinking about it?"

"It must be difficult to get the right temperature. One that suits everyone," I volunteer.

"When you get back to your office, look at the back of the picture. There should be a number there."

"There is no number," I say.

"You sure?"

"Yes, I looked to see if it had a number like the other documents in the files."

"Maybe someone forgot to put a file number on it."

"Would it be thrown away if it had no number?"

"Not if it seems related to a case. Anyone looking at the picture would know that it had to be connected to a Vidromek case. Nothing is thrown away on purpose, but maybe it was thrown away by accident. But you don't believe that was the case?"

"No. Only copies were in the box. I checked. And there were no other envelopes like the one that contained the picture."

Jasmine pushes the soup away from her. She grabs her head with both hands. When she speaks, her tone of voice is different. It is a tone of voice one uses when it is not important to be logical. "Why are you so interested in the girl?"

I notice that my hand is opening and closing automatically. I stop it from doing that. "I felt something," I say. "I felt something I have never felt before. It was like a fire. Here. And here." I touch the top of my stomach, where my rib cage ends, and then the middle of my chest. "It was like I wanted to fight the people who hurt her. But then I realized that might include my father. It was confusing. And. . ."

"Go on, tell me. I want to know."

"There was the girl herself. Not anger. Something else."

"Ahh."

"I don't have a name for it."

She is looking at the untouched soup. I feel I need to explain to Jasmine what I felt for the girl, but how can I when I don't know myself? "It was like a question. Like a question that had to be answered."

"What question?"

"There are no words for it."

"But if you could put it into words, what would the question ask?"

Is there a way to articulate what I feel? It seems like a long time passes before I speak. "I guess it would be something like, 'How do we go about living when there is so much suffering?' Does the question make sense? Is it the type of question that is ever asked?"

I wait for her to answer. After a few seconds she says, "We should go back."

"Do you think Arturo ever saw the picture?"

I can see her hesitating. Then she says, "If it was part of a lawsuit against Vidromek? Yes. Vidromek is the firm's biggest client. About eighty per cent of the firm's money comes from them. Your father insists on seeing every document related to a Vidromek case."

"But an error could have been made — a document could have been received and filed without Arturo seeing it."

"Yes, that's possible." She looks away and I see her bite the bottom of her lip. "Do you want to talk to him? About the picture?"

"I am afraid that if I talk to Arturo, he will not let me help the girl or maybe the girl will get more hurt."

There must have been a look of guilt on my face, for I hear Jasmine say, "That's OK. There's no need to feel ashamed. We feel what we feel."

"My father always does what is right." I can almost see the words in front of me, floating in the air like solid objects.

"You shouldn't feel bad about not telling him. It's OK to want to get more information before you approach your father."

I wrap the uneaten sandwich in a piece of wrinkled foil. I smooth the foil as best I can and place the sandwich in the paper bag next to the cookies and apple. I want to change the subject of my thoughts, so I say, "I have something I need to confess to you. You may not like it."

"What?" I see on her face the look of nervous anticipation I hoped to see.

"This morning I listened to the CD you lent me: Keith Jarrett's version of the *Goldberg Variations*. On my laptop, with the headphones."

"Instead of doing Wendell's work?" She is dismayed at my transgression.

"No, Wendell was not in this morning. There was nothing for me to do, so I listened to the CD."

"Oh, no. How could you? You failed to exercise the immense skills required in your new job."

"I know," I say. I try to look as if I'm sorry to be so irresponsible.

"You're right. I don't like it."

"No, that's not what I thought you wouldn't like," I say.

"Then what?"

"I have a CD of the *Goldberg Variations* at home. It is by a pianist named Glenn Gould, and I think Glenn Gould plays the *Goldberg Variations* more correctly than Keith Jarrett."

"More correctly? More correctly? Is there such a thing as more correctly?"

"Yes," I say. But in fact I'm not sure "more correctly" is grammatically correct.

"OK, fine. I'm going to skip the 'more correctly' discussion for the time being. I can't believe you said that. You are so, so wrong. But let's leave that aside for now. I want you to answer me this: who is the better artist, who has the most talent? Your Glenn Gould *interpreting* Bach's *Goldberg Variations* 'more correctly', as you put it, or my Keith Jarrett *improvising, creating* on the spot? Answer that for me."

But I can't. I am unable to answer her question. I am at a total loss. I see the skills and talents required for both types of playing and I am stuck. She waits for me to answer, beaming warmth. I can feel the warmth coming from her all the way across the table. And the warmth reminds me of the fire I saw in the girl's eyes.

"I must help the girl somehow."

"I know." She is still beaming.

"But I don't want to hurt my father."

The warmth coming from her fades now. "I know."

"What would Jasmine do if she were in my place? Would she forget about the picture? Does Jasmine think that I am acting strange?"

"That's one of those questions that can only be answered by you."

"I know. But why can't Jasmine give me her opinion?"

"Because my opinion would not be based on all the factors that need to be taken into account. I'm not you. I don't feel what you feel for your father or for the . . . girl. I am not situated to lose what you might lose. Every time you decide, there is loss, no matter how you decide. It's always a question of what you cannot afford to lose. I'm not the one playing the piano here. You're the one that needs to decide what the next note will be."

"But how do I know the next note is the right one?"

"The right note sounds right and the wrong note sounds wrong."

We do not speak on the way back to the firm. In the elevator, as we ride alone and in silence, I ask myself: *If I do nothing to help the girl, if I let things be, what do I lose?*

Chapter 18

On my way back to Wendell's office after lunch, Juliet says to me, "I hear you got promoted."

At first I decide not to answer her but then I ask, "When is Wendell returning?"

She opens the top drawer to her desk and hands me a note. I recognize Wendell's handwriting. "He came in while you were at lunch," Juliet informs me.

Hey Marcelo,

What did I tell you? Ask and it shall be given. I'm out for the rest of the week on a little relaxation cruise. Juliet will tell you what to do. Remember: Sandoval and Holmes above all. Stay out of Juliet's clutches if you can.

Wendell

I fold the note. "You are supposed to tell me what to do," I tell Juliet.

"Is that it? Does he tell you anything else?"

"He says I should stay out of your clutches."

"Is that supposed to be funny or something?"

"I believe he was talking figuratively."

"I've never clutched anybody in my whole life."

She seems upset, but not at me. She doesn't like that Wendell said that about her. It means that Wendell thinks about her in a way that is different than the way she would like him to think about her. This is how I interpret her sudden grouchiness. But then again, Juliet is always grouchy. I have never seen her smile. Suddenly I realize how pleasant it was to work in the mailroom. Jasmine didn't smile that much either, but it was different.

"Has Juliet ever seen Wendell's yacht?" The question pops into my head.

Juliet sits back in her chair with a jolt. I look up long enough to see a momentary look of fear. "Why do you want to know?" She asks this as if she's afraid of what I am going to answer.

"I wanted to know what the boat was like."

"It's a boat."

"Wendell invited Juliet."

Her usually pale face is turning pink. I am making her upset and I don't mean to.

"For your information, and not that you need to know, Wendell has invited me to the boat like he has invited many others in this firm. And for your information, I know what the boat looks like, but I did not go there at Wendell's invitation. I am not into little boys."

She is flustered and now she turns towards her computer and begins typing. I believe that she regrets telling me so much. It seems that lately I have been interpreting people's gestures correctly with more frequency than ever before. But how does one ever know if those interpretations are truly correct without actually testing them out, either by asking how a person feels or by doing something else that reveals their state of mind? I decide not to pursue this line of questioning any further. I don't know why I even asked Juliet. And why did I lie when I told her that I wanted to know what the boat was like? What was it that I really wanted to know? There was a sense of relief when Juliet said that many others had been on the boat. There is something about Jasmine not being singled out by Wendell that is comforting.

"Are you going to stand there all afternoon?"

Jasmine used to ask me that question when I got lost in thought in the middle of a task. But there was humour in the way Jasmine said it. In Juliet's voice there is only annoyance.

"The note said that Juliet was going to tell me what to do."

"And I'm a babysitter too?" She stands up and walks to Wendell's office. She doesn't tell me to follow her, but I suppose that's what she wants me to do.

She stands at the doorway. "Wendell wants all the boxes out of here. Move them down to where you are going to be."

"Where I am going to be."

"Do you always repeat what people say?" Before I can answer she starts walking again. Juliet walks as if she had a stack of plates on her head. We stop three offices down from Wendell's office.

"The lawyer here is out on vacation, and when he comes back he's going to be fired, so you can use this office. Just put the pictures and stuff on his desk in a box. Don't go through any of his drawers. He can do that himself. He's going to get axed the minute he comes in."

I stand there looking at a desk full of pictures of children. "Fired. Axed." I am not sure what these words mean, but because I am going to use his office, I suspect that it means that the lawyer will be dismissed from the law firm.

Juliet is looking at me as if I were an idiot. I probably am in her eyes. She has told me so before. "Fired. Axed. As in you're out of here. As in, to put it in a language that you would understand, *hasta la vista,* baby."

"Why?"

"He didn't have what it takes. He did not measure up to expectations. He was too soft."

Listening to Juliet talk requires additional effort. At the risk of getting her upset again, or more upset than she is, I ask, "What does it mean when a person is too soft?"

She starts to walk back to her office. I walk behind her, thinking that she is not going to answer my question, but then I hear her speak and I speed up so I can walk next to her. "People hire Sandoval and Holmes when they want the meanest and the toughest. When other firms know that we are on the case, they know our client is out to win. You want to succeed here, you need to be merciless, go for the jugular. The guy in that office didn't have it. He thought too much. He was always in Mr Holmes's office, bugging him about whether a course of action was correct. He had nerve to question Mr Holmes, I'll give him that. But he was soft."

Juliet is looking at me with a look of disgust. I know she thinks I am soft as well, as she has just defined it. After all, doesn't Marcelo think about things too much? "Is being soft the same as being meek?"

"I don't know what that means. What is 'meek'?"

I hesitate. Should I break the rule and tell her the religious uses of this term: "Blessed are the meek for they shall inherit the earth" from Jesus's Sermon on the Mount or "the meek shall possess the land and delight themselves in abundant prosperity" from Psalm thirty-seven? I decide not to respond, even though Juliet is waiting for an answer. For the first time I have doubts that the meek will ever inherit or possess anything.

Juliet goes on, "Meek or weak or whatever, he's gone. You need to move all the boxes in Wendell's office to his office. When you finish that, come see me. I have some filing for you."

I move all the boxes into Robert Steely's office. The good thing about this is that, in the privacy of Robert Steely's office, I will have the opportunity to look for a file that goes with the girl's picture. But how do I go about doing this? There are so many files. I decide to look first in the two boxes that I used when working with Wendell's assignment.

I find the boxes. I place them on top of the desk and proceed to go through each file. I don't know what I am looking for. Another picture of the girl? Maybe the picture ended up in the trash box because it truly was a duplicate. There are twelve files in each box, each one full of hundreds of pages. I go through every single file, every single page in that file. Nothing. I look for pages that have paper clips with nothing attached. None.

I sit down in Robert Steely's chair to think about what my next step should be. Now that I started looking for the file, the need to find out about the girl has increased. It is as if the act of looking has confirmed the rightness of my quest. I look at the pictures on the desk. In one picture, two small children sit underneath a beach umbrella. In another, the same children, but older, are wearing Mickey Mouse hats and holding on to Robert Steely. Seeing his picture reminds me of the times I saw him in his office on my mail delivery runs. Juliet said he thought too much. He questioned Stephen Holmes about what was correct. I wonder if that included what was right or wrong. I never noticed anything different about him other than that he was one of the few lawyers who was not afraid to talk to me. For some reason he and I would find ourselves going to the bathroom at the same time. "We seem to be on the same kidney schedule," he said to me once.

I am not supposed to, but I open the top drawer of his desk. There are pen refills, paper clips that have been extended and can no longer serve their function, lots of pennies, business cards, a menu for a Thai restaurant, a small ball made from rubber bands, a drawing of a spider's web on a sticky, a magnifying lens, three plastic spoons, a napkin, dental floss, a cough drop that is stuck to the bottom, a dozen Pepto-Bismol tablets.

I take out the picture of the girl again. I wish so much that she had a name. I want to call her by her name. Her hair is black and short like Jasmine's. Her eyes are black. The eyebrows are thick and form arches over her eyes. It is not a colour picture, but her skin is dark brown like Abba's or Aurora's or Yolanda's. My skin is more like Arturo's, a beige colour, a little browner than white but not dark brown. Abba came from Mexico and Arturo's great-grandparents did as well. I wonder if the girl or her parents are from there too. Maybe the fact that she is like me in that respect is what is drawing me to her.

I had not noticed the background behind the girl. The picture was taken inside. It looks like an office because I can see the edge of a filing cabinet on one side of the girl and on the other side, behind her, there is a calendar. I can tell because I can make out the sequence of dots that represent the days of the month.

I remember the magnifying glass in Robert Steely's top drawer. I take it out now and look closely. It is a calendar. The girl's face covers most of it but I can tell it is a month with thirty days. On top of the numbers there seems to be a picture of a tree in autumn. Below the calendar days there are some letters. Maybe it is like the calendar that Aurora gets from the hospital every year — at the bottom is the name of the hospital, the address, and a statement about the excellent work they do. Here all those words are obscured except for two words and five numbers. Even with the magnifying glass I cannot make out the words or numbers, but maybe I can take the picture to the mailroom and enlarge it. I grab the picture and am about to go out when suddenly the door opens.

All of the following happen simultaneously: my heartbeat accelerates. I quickly do what I can to turn the picture against the side of my leg. I expect to see Juliet. I start to think of what I can say to explain what I was doing with the door closed in Robert Steely's office.

But it is not Juliet. It is Robert Steely. "Oh," he says, jumping back. "Oh," he repeats again. He is speechless and so am I. Then he sees the boxes occupying almost every inch of his office. "What is this?" he says without any surprise in his voice. He is expecting to receive a rational explanation. He is carrying a briefcase in his hand and it is clear he just arrived at the office.

Juliet said that he would be fired as soon as he returned. I don't know how getting fired works. I imagine someone tells you that you can no longer work at the law firm. It is not something that I would mind happening to me, but maybe it would be different for Robert Steely. Where will he get the money to feed his children?

"The Vidromek boxes," I respond.

I look around the office just as he does and see that I left his magnifying glass on top of his desk. He will know that I opened his top drawer. I am about to say something about that, but then I see him drop his briefcase on the floor. He turns around and sits on the edge of the desk, looking at the door. His shoulders are slumped and he has turned white. "Bastards," he says under his breath.

Now he is hiding his face with his hands. I wonder if I should put my hand on his shoulder, but I have never done this before and am afraid. Then he shakes his head and rubs his eyes with his coat sleeve.

"You know," I say.

He nods. "I didn't think it would happen this soon. I thought I had at least until the end of the year. I thought I'd get a few months to look for another job."

We both look up when we hear the sound of Juliet's high heels. She is at the doorway, standing very straight, her hands on her hips. "We didn't expect you until Monday."

"Obviously." Now for the first time I hear anger in his voice.

"The person at the reception desk was supposed to direct you to Mr Sandoval's office."

"She must have been taking a break, because I walked right in."

"Mr Holmes is not in, so you should go see Mr Sandoval."

Robert Steely looks at me and raises his eyebrows. How am I to interpret that look? *Look, see, this is who your father is?* He straightens himself up, takes a deep breath and walks out.

"What's that?" I see Juliet looking at the picture in my hand.

It has always been almost impossible for me to lie. The synapses in my brain usually travel faster than they should, but when it comes to lying, the same synapses freeze in place. I cannot think fast enough to come up with an alternative to the truth. So I answer Juliet's question truthfully: "A picture." Then I say something that comes as a surprise to me. "I found it under the desk. It belongs to Robert Steely."

The deception works. Juliet does not ask to see it. She says, "I'm going to get someone to watch him while he collects his personal belongings. You should go to the mailroom and find him a couple of empty boxes so he can take his stuff."

"I can help Robert Steely pack his things."

"No. We need someone to make sure he doesn't take any files that belong to the firm. He is only allowed to take his personal stuff. You can't tell the difference."

I think I can. Juliet actually thinks that I am stupid. I put the picture face down on the desk, pretending that I am going to leave it there, and wait for Juliet to turn around before I grab it again. I can get to the mailroom without passing by Juliet's desk.

"Hey, you back to work in the mailroom?" Jasmine asks. It feels like years since I last saw her.

"Juliet sent me to get empty boxes for Robert Steely. He is fired."

"Gosh," she says. "It seems like the nice ones never stay for long."

"Juliet said he was soft. That's why he is fired."

"Juliet's the one that's soft." Jasmine taps her head with her index finger.

I nod my head in agreement. I remember the picture in my hand and hold it out to her. "On the wall behind the girl there is a calendar. It is mostly covered by her, but I can make out two words and five numbers. Maybe the words and numbers can help us find the girl."

She takes the picture from me and goes to the copying machine. I follow her. "Let's try enlarging it one hundred and fifty per cent." From the side of the copying machine a blurry picture of the girl emerges. But now the words behind her are clear.

SU TAQUERÍA
02130

"*Taquería* is a place where they sell tacos, right? Like a *cafetería* is place where they sell coffee," Jasmine says.

"You know how to speak Spanish?"

"Three years in high school. Besides, I hate to tell you, but *taquería* is not that hard to translate. This picture could have been taken in any of the countless places in Spanish-speaking countries where Vidromek does business. Except that. . ."

"Except that."

"Except that we only represent Vidromek in accidents that took place in the US. So if this picture is somehow related to a case we are handling, then this *taquería* is in the US, which doesn't narrow the options all that much. Mmm."

"What is it?"

"The numbers. So this is a calendar advertising a *taquería* somewhere in the United States. The advertisement would have an address for the *taquería*, right? And what usually goes in an address?"

It seems like an easy question to answer, but my mind is a total blank.

"Either a street address or a zip code. But since there are no words following these numbers, this is probably a zip code. Zip codes have five numbers," Jasmine says.

"A zip code," I repeat. I probably should feel dumb but I don't. Probably because I'm so thrilled by the sound of excitement in Jasmine's voice.

"Do you have to get back to Juliet?"

"I have to bring Robert Steely two boxes. To pack his personal belongings."

"Do that. I'll do a search of *taquería* and 02130 and see what I get. Take the boxes, and when you come back I'll know more."

I grab two empty boxes, the kind used for the copying paper, and I go to Robert Steely's office. I put the boxes in the office. Robert Steely is still talking to Arturo, I suppose. How long does getting fired take? Perhaps Arturo is trying to be as kind as possible.

"That took you long enough," Juliet says to me on my way back to the mailroom. "Now where are you going? Look, Jasmine and I worked out a schedule and you're now operating on my time. I need you to fold and stick these letters in the envelopes and then seal the letters. You can use this bottle with a sponge to seal the envelopes or you can lick them if you prefer."

I look at the stack of paper. There must be two hundred letters. Juliet hands me the stack, and she places a box of envelopes on top of it. Then with her chin she points in the direction of Wendell's office. That's where she wants me to work.

It is the first assignment at the law firm that I do not perform as well as I can. I am rushing and I can see that some of the letters are getting folded in uneven ways. Then when all the folding and inserting is done, I wet the envelopes with the bottle of water that has a miniature sponge attached to the end. It is hard to control the exact amount of water and some of the letters look as if Namu had licked them.

I wait for Juliet to leave her desk, then I head towards the mailroom. The letters need to get stamped by the machine in the mailroom anyway. Jasmine is intent on the screen of her computer. At first I think she does not notice when I come in.

"Listen to this," she says without looking at me, "I typed in *taquería* and 02130 and found a site for Mexican restaurants in Boston. Then it hits me, 02130 is a Boston zip code! Anyway, I click on this site for the Boston restaurants and I see all these restaurants that have the zip code 02130. I get about thirty restaurants, all in Jamaica Plain. It's a neighbourhood that has many Latino residents and businesses. So then I narrow the search by clicking *taquería* and Jamaica Plain and I come up with ten restaurants."

"What do we do now?"

"We call the restaurants. How many of those ten restaurants send out calendars? And then, I don't know, maybe we go and show them the girl's picture to see if they know her. This picture was taken in an office. You see the file cabinet?"

"It looks like a file cabinet in this law firm."

"Right. That's what I was thinking. Like the picture was taken in a lawyer's office, which makes sense, since the picture ended up here and is probably tied to some kind of legal action."

"A lawyer that eats at a *taquería* in Jamaica Plain."

"You took the words right out of my mouth."

"Oh."

"It's a figure of speech. Look, here's the plan. We look up what lawyers work in Jamaica Plain, and when we call the restaurants that send out calendars, we read them the names and ask if the lawyer is on their mailing list or if they know him or recognize the name. I mean, how do people get calendars? They get them in the mail or they pick them up when they shop at the place that's giving them out."

"We."

"We what?"

"It was I who needed to find the girl and now it is we — Jasmine and Marcelo."

"I don't *need* to find her like you do." Jasmine's voice sounds serious. "I don't know, it makes me feel kind of alive, playing detective in your good cause."

"Like Sherlock Holmes."

"Yeah."

"Jasmine is logical in her thinking. One step leading to another. Analysing probabilities and discarding them."

"You look surprised. Didn't you know I was smart?" She pretends to be angry.

Even though I know she is teasing me, I feel my face get red-hot. How can I tell her that I knew but I didn't know — like seeing the sunset every evening but not seeing it.

Chapter 19

It turns out that Cielito is the only *taquería* in Jamaica Plain that hands out calendars. They didn't have a mailing list but gave them to their customers starting in early December. It turns out also that there are thirty-seven lawyers that practice in Jamaica Plain, and when I called Don Ramon, the owner of Cielito, and asked him if he knew any of the names I read to him, there was only one he recognized without any hesitation. His name is Jerry García and, according to Don Ramon, he practically lives at Cielito. Jerry García's office is half a block away. Jasmine and I are certain that the picture of the girl was taken there.

Jasmine walks me to the entrance to the subway on Washington Street but doesn't want to come with me. She thinks it is something I should do on my own. I have a detailed map showing exactly what to do in order to get to Jerry García's office once I get off at Jackson Square. I have a cell phone that I can use if I get lost. "You can do it," Jasmine said just before I descended the stairs of the subway station.

I am on extreme alert on the subway, standing up, holding on to the back of an empty seat.

I get out at the Jackson Square station and walk east on Centre Street. Jerry García's office is only five blocks away. I block out the traffic on the street, the people on the sidewalks, the words and noises that come flying at me. I touch the sides of buildings for reassurance and then continue.

I look for and finally find the number to Jerry García's building. His office is in Suite 3A. I look up and see a window with white lettering:

GERONIMO (JERRY) GARCÍA ESQ.
SU PROBLEMA ES MI PROBLEMA

I walk up three flights of stairs. Suite 3A has a wooden door with the same name and logo as the window. The door is partially open. Inside there are a dozen people, adults and children, sitting in a parlour. There is a small desk with a telephone in the front of the room but no one at the desk. A tall fan in the corner is whirring left and right. Some of the children are playing on the floor with plastic cars and trucks. I see a box of toys in another corner. I may be in the wrong place. This looks like the doctor's office where Aurora used to take Yolanda and me when we were children. Everyone is staring at me as I stand in the doorway, not knowing what to do or say.

"*¿Busca a Jerry?*" an elderly woman is asking me.

"*Sí.*" I remember the Spanish that I learned from Abba.

"He's here. Sit." She makes a small space on the crowded sofa. I remain standing.

A door next to the desk opens. A man with a white shirt and blue jeans holds it open as a young woman comes out, dabbing her eyes with a handkerchief. The man looks at me. I must seem out of place in this room, standing with my backpack and my hands in my pockets.

The man with the white shirt and blue jeans is Jerry García. I know because Jasmine and I found a picture of him on the Internet. He has an ad in a Spanish-speaking newspaper, telling people to call him if they have an accident.

He motions to the lady who first spoke to me. She gets up slowly, holding on to the side of the sofa. He comes over and takes her arm. "Sit, please." He is talking to me. "I'll be with you as soon as I can."

I wait three hours. Every time he comes out he tells me he will be with me in just a little while. Everyone who was there when I came in is gone but more people have come in so that the room is full again. I stand up so as not to be squeezed on the sofa.

"OK," he says. "Come in." It takes me a while to understand that he is finally talking to me. I walk in and he closes the door behind us.

"You're in the autism spectrum, aren't you?" Jerry García asks me.

This question has become even more difficult to answer accurately as the summer has progressed. There are times when I wonder whether I ever belonged at Paterson. Here I am functioning in the real world, having conversations with people, detecting what is on their minds, imagining what they must be feeling, in a way that many autistic kids are never able to do. But I like it when people do not walk on eggshells (one of my favourite figures of speech) and say what is on their minds, the way he has just done. It makes me like him almost immediately.

"The closest description of what I have is probably Asperger's syndrome. It falls on the high-functioning end of the autism spectrum." It is as good an answer as I can give.

"I could tell. Sometimes I represent autistic kids and their families, trying to get the schools to comply with federal law and provide the special services they need."

"Why did you ask?"

"Something in your eyes, you know, kind of looking sideways when you speak." Then when I look at him and rest my eyes on him, he adds quickly, "But to a much lesser degree than the kids I've met. Also the way you stand and sit: very formal, very still. Most kids your age slouch and fidget."

"Arturo says I stand like a lead soldier."

"Arturo?"

"My father."

"What's your name?"

"Marcelo Sandoval."

A big grin appears on his face. "I knew you reminded me of someone. I was a classmate of your father's in law school."

"I know."

"You know?"

"I did not know you knew my father but I knew you graduated from Harvard Law School the same year he did. I found that information on the Internet."

"Oh."

Now comes the hard part. He is going to ask me why I am here to see him. I have rehearsed the reply to this question many times, but I keep changing my answer. Despite the fact that I am here in front of Jerry García, I am still not sure why I am here. Despite all the planning, the lying to Juliet about how I had a doctor's appointment, the studying and memorizing the directions to Jerry García's office, despite all that, this feels as if I were being asked to enter a dark room. I cannot remember a single time in my life when I have not known where I was going. I have always been sure I could see what was ahead before I stepped towards it.

So now I see him moving about his cramped office, making room for me to sit on a blue sofa that has pieces of cotton sticking out. As I sit, I hear him saying something about how he wishes he could be more organized and how there is just too much work for one person to do and something about how much I look like my father, how I have the same determined, intense look. I hear all these things but only pieces of them because I am wondering what I will say when he asks me why I am here. Different words from different people play in my head along with the chatter of Jerry García. *"The right note sounds right and the wrong note sounds wrong,"* I remember Jasmine saying. And so I listen carefully now and try to detect what I hear inside, trying to listen for the note.

Jerry García pulls a wooden chair in front of me and crosses his legs and asks, "What I can do for you?"

Although my eyes have been open all along, it is at this point that I begin to truly see where I am. Jerry García works out of a desk cluttered with files and papers and boxes. There is a table behind his desk with a computer, a printer and a fax machine. To the side of the room is the sofa where I'm sitting. This room too is full of shelves lined with books and brown folders. Except that on one of the shelves, the one that is closest to me, I see a picture of Jerry García, his arms around an older man with dark sunglasses, who I know is blind because he is holding a German shepherd on a harness.

After I don't know how long, I say, "I have a German shepherd. His name is Namu."

"Namu. Nice name. As in *Namu Amida Butsu*?"

"Yes." No one has ever recognized the source of Namu's name before. "Do you think it's wrong to name a dog after a Buddhist prayer?"

"Of course not. That way every time you call Namu you can say the Nembutsu."

"That is what I thought also. I thought the Buddha would be OK with that."

"I have no doubt he would."

"My uncle Hector brought Namu and Namu's brother, Romulus, from Texas when I was twelve years old. He gave Romulus to Paterson, the school I attend."

"Your uncle Hector lives in Texas?"

"In San Antonio. He is the head of Furman, a reformatory school for delinquent boys. They breed and train the dogs there. The contact with the animals helps the boys. And the dogs raise money for the school."

"A good idea. A very good idea."

"We have Haflinger ponies at Paterson, where I go to school, for similar reasons. The ponies — we call them ponies but they are not technically ponies, they are small horses — help the kids with coordination and with their confidence."

"Yes, I can see they would."

There is a pause. I breathe slowly one, two, three times. I speak. "I helped with the Vidromek litigation. I found a picture. In the picture I saw that." I point to the calendar hanging on the wall behind his desk. "That's how we found you."

"We?"

"Jasmine works with me at the law firm. She helped me."

"Ahh." Jerry García smiles, as if he knew that was the reason for my visit.

I remove the picture from my backpack.

He takes it in his hand but hardly looks at it. He is obviously familiar with the picture. Jerry García smiles and returns it to me.

He sits back on the chair he has placed in front of me and begins to speak so softly I can barely hear him. "When your father and I were in law school, there was a poker game every Friday night without fail. There were seven of us, the seven Mexican-Americans at Harvard Law School. Your father, myself, this guy Rudy, and I don't remember the names of the other guys. These poker games were unbelievable. There was so much hostility there. When I went there, I thought, well, this will be a nice support group with my *carnales, mi raza* — you know, my brothers. But all everyone did was openly envy and insult each other. I kept on going because I needed the money. I could eat for the next week with that money. So in that sense my *carnales* helped me out despite themselves." Jerry García laughs and slaps his knees at the same time. "Do you play poker?"

"No."

The phone rings. Jerry García gets up and pushes a button on it. "My secretary left me last week," he says when he sits down.

"She went to work in a law firm like your father's. Imagine, after I trained her and everything." He shrugs. This shrug means, *What can you do?*

"Where was I? My brain is like one of those balloons that you untie and they go *prrrrr* all over the place. You know what I mean?"

"I do." Every time I have to do more than one thing at once my brain feels like that. "What happened with the poker game?"

"Wow! They were something, those poker games. Where was all the anger and downright meanness coming from? I mean, it wasn't gentle ribbing. I could tell that people were really pissed when one got an A and the others didn't or when one got a job offer with a bigger law firm. It was craaaazy-*loco*! When I walked out of there, I felt like I needed to take a shower. Only I needed the money. It made me sad. Really, they'd ask me what I wanted to do after law school and I told them my plan. First, I'm working with the US Attorney's office to get some experience in litigation and then I'm opening a solo practice in a poor neighbourhood. They'd look at me like I was from, I don't know, like I was from. . ."

"Mars."

"Yeah. Exactly. Except . . . except your father. He never made fun of me. Then one evening he and I got to walk together back to our dorms and, I don't know, I guess he had a couple of tequilas in him, I did too, so he said to me, 'I hope you make it through law school still feeling like you do.' 'Why wouldn't I?' I asked him. And he answered, 'Sometimes you start off going one way and you end up going another way and you don't know how it happened. It's kind of like a current veered your boat.' When he said this, I knew he was talking about his own life, about a decision he had made that he wasn't sure about. 'Veer it back,' I said to him. 'It's never too late.' But he patted my back and walked off towards his dorm. We were about to graduate and your dad had already received an offer from one of the most prestigious law firms in Boston."

"My father said that to you?" It was a different image of Arturo. Arturo, only eight or so years older than my present age, a young man, wondering about the path he was about to take.

"So, what does all this have to do with the picture you found? When the Sisters came to see me about Ixtel, that's the name of the girl in the picture, and when I found out that your father's law firm was handling the case, I remembered those poker games and the conversation we had that night. I thought I'd try the personal letter approach. Give it a shot. Oh well."

"You wrote Arturo a letter."

"Didn't you see the letter when you found the picture? The picture was attached to the letter."

"No." I decide not tell him that I found the picture in the box marked "Trash".

"Hold on. Let me see if I can find the copy." He opens up the file cabinet, the one that partially appears in the picture. Then he returns to where I'm sitting and gives me the letter. "Take your time reading it. I need to step outside and tell the folks to come back later this afternoon, and then I'm going to go down the hall and pee."

This is what I read:

Dear Art:

Do you remember me? Harvard Law. Poker games at Rudy's (I forgot his last name) apartment on Friday nights? You guys always got mad at me because I came in with only twenty bucks and walked out with a hundred or more?

You've done well. I was floored when I saw who was representing Vidromek. Sandoval and Holmes. Your own firm! Cabrón! I got this solo practice here in Jamaica Plain making a buck here and there. You or any one of your lawyers ever caught driving under the influence, give me a call.

I tried to phone you but your secretary wouldn't patch me in to you. You're an important guy, I understand. I'm better at writing anyway. Here it goes. I represent a sixteen-year-old girl by the name of Ixtel Jaetz (great name, huh?). She and her mother were driving a car with a Vidromek windshield. A Coca-Cola truck in front of them suddenly stopped and they rammed into it. They hit it at about twenty-five miles an hour. The car did not have airbags, but both mother and child were wearing seat belts. The Coca-Cola driver says he hardly even knew his truck was hit. But Ixtel was pierced on the side of the face just below the left cheekbone with a shard of glass from the windshield. The mother was OK. The windshield, as you know, should not have done this. Ixtel was taken to Mass General Hospital where the shard and fragments of window were removed and her face was temporarily patched up.

I am enclosing for you a picture of the girl that I took a couple of weeks ago. When I saw you were representing Vidromek, I thought I'd try a personal appeal here. I could sue you, but why fool ourselves? You'd kill me with depositions and other bullshit discovery that you know a solo practitioner like me can't handle. So I'm proposing something radical here: let's do the right thing! I won't go after pain and suffering and all those other damages that I might be entitled to, and in return your client pays for the cost of the reconstructive surgery plus my twenty per cent contingency fee, which comes to about sixty-eight thousand dollars. A drop in the ocean for Vidromek, wouldn't you say?

These are poor people, Art. Mass General waived the hospital charges under their Good Samaritan programme. The girl is with the Sisters of Mercy at a home in Lawrence. Ixtel's mother died a few months after the accident from liver cancer. The father, who was from Hungary originally (hence the name Jaetz), died when the girl was two. The Sisters were named legal guardians since there was no other family. They're only asking for the cost of the surgery. By the way, the reconstructive surgery will not only somewhat restore the girl's beauty, it will also allow her to speak clearly, chew and alleviate the pain she feels whenever she eats or tries to speak now.

What do you say, Art? You want to do the right thing? Call me.

Yours truly,
Jerry García

I look up when I finish reading and see Jerry García sitting in front of me. "Ixtel. What is she like?"

"She's been through a lot." Jerry García frowns. "No father. Face gets disfigured. Loses her mother. She went kind of wild there for a while, but now she's on the right track. I don't know, even with her face there's kind of an inner beauty that shines out."

Jerry García's words jolt me. It is as if he has given a name to what I could not name.

"Would you like to meet her? Lawrence is about an hour from Boston. I can take you there. I try to go at least every other Saturday. I get a kick out of the girls who live there and the Sisters are a blast. Most of them are from El Salvador and they barely speak English."

I am silent. If the picture had such an effect, what would the real person do to me? Finally I say, "Yes, I would like to meet her someday." I feel at that moment that I already know her.

"Well then, I'll arrange it." The phone rings again. "Don't worry, it'll go straight to my secretary." He winks at me.

I realize that the telephone has been ringing constantly since I sat on the sofa. It rings once (that must be when it goes to voice mail), then after thirty seconds, another ring. Behind every one of those rings there is a person with a *problema*.

"You said you got a response from my father to your letter?"

"Yes, he wrote me back."

"May I see the letter?"

I can see Jerry García hesitating, but he gets up and takes a piece of paper from a folder on his desk. He hands it to me. This time he sits in front of me while I read.

Dear Jerry:

I see you are still doing God's work (?). Please consider this a response to your "personal" letter. Vidromek will <u>not</u> pay for any injuries to your client.

Regards,
Arturo Sandoval

I understand now beyond any doubt that my father knows about Ixtel. He saw her picture and read Jerry García's letter. If the letter came to him and the picture was attached to the letter, it is through him that the picture found its way to the box labelled "Trash".

"What does a question mark in parentheses mean?"

He laughs. "I think he's questioning whether I'm really doing God's work or just trying to make a little money."

"Which is it?"

"What can I tell you? I have to live."

"You never asked me why I came to see you," I say after what seems like a long time.

He waves a hand at me. "I know why you came." He waits until my eyes meet his. "I know. Trust me. I know. The other day I called again and talked to Holmes's son, what's his name?"

"Wendell."

"An arrogant little prick. A shame. For one so young, I mean. I understand they get that way eventually, but usually not before they graduate from law school."

"I'm sorry," I say.

"I deal with people like him a hundred times a day. They look at me and naturally assume I'm not as smart as they are. God help us. But think about it, it's a tremendous tactical advantage, not to mention personally liberating, to have others think I'm a dummy."

"I found the picture in a box marked 'Trash'."

Jerry García raises his hand for me to stop. "You saw the picture of Ixtel and you wanted to find out more about her. That is why you're here." He stares at me. "I'll take care of Ixtel, don't worry. I'll make sure she's OK."

The telephone rings again. I stand up and stretch out my hand. I am not sure what just happened, but there does not seem to be a need for further talking. "I should go."

Jerry García stands up as well and takes my hand. "Marcelo," he says, "if you want to help Ixtel, all I need is a clue."

"A clue?"

"Vidromek and . . . its lawyers, they claim they shouldn't pay because they had no knowledge that the windshields were defective when they made them. Even now, they are still making them the same dangerous way, because if they fix the problem they would be admitting there was a problem. What we have to do to stop this is find a document that shows they *knew* the windshields were not safe and they kept on making them nevertheless. They have to have known. It is impossible for them not to. Somewhere in the Vidromek documents there is a document proving this prior knowledge."

"There are boxes and boxes of documents."

"I need something that will take me to the document or something that will show them that I know it exists. If there is such a document, and I know that there is, it's not right to hide it. Whoever's working on the Vidromek litigation knows about it."

I think of Stephen Holmes and Wendell and Robert Steely. I remember Jasmine telling me that Arturo looked at every document associated with Vidromek.

"If you find a clue and you decide to give it to me, I'll do what I can to protect you and your father, but I can't make any guarantees."

"He would lose the case."

"Maybe. Most likely his client will lose some money."

"Sixty-eight thousand dollars."

"It'll be more now. They'll have to pay more for playing games with me."

"Your fee will be higher." As soon as I say this, I wish I hadn't.

"You better believe it. Maybe I can get my secretary back. Think about it."

"I will need to decide."

"Hey, whatever you decide, you would still be able to help Ixtel. You can take her and the other girls to your school to ride the ponies. I'm going to give you the address of the Sisters in Lawrence in case you can go see her. I'll let her know about you and let the Sisters know you may be coming. This friend of yours at work, Jasmine you said, does she drive?"

"Yes." I know because Jasmine has told me that she drives to Vermont to spend weekends with her father.

"She can take you then. Or give me a call and I'll take you. Or, you know, it would be great if you can get your father to take you."

We smile at each other. We know this is not likely to happen.

Chapter 20

I get back to the office around one o'clock. I just completed a trip in the city on my own and I should be happy but I am not. Deflated. That is the word that comes to mind.

"That was some doctor's appointment," Juliet says when I walk past her.

For a moment I do not know what she is talking about. Lying requires an incredible amount of mental effort. "There were many people waiting," I say.

"Speaking of waiting, Wendell has been waiting for you. He needs you to do an errand for him."

I have seen very little of Wendell in the past two weeks. He calls Juliet from somewhere, his boat perhaps, and dictates to her what I am supposed to do. I now understand that I have been doing his work. Still, I am glad that he has been away. Every time I do see him, he asks about the boat ride. I have not brought myself to tell him no. It is such a simple word, but uttering it means that Wendell will be my enemy. I am afraid of what that will feel like — to be hated by someone. Then there is Paterson. To say no to

Wendell is to say goodbye to Paterson. Wendell will make sure of that.

So I keep stalling and he keeps insisting. He is losing patience. But now I have another reason to stall. I need to be around the Vidromek documents so that I can look for the document that will help Ixtel. But to find such a document would also mean the end of Paterson.

"Marshello, Marshello, where have you been? I leave you alone for a few days and you lose all your good work habits." Wendell is typing very fast and hardly looks up at me. His arms are golden-brown from the sun. There are small flakes of skin peeling from the top of his forehead.

"I had a doctor's appointment."

"Yeah, sure." He looks up and winks at me. "Listen, I'm only here for a few minutes. I gotta take advantage of Daddy-o being away. You need to do something. Do you know that guy Robert Steely, the one that got canned last week?"

"Yes." Canned. Another mysterious figure of speech. I think of fruit being put into cans. What is the relationship between "canned" and being asked to leave a job?

"You need to take this letter I'm typing to him. Father just called from someplace in Italy and asked me to do it. He wants me to deliver it personally. But you can do it. All you need to do is make sure that he signs a copy of the letter where it says, 'Receipt acknowledged.'"

Another trip? Today? And this one without all the preparation that went into the trip to Jerry García's office? "I don't know. I do not know where Robert Steely lives. We could get a messenger. We can ask Jasmine to call a messenger."

"Relax. Juliet is going to get you a cab. The cab will take you there and the cab will bring you back. Father wants someone from the firm to witness that this letter was given to him and that Robert Steely signed it. He's being overly cautious as usual, but what are we going to do. We need to send someone who knows Robert Steely. And what better person than you? Who would ever doubt someone like you? There. Let's print it, make a copy, and off you go."

We walk to the printer located in front of Juliet's desk. "Juliet, if you can do us the favour of calling this gentleman a cab," Wendell says. Juliet immediately picks up the telephone. She has the telephone number for the cab company memorized. Wendell takes the piece of paper from the printer and throws it on Juliet's desk. "Make a copy and put it in an envelope, will you, sweetie?"

Then Wendell looks at me. He looks stern. The jovial Wendell has disappeared in a matter of seconds. "Do you have an answer for me?"

I know what he is talking about. It suddenly occurs to me that I am afraid of Wendell and that my refusal to say no to him is cowardice. "I don't have an answer for you," I say. I tell myself that I need to stall in order to be able to help Ixtel. But I know that I am lying to myself about this.

"Next week. Any day next week. Jasmine needs to be on that boat next week. That's it. If it doesn't happen next week, the bond is broken. You do not want that to happen. Do you understand?"

"Yes." I feel Wendell's index finger on my chest and I swat it away. I have never ever in my life thought I could hit another human being, but just now I realize I can.

Wendell glares at me and then, as if nothing happened, breaks into a smile. "Next week. Remember." Then he looks at Juliet, who has been staring at us the whole time. "Make sure he brings back a signed copy of the letter."

I put the letter in my backpack. Juliet tells me that a cab will pick me up in the back of the building. All I have to do is stand there like a dummy, she says, and the cab will honk at me. I want to stop by the mailroom to see Jasmine but I am still breathing hard from the encounter with Wendell. "People will run over you if you don't show anger," Jasmine told me once. That's what I feel like now, run over. Now I know why words like "hatred" and "enemy" are used at the law firm.

It is only a few minutes before a cab pulls up and honks at me. I show him the address on the envelope that contains the letter to Robert Steely and we are off. There is a plastic divider between the cabbie and myself. It is not possible here in the real world, as Arturo calls it, to be protected by a shield of plastic. There does not seem to be a way to maintain throughout the day the peace I found when remembering. "Be in the world but not of the world." The words are from Jesus. But I have not the slightest idea how to accomplish that or even if it's possible. The world will always poke you in the chest with its index finger.

Fortunately, Robert Steely lives a long way from the law firm. I say fortunately because it gives me time to breathe steadily again and to stop thinking about Wendell. I am thinking now about Jerry García and the calmness that he showed while he was talking to me. I see him taking his time with each of the people waiting for him. I think of his voice and how he spoke with a fire that did not contain any hatred.

Robert Steely lives in a neighbourhood where the houses are closer together than where I live. We travel slowly through streets with children riding bicycles. The cab driver stops to ask directions from a woman pushing a baby carriage.

The cab driver points at a house. "That's it."

Robert Steely's house is a one-storey house painted light green with shutters that are darker green. The door is red. I knock on a brass knocker shaped like the head of a lion. Robert Steely opens the door.

"Marcelo." His voice is flat. There is no surprise in his face. "Come in."

"Wendell asked me to bring you this," I say as I hand him the envelope. "I am supposed to watch you sign it and bring it back."

He tears an end, blows into the envelope, and takes out the letter. He shakes his head as he reads. "Unbelievable." He looks at me. "Do you know what this is?"

"No."

"Come sit down." He is gesturing towards a room cluttered with the kind of toys that small children play with.

"There is a cab."

"Oh, the cab driver is getting paid for waiting. This will only take a second. I just need to read this carefully. Sit, please."

In a corner of a room I see a red battery-operated keyboard that contains only eight keys. The sight of it reminds me of Jasmine and the conversation that we had in the cafeteria. She asked what takes more skill, to play music composed by someone else or to improvise. There are events that happen by coincidence, that appear out of the blue, unexpected. Here is one. I am here not because I thought of coming to see Robert Steely but because Wendell sent me. Robert Steely is the lawyer who did the most work on the Vidromek litigation. He is the most familiar with all the Vidromek files. He is sitting now in front of me and I see this now as a sign. Will he help me? Will he help Ixtel? The question is, do I have the skill to improvise?

Robert Steely puts the letter on the coffee table. "In their hurry to get me out of the law firm, they forgot to get me to sign an agreement that I will not use any information I learned while working at the firm. As soon as I sign this, my last pay cheque will be sent. In other words, if I don't sign it, I don't get my pay cheque. Excuse me, I'm still a little bitter. I shouldn't talk that way in front of you. You're the boss's son."

"My father canned you."

"Well, I worked with Stephen Holmes, but since Holmes was away, it fell upon your father to do the honours."

"Honours."

"To tell me, you know, 'Please pick up your things now and go.'"

"It happens fast. When one gets canned."

"That's the way it goes. They don't want you to hang around and think of ways to get back at the firm for canning you."

"I have a question for you." I am going to improvise. How can I say what I want to say?

"Go ahead. Hold on, let me get a pen so I can sign this." He goes to another room and returns with a pen. He signs the paper, puts it back in the envelope and gives it to me. "What do you want to know?"

"Is it Vidromek's fault that the windshields don't break into little pieces?"

"Woo! Where is that coming from?"

"I need to know."

He moves to the edge of his chair. "What do you mean by 'fault'?"

I search in my mind for what Jerry García said to me this morning. "Did Vidromek know the windshields would not break into little pieces and made them anyway?"

"Very good." Robert Steely begins to rub his right arm as if he had ants crawling on it. "Why are you asking me this?"

"I need to know . . . so that I can help someone."

"Who?"

I reach down in my backpack and take out the picture of Ixtel. "Her name is Ixtel. She was hurt by a windshield. I don't know her." He looks at the picture and gives it back to me.

"I have never seen that picture." He turns it over. "It's not marked as part of a case. This didn't come with any official papers, did it?"

"It came with a letter to my father."

"I see. And your father said there was nothing that could be done."

"Yes."

"You shouldn't blame your father. That's the nature of the business. He had to say no. Even if he personally wanted to say yes, even if the picture came with a letter from your mother asking him to do something for the girl, he would still say no. You can be the kindest person in the world, a saint, but once you step into the world of defending corporations, you operate by different rules."

"If we can show that Vidromek knew about the windshield we can help Ixtel. Maybe others like her."

"You've been talking to someone about this. Don't tell me. I don't want to know who. Do you know why Stephen Holmes canned me?"

"You thought too much."

He chuckles. "I tried to show Holmes how admitting responsibility would actually save Vidromek money. I had the numbers to show that fixing the windshield was better business in the long run. He told me to leave the numbers to the accountants."

"Can you help Ixtel?"

"You don't know her?"

"No."

"Does your father know you want to help her? Have you talked to him?"

"I have not." I am at a loss to explain why. I am doing something that Arturo would disapprove of, I know. Deep inside of me I hope to find a way to persuade him that helping Ixtel is something he should do, we should all do. But right now I don't know how real that hope is.

Robert Steely stands up and walks to the window. "You should go. I think your cabbie is getting impatient."

I stand up before I understand that he is telling me he does not want to help me. I have the strange sensation of not knowing where I am. Then I recognize Robert Steely's house. I want to shake his hand, but he is still looking out the window. Just as I open the door to step out, he says, "Are the Vidromek boxes still in my office?"

"Yes."

"All thirty-six of them?"

"Thirty-five," I say, correcting him.

"Hmm," he says. "I wonder what happened to the thirty-sixth box?"

"Thirty-sixth?" I am confused. I am certain there are only thirty-five. It is not the kind of thing I am likely to be mistaken about.

"Goodbye, Marcelo. I wish you luck in your quest."

He closes the red door behind me.

By the time I get back to the office I can feel my body shake. "Stimuli overload" is what they call it at Paterson. I walk directly to the mailroom.

The look on Jasmine's face is one I've never seen before. She is happy and angry at the same time. "Where have you been? You've been gone all day." She thinks that I just got back from Jerry García's. "Did you get lost? I thought something happened to you."

"You were worried."

"I wasn't *worried*. I was just . . . wondering. I thought maybe something happened to you and then I'd feel guilty the rest of my life for not going with you like you wanted me to."

"The minute I returned from Jerry García's, Wendell sent me on an errand — to take a letter to Robert Steely."

"Why you? Why not a messenger?"

"Robert Steely had to sign a copy of the letter. Wendell thought I would be a good witness. Who would doubt me?"

"You could have just stepped in the mailroom to say you were all right. I called Jerry García and he said you left two hours ago. I tried calling you on your cell but there was no answer."

"I must have turned it off by mistake while I was waiting for Jerry."

"Wonderful."

"Jerry knows about you. I told him."

"He told me about your visit."

I walk over to my desk and sit down. I can feel my hands tremble. "He showed me the letter he wrote to my father. Arturo knows about Ixtel. He said no. He said Vidromek would not pay for the surgery."

"Why are you trembling? Hold on a second." She disappears and comes back a few seconds later with a paper cup full of water. I drink.

"It is not possible to process everything one hears and sees and thinks no matter how hard one tries. In order to process, it is necessary to block out what is not important. For this, time is needed."

"Marcelo, you are babbling."

"There is a thirty-sixth box. Somewhere in the firm there is a thirty-sixth box." I try to stand, but she pushes me down on the chair.

"Just sit down for a second. You only have a few minutes before you have to catch your train."

"Jerry García said that there must be a document that shows that Vidromek knew the windshields were not safe. He said the person who worked on the litigation has probably seen it. Then Wendell sends me to see Robert Steely, the exact person who worked the most on the Vidromek case. I asked Robert Steely to help me. I thought of you because I improvised and then when I was leaving Robert Steely gave me a clue. He said there were thirty-six boxes, but I have only seen thirty-five. It is not the kind of thing that Marcelo would be mistaken about. Why is

Jasmine smiling like that?"

"Because look at you. You went to Jerry García's and then to Robert Steely's and you put all this together because you want to help a girl you saw in a picture. It's good to see you with some fight in you!"

"It is not normal to act this way from just looking at a picture."

"It's not common, let me put it to you that way. But it's kind of neat."

"We need to find the thirty-sixth box."

"Tomorrow. Right now we're walking to the station."

"Jasmine can look tonight after everyone leaves."

"Oh yeah?"

"She knows all the places in the law firm where a box could be hidden."

"This is your quest, not mine."

"Quest. Robert Steely called it that as well. He said, 'Good luck with your quest.'"

"The key word there is *your*."

"Jasmine will look tonight. Please."

She shakes her head, but I don't think it means that she won't do it. "Sure. And then I'll be out there with Robert Steely looking for a job. Come on, I'll walk with you to the train."

Chapter 21

All morning I have been making up excuses to go to the mail-room. Every time I find my way there, Jasmine is either on the telephone or away from her desk. When she made the first mail run, she lifted up her right thumb as she went by. I think that means she found the thirty-sixth box. Or else it means something I am not aware of.

Finally at noon, I am on my way to the mailroom to meet with Jasmine when I see Arturo walking down the hallway towards me. He smiles and I can see that he is glad to see me. I on the other hand want to turn around and avoid him. I cannot imagine Arturo writing the letter that he wrote to Jerry García. I cannot imagine him seeing the picture of Ixtel and reading Jerry's letter and saying no. These facts stand in contrast to the father who said yes to the tree house, who said yes to Paterson, the man who likes to grab Yolanda in a headlock and pretend he is knocking on her head. I lower my eyes and pretend I'm on important law-firm business.

"Hey, how about a hello for your old man?"

"Hello."

"Is everything OK? You look like you're down in the dumps."

"I am not in the dumps," I say. I can hear the irritation in my voice.

"OK, you're *not* in the dumps. I'll take your word for it. How about lunch?"

"I have lunch."

"We'll save your sandwich for tomorrow."

"No."

"No? Why?"

"I am having lunch with Jasmine."

"Oh, I see. Where?"

"We go to the cafeteria."

"You do? How often?"

I start to walk away.

"What's wrong? Why are you in such a hurry? Jasmine can wait a few minutes. Are you still upset because I reassigned you to Wendell? Come on, get over that. Wendell is who you should be having lunch with."

"Marcelo is not upset at that. Goodbye." I don't raise my voice when I say this. I don't think I do anyway. Still I walk away from my father while he is not finished talking to me. I have never done that before. I can almost feel his eyes on my back. It feels good to walk away from him but I am also afraid. Of what? Of making him angry at me? Of losing him?

No pea soup for Jasmine this time but clam chowder. Clam chowder does not come as piping hot as pea soup. She puts a brown folder on the table.

"You found the box," I say.

"You need to think a little more about what you're doing here."

I don't know what to say. Jasmine seems afraid.

"I mean," she goes on, "you need to take some time and think about all the people who could be affected by what you're doing."

"Marcelo has thought about it."

"Maybe in the abstract. But" — she places her hand on the folder — "it's going to get real."

I reach out for the folder but the force of her hand prevents me from moving it towards me. "Look at your hand, you're still shaking," she says.

"I saw Arturo. On my way to the cafeteria."

"And?"

"Marcelo has never felt confusion before. It is painful. There is no peace. No certainty. Am I supposed to put my father ahead of everything?"

"Let's talk about what is in this folder, just so we are all clear on what we are doing."

"Yes."

"What is in here is bad, as far as Vidromek is concerned. If it's made public, Vidromek will have a very difficult time proving they were not at fault. Then there's what this may do to the firm. Vidromek is the firm's biggest client, and if the firm is responsible for Vidromek's losses, then. . ."

"What? What happens?"

"Vidromek has dozens of ties to other businesses in the United States and we, the law firm, do all their legal work. It would be like dominoes falling. If Vidromek goes, they all go. I see the money that comes in from Vidromek and the salaries we pay and the rent we pay. Without the Vidromek money, there will not be enough money to pay all that."

"Jasmine could lose her job."

"And Marcelo could end up going to public school."

I had never thought about it in that way, but it is true. Paterson is expensive. I have heard kids say that they are attending the school on a scholarship because their parents cannot afford to send them otherwise. Without the money Arturo earns from Vidromek, we may not be able to afford Paterson.

"That is why I will show you what is in here only if you agree to one condition."

"Yes."

"You haven't even heard what I was going to say."

"I meant 'yes' as a question. But also probably I will say yes to your condition."

"Because I'm usually right?"

"Because if I don't say yes, I will never know what Jasmine found."

"Fine. Here's my condition. You go with me to Vermont next weekend and think about everything we're doing here. I have to take Dad to the doctor anyway and you need to get away from here. Things are happening way too fast. There you'll have time to weigh all the repercussions and sort through all the facts and feelings that are so confusing. You might even stop trembling after a day out there in the hills."

"Vermont."

"Yeah, it's the perfect place to ponder."

Ponder. I would like to slow down and ponder.

"When you get back you can do with this as you wish."

"Is it so bad, what is in here?"

She lets go of the folder. I open it and take out a single sheet of paper.

It is in Spanish. I read it as best I can.

MEMO
Importancia: Urgente

Dirigido a: Sr. Reynaldo Acevedo, Presidente
Por conducto de: Lic. Jorge Baltazar
De parte de: Ing. David González, Jefe de Control de Calidad
Fecha: 21 de junio de 2005
Re: Pruebas de Impacto Modelo 285X

Se adjuntan Pruebas de Impacto — Parabrisas Modelo 285x. Pruebas demuestran fragmentación diferente a la especificación de diseño. Se recomienda descontinuar fabricación de dicho Modelo 285x inmediatamente.

"I don't know all the words," I say. "What is *parabrisas*?"

"It means windshield. I looked up the words I didn't understand, but most of them are not much different than the English words. It is a memo from the engineer who is in charge of quality control to the president of the company."

"He is recommending that the manufacture of the windshield be discontinued."

"A whole bunch of charts which were probably the test results were attached."

"Vidromek knew." I realize my hand is shaking again.

"There are so many things we don't know about this. Sometimes it is not as simple as it seems."

"Where did Jasmine find the memo?"

"Some of the lawyers keep the important files in their offices."

My heart stops and then begins to race. "Arturo's?"

Jasmine ignores me. "The question is, now what? You give that to Jerry García and then all kinds of things will happen."

I put the memo back in the folder. If someone asks me where I got the memo, I will have to lie — otherwise Jasmine will lose her job. "Jasmine could have told me that she looked and did not find a thirty-sixth box. Why did she give me the memo?"

She crumbles tiny round crackers into her clam chowder without looking at me. "OK, so, if we're going to Vermont, we leave early Saturday morning and get there in time to take Dad to the doctor. We can go camping on Sunday and come back on Monday. Have you ever been camping?"

"I live in a tree house. Is that like camping?"

"Look at you. You're a mess, mentally speaking. Out there in the middle of the wilderness you see more clearly. There is less confusion."

"OK."

"OK, you'll come?"

"Yes."

"Fine." She smiles. Going to Vermont has made her happy. "Belinda will take care of the mailroom on Monday. You don't have to look so glum. It might even be fun."

I lift the folder with the memo. "Now Jasmine is involved in all of this."

"Yup. That's what happens. I'll keep this. When we return from Vermont it will be yours to do with as you wish. But not until we return."

She is already up from her chair and going to dump her almost full cup of clam chowder. Another lunch where neither of us managed to eat anything.

Chapter 22

Jasmine's battered Jeep turns into the driveway. The top of the Jeep is down. Namu acknowledges her by a simple pricking of his ears.

"Ready?" she asks.

I nod. I am putting my backpack in the back seat when Aurora comes out with a plastic bag full of sandwiches, assorted fruits and juice drinks. The trip to Vermont is three hours if there's no traffic on I-93, but Aurora always packs a lunch regardless of how long or short a trip is.

Namu climbs into the Jeep by the side door and makes his way to the back seat. This he does on his own accord.

"Someone's looking forward to this outing," Aurora comments.

"He'll have lots of fun," Jasmine responds.

Aurora was thrilled when I told her and Arturo about the trip. It was Arturo's reaction, however, that surprised me. Just when I thought I was getting good at understanding the feelings behind most facial expressions, a new one presented itself for deciphering. Arturo, who has been pushing so hard for me to be independent, suddenly dropped his jaw and turned stiff when I mentioned the trip. What was that look of his, what did it mean, where did it come from? Suspicion? Resentment? I have never seen that look on Arturo's face before.

"I don't think that's a good idea," Arturo said.

We were sitting at the kitchen table. Aurora and I stopped eating when we heard his words.

I repeated what I had just said in case he misunderstood my description of the trip. "We are going to take her father to the doctor's on Saturday. Then on Sunday we will go hiking nearby for a few hours. Jasmine says she can drop me at home Monday evening around eight."

There was silence at the table. I looked at Arturo and saw that look I had never seen before and I felt fear.

Aurora spoke, ignoring Arturo's objection. "That sounds good. But I want you to take Namu with you. He'd be good company on the hike."

"OK," I said.

"I don't think so." Arturo was firm, but there was something unusually shaky in his voice.

"Why?" Aurora asked. She was now the one with a suspicious look.

"I was going to ask Jasmine to work this Saturday. We are working on a merger of two of our Mexican companies that needs to be done next week. And she never asked me if she could take Monday off."

I said, "Jasmine does not know about the merger."

"Arturo," Aurora said, "she needs to take her father to the doctor."

"Jasmine did not mention anything to me," Arturo said.

"Does she need to tell you how she spends her weekends? What are you afraid of?" Aurora asked. That was a first too. I had never seen Aurora speak so bluntly to Arturo.

Arturo was silent, confused, speechless, for the first time ever.

"It seems to me that the plans have already been made. I'm sure you can find someone else to help you if you need to," Aurora said. And it was the final word.

Aurora now takes me by the arm over to the side of the house to say something to me alone. "Listen to me," she says. She waits for my eyes to meet hers. "You call me immediately if anything happens to you or Jasmine, if the least little thing in your trip does not go as planned. Your cell phone is equipped to handle long-distance calls from absolutely anywhere in the world. If you or Jasmine are in danger, large or small, you call. It will not matter one bit how or why you got into trouble. Am I clear?"

"Yes," I say. I sign *I love you* with my hand, the way I learned at Paterson.

She touches her heart with her hand and then touches my chest.

By the Jeep, Jasmine hands Aurora a slip of paper. "My father's phone and address. He's getting old and his mind doesn't work as well as it used to, so I also gave you the phone of a neighbour. Jonah will know exactly where we are and can come find us if you need us for anything."

"Thank you. Did you say goodbye to your father?" Aurora asks me, as if suddenly remembering.

"Yes," I answer without looking at her. But I am not telling the truth.

Namu barks a solitary bark. *Enough with the goodbyes already. Let's go,* is what I think he's saying.

When we reach the highway, I ask Jasmine, "Is your father proud of you?"

"Where is *that* coming from?"

"The dictionary defines pride as 'pleasure or satisfaction in one's work or achievement'. According to that definition a person needs to do something before you can be proud of them. You could not be proud of them simply for who they are. I'm not sure I know what pride in another person feels like."

"I talked to your father late yesterday. He stopped by the mailroom before he left. He wanted to know more about our trip." She shakes her head and smiles at the same time. "Your father is proud of you, if that's what's bothering you."

"What else did Arturo say, when you saw him?" I feel strange as soon as I finish asking her. I am trying to find out why Arturo did not want me to take this trip. I feel ashamed for thinking that maybe Jasmine knows and she is not telling me.

She looks at me in a peculiar way, as if trying to figure out the real motive behind my question. Then she says, "He wanted to know where we were going to go camping, whether anyone else was coming with us. It was kind of weird. Like he suddenly had doubts about whether you could handle all that. You can, can't you?" I know that she expects me to laugh or at least smile, but I don't.

"Does your father know you play the piano?" I ask.

"Of course. I grew up playing it at home. My mother brought the piano from her home when she got married and sat me at the keys before I could walk, it seems."

"But does your father know that composing and playing your music is what you want to do?"

"I suppose he does. We don't talk about it much. You'll see when you meet him. Amos doesn't much care what you do with your life so long as you're keeping busy and you're earning your keep."

I close my eyes and remember the time when I was eight and Arturo enrolled me in the town's soccer league. Within five minutes after I took the field, it became obvious to all that I could not play. I stood there lost, not knowing what to do, taking a few disoriented steps every which way except in the right direction. When the ball came to me I kicked it to the sidelines or to one of the opposing players. I remember the look on Arturo's face as we drove home, the father's realization that his son would never be able to participate in any sports. Then, a few seconds later, remembering what Jasmine said to Aurora just before we left, I ask, "Who is Jonah?"

"You'll meet him today. Jonah and I grew up together. His mother and my mother were best friends until my mother died. My brother and Jonah's little brother, Cody, were the best of friends too. You'll like him, you'll see."

We travel the remaining two hours mostly in silence. Jasmine asks me if I mind if she puts some music on. I know she is doing that so that I don't feel like I have to talk. She hasn't asked me anything about Ixtel or about the memo. It's not that she doesn't care. I can tell she wants to let me be alone with the decision. But I decide not to think about the memo just yet. Instead, I close my eyes and feel the cool air rush past my face.

"There it is," she says.

I open my eyes and see Jasmine's house down a dirt road and up a green hill. It is a white house with a red-brick chimney, a tall black pipe and a crumpled television antenna on the roof. An unpainted barn behind the house seems to tilt slightly to the right. As we get closer, we see an assortment of plastic animals on the front lawn: a family of deer, two white swans (now greyish), a mother duck with six ducklings behind her (one tipped over), two rabbits kissing each other, a brown fox, a groundhog up on his hind legs, a flamingo that could have been pink at one time but is now a whitish colour.

"My mother used to collect them," Jasmine says by way of explanation.

We pull up and park beside the house. Namu is the first to get out. He leaps out of the back seat but stops as soon as his feet hit the ground. I immediately see what made Namu stop. Sitting calmly by the front door of the house is a large black-and-white dog. The dog stirs and begins to walk towards Namu, who sits down. It is Namu's way of telling the other dog that he knows he is only a guest.

"Gomer! It's good to see you," Jasmine says to the dog.

Gomer shakes his head and his tail and allows himself to be petted by Jasmine. Then he goes over to Namu and the two dogs sniff each other's private parts.

"Look," Jasmine says.

I follow her hand and see a field of tall grass and purple flowers. Between the house and the paved highway in the distance is a patch of brown and black cows. One of the cows is walking up the hill towards us and I can hear the clang of the bell that hangs around her neck.

"That's Eleanor," Jasmine points out. "She's the grandmamma of them all. I birthed her and raised her and she still thinks she's a house pet. She can't see farther than her nose but she knows I'm here and she's coming to say hello. Gomer, where's Pops?"

Gomer removes his cold nose from my hand and waddles towards the barn. Namu is staring at the cows, whimpering.

"He wants to go see the cows," I say.

"They don't call them German *shepherds* for nothing," Jasmine says. She is taking the backpacks out of the Jeep.

"Is it all right?" I ask.

Namu tilts his head towards Jasmine and awaits her response. "Of course," she says.

As soon as he hears that, Namu begins to lope towards the cows.

"Let's go see what the old man is up to," Jasmine says. "What are you carrying in here?" She drops the backpacks by the side of the house and rubs her arm. Then before I can answer her question, she warns, "Don't pay attention to what he says. His mind is half gone with dementia. It makes him forgetful and hostile, which means you can get verbally assaulted multiple times and he'll think he's doing it for the first time."

The space between the house and the barn is strewn with rusted farm machinery and tall milk cans. The closer we get to the barn, the more my nostrils fill with a sweet, pungent smell. "Cow shit and cow urine. Some of it very old and some of it brand-new," Jasmine explains when she sees me breathe in deeply.

The sliding door to the barn is open. In the back, I see a small man with black rubber boots up to his knees shovelling manure into a wooden wheelbarrow.

"Shit, goddamn, shit," I hear him say.

"That's Amos. Dad, we're here!"

The man stops shovelling and walks towards us to investigate. His face is wrinkled and his white hair is strong and bristly.

"About time you woke up," he says to me.

"He thinks you're my brother James," Jasmine explains. "It's me, Jasmine. This is Marcelo."

"I suppose you're going to cover up for him again. As if I didn't hear him come in early this morning from drinking and whoring."

"This is Marcelo, Dad. Remember I called you last night to tell you we were coming up."

Amos walks back to get the wheelbarrow. I can see his thin arms tremble as they lift the load. "Drinking and whoring all night long."

"Where in the world do you think he could go whoring around here?" Jasmine asks him. Then to me, "Sometimes it's just easier to go along with him until he snaps to."

"There's plenty of places to go whoring. Man's got a dick, he'll find a hole to put it in."

"James just went out and had a few drinks over with Cody. Just a little boys' fun, that's all." Jasmine is shaking her head and throwing her arms up in the air.

"Shit!" Amos mutters in front of us. He dumps the contents of the wheelbarrow in a pile on the side of the barn.

"Eleanor!" Jasmine shouts. A tan cow is walking tiredly towards us. Her large black eyes seem sleepy. "You walked all the way up the hill to see me!"

"Should have turned her into stew while her meat was still soft enough to chew," Amos says.

"What are you talking about?" Jasmine objects. She is stretching and holding the cow's ears as if they are bicycle handlebars. "She's still milking, isn't she?"

"Five squirts. Thin, watery stuff, clear as widow's piss," Amos retorts. He turns towards me. "Borrowed Bruno from Shackleton last year to fuck her for old times' sake. Took four of us — me and the three Shackletons — to lift him on top of her."

"Dad! She's too old for breeding. She gave you at least one calf a year for twelve years. Let her be now. She's earned her rest."

"Didn't want a calf. Wanted her to get it good one last time." He winks at me. "Couldn't get Bruno to agree. His pecker stayed soft as a hose."

"You got any coffee in the house?" Jasmine asks. I can tell she is trying to change the subject.

"And pancakes too. Made them last night as soon as I heard you were coming. We'll put them in that gizmo you bought me and zap the living shit out of them." He takes a squashed pack of cigarettes from his front shirt pocket, lifts a cigarette out of the pack with his lips, and then begins to search his other pockets for a light.

"Smoking is bad for you," I warn him.

"So is living, but I'm not going around telling *you* not to do it." He locates a book of matches in the back pocket of his overalls.

Somehow, after lunch, Jasmine is able to cajole Amos into the bathtub. She ignites the water heater, which is only turned on for baths, waits half an hour until the water is coming out of the spigot hot, and then she pushes Amos into the bathroom adjoining the kitchen.

"If I don't hear the water splashing in one minute, I'm coming in. I'm putting a chair right here so there's no use in you coming out."

"I took a bath last month," Amos grumbles from inside the door.

"After you're done with the bath, I'm taking you to your doctor's appointment."

"The hell you are," Amos answers.

"Then after the doctor we'll go to the co-op and get you your cigarettes, and then maybe we'll stop at the liquor store after that."

Silence follows. After a few moments I hear the sound of water splashing. Jasmine comes out to the living room where I am standing by an upright mahogany piano. I touch middle C and hear the note's mellow sound. Then I play C, E and G together.

"It is in tune," I declare.

"Wish everyone was in tune," she responds. Her eyes motion towards the bathroom.

I am looking at a picture in a silver frame that stands on top of the piano. Jasmine is next to a boy with wild blond hair that covers most of his face. In back of the two children stand Amos and a woman. The woman is the only one smiling in the picture. Jasmine sees what I am looking at.

"That was taken when I was eight and James was ten. It's the only time Mother was able to get the two of them to pose for a formal photograph. That's what she wanted for her birthday."

"Your mother?"

"That's her. Listen, after he gets out, I'm going to drag him to the doctor. You want to come with us?"

I'm staring at the picture.

"If you come with us, I'll show you around. Hold on one second."

She goes up to the bathroom door and places her ear on it. "How you doing in there? Make sure you wash inside your ears," she says.

"For Christ's sake, I know what holes to wash!"

"I left you some clean clothes there by the chair."

"I see them."

"Don't put the dirty ones back on."

"All right already."

She says to me, "He'll be in there until the water gets cold. Let's go outside, I want to show you something."

We walk out the front door. Just beyond the plastic animals' preserve we take a footpath that leads up to a green knoll overlooking the house. Behind the knoll, a mountain of maples and pines rises up to meet a blue sky. The deep blue of the sky reminds me of the word azure — like Jasmine's eyes.

"If we climb to the top of the mountain, we can touch the sky," I say.

"That's not a mountain. That's just a hill. Over there, those are mountains."

I turn and let my sight go as far as it will go. In the distance, I see the white-capped mountains, the same ones in the picture that Jasmine has in front of her desk.

"Look at Namu and Gomer," she says, pointing.

In the pasture below us, Namu and Gomer sit among a dozen cows.

"He likes it here," I say.

When we reach the top of the knoll, she points to the "hill" that rises above us and says, "That is Amos's hill."

"Amos Hill," I repeat.

"No, Amos is not the name of the hill. The hill belongs to Amos. He owns it, as well as thirty acres of land down there all the way to the road. Amos grows hay down there for the twelve or so cows he keeps. He used to have eighty acres, but he sold fifty after Mother died to pay the doctor's bills. The hill and the eighty acres, when worked right, took care of a family of four. When Mother was alive Amos had forty cows, half a dozen hogs, chickens. They used to harvest maple syrup and wood from the hill. They grew their own hay for wintering the cows. Mother sold enough honey to pay for 'February's groceries', as she used to say. She gave piano lessons to a couple of kids. Amos sold the milk to some ice-cream place in Montpelier. A hundred dollars here, fifty there. The hill gave them all the wood they needed to keep everybody warm during winter. It doesn't really take that much to live here, if you work hard at it."

From the top of the knoll we see Amos come out the back door of the house. He is wearing only a pair of blue jeans and has not put on a shirt or socks or shoes yet. He takes a few steps out the back door and begins to urinate. A chicken pecking the dirt near the flow steps out of the way.

"There's a toilet next to the bathtub," Jasmine says, shaking her head. "I don't think he's peed inside in his life. We didn't get a septic tank built till I was five. I still have memories of those little white chamber pots we used so we didn't have to go outside in the middle of winter."

"Your mother taught you to play the piano," I say.

"She had me sitting on that stool before I could walk."

"James played also."

"She gave up on him after a couple of tries. During the winters you spend a lot of time inside. If you have something to keep your mind busy, it helps. James was not much for piano playing or staying inside, winter or no winter. As soon as he was able, he was climbing up the hill, going fishing, hunting, raising all kinds of critters, rabbits, hamsters. He sold them to pet stores. When he was ten he started a chinchilla farm out in the barn. I hated it because I knew what was in store for the little creatures. Chinchillas are like these long, skinny rats, but people like their fur because it's warm. Fortunately, a fox got in the barn one year and put everyone out of their misery. Careful," she says as I trip over a shovel. She bends down and picks it up.

We are on top of the knoll, looking at a hole in the ground the length and depth of a backyard swimming pool. The flat top of the knoll is in the shape of a circle. The hole is located exactly in the middle, equidistant from all points. Jasmine leads me away from the hole towards the front of the knoll. We see a fuel truck travel down the paved road below. I strain to hear the sound of the truck's motor but am unable to do so. All I can hear is a swooshing sound coming out of the trees. Below us, to our right, on a smaller knoll I notice two crosses.

"Mother and James," Jasmine says, anticipating my question.

"Is that Kickaz over there?" I point at the two horses below in the pasture, a short distance from where the cows are bunched up.

"The sleek black one. That's Kickaz." Kickaz lifts his head up in the air as if he heard his name. Jasmine takes a few steps and gestures towards a smaller field below us. "See that field? In the winter, Amos ploughs an oval through the snow the size of a football field. He goes out every afternoon right after lunch — when the sun is hottest, if you can call it that — and walks Kickaz around for an hour, sleet or snow. He won't be able to do that too much longer," she says, mostly to herself. Then to me, "We better head back. Do you want to come with us to the doctor or stay here? Either way is OK. It's half an hour to the doctor and half an hour back and it's usually a couple of hours of mostly waiting at the doctor's, so, all told, we'll be gone about three hours."

I whistle softly and watch Namu immediately stand up and turn around. "I will wait for you here," I say and start to walk down towards the pasture where Namu and Gomer are guarding the cows and horses. It is almost noon. I can tell because the sun is halfway through the arc of the horizon. It strikes me that a house built on that knoll would receive sunlight from dawn to dusk.

"Your mom's sandwiches will be on the kitchen table if you get hungry," Jasmine says.

I stop and begin to climb back to where she is still standing. "Where are we going tomorrow?"

"We'll load up Kickaz with camping gear and the four of us — Namu included but not Gomer because he's too old — we'll hike up Amos's hill and down the other side and over a few more hills until we get to Hidden Lake. About a three-hour slow hike. Amos has a shack he slides to the middle of the lake for ice fishing and a canoe he uses in the summer. We'll fish and canoe on the lake and on the stream that feeds it." She sounds excited. "We'll head back Monday morning and then we drive home."

"OK," I say. I take a deep breath. Monday's drive home will get here much too soon.

Halfway down to the pasture where the cows are grazing, I change direction and walk towards the two white crosses. I sit in front of them and read out loud the names and dates inscribed on the granite. Lila and James. Mother and son. One lived fifty-five years, the other eighteen. I hear the sound of Jasmine's Jeep and then it comes into view and I follow it until it becomes a green dot down the road and disappears.

I remember why Jasmine brought me to Vermont. She was worried about me and thought this was a good place to sift through all that has happened, to decide. I promise myself that I will do so. Tomorrow when we get to the camping place, I'll make sure I find the time and place to weigh all of it. But today — today I will just be.

Chapter 23

In the evening Jasmine and I are washing the supper dishes when we hear the motor of a car. Amos is stuffing a pipe with tobacco that smells like chocolate. He asks, "I wonder who that could be?"

"Oh, Dad. You asked them to come, didn't you?"

"I did not," he says. "Busybody Shackleton took it upon himself to come and check out the boy as soon as he knew you were here."

Just then the kitchen door opens and three men walk in. They come the way people come into a house they've entered many times before. The oldest man, the one I believe to be the father of the other two, looks like a younger, less bent version of Amos. The one I believe to be Cody is carrying a box of Bud Light. The one that I believe to be Jonah has two bags of potato chips in his hands.

"Oh no," Jasmine exclaims as soon as the three are in. "There's not going to be any carrying-on tonight. We have to get up early tomorrow."

"Oh yeah?" the father says as Jasmine leans over to receive a peck on her cheek. "Going camping, are you?"

"Jonah?" Jasmine asks.

He points at himself and shakes his head. The gesture means *I didn't say anything.* "I'm Jonah." He stretches his hand towards me. I feel my hand gripped by a much larger and stronger hand than mine.

"And I'm Cody." The grip of this hand is only slightly softer.

"So you're the young fellow. I'm Samuel Shackleton." The older man holds on to my hand while he studies me. "He's strong for a city boy," he says to Amos, who is having trouble getting the fire in his pipe to catch on.

"Wouldn't know," Amos answers between puffs.

"We're not staying long," Jonah says to Jasmine. "I couldn't keep them from coming. Mom wanted to come but I talked her out of it. She would have killed him with questions."

"Where do you want us to sit?" Samuel Shackleton asks. "On these backbreakers or in there in the comfy chairs?"

"Here," Jasmine responds quickly, "since you're only going to be here a *short while*."

"There's no room in the fridge to put these in," Cody complains.

"Full of cereal boxes," Amos says.

"You don't need to put them in the fridge. Just put the box there on the floor. They'll keep cold." It's Jonah speaking.

"But we got them lukewarm at the store," Cody says. "I'll put a few in the freezer. Just enough to last us for a couple of hours."

"What?" Jasmine yells.

Samuel Shackleton pulls out a chair across from Amos and sits down slowly. He is a large man and it does not seem as if the wobbly legs of the kitchen chair will support him. "How you doing, old man? Found that lost marble of yours yet?"

"I got all the marbles I need," Amos says. Finally, a red dot begins to glow from his pipe bowl. "They're still wrinkled from the soaking they made me give them today." He shoots a glance at Jasmine. "But I suppose they're still working just fine, wrinkled and all."

"How the heck would you know?" Samuel Shackleton asks him.

"Here we go," Jasmine says.

There's a whoosh from a beer can opening. "Who wants a beer?" Cody is asking.

"Why don't you get some of the good stuff you hide under the seat of your car?" Amos suggests.

"No way," Jasmine pleads.

But it is too late. Samuel Shackleton nods to Cody and Cody is out to get the good stuff, whatever that is.

I resume scrubbing the frying pan Jasmine used to cook the corned-beef hash. Jonah stands beside me and says, "I always find it better to let the pan soak. After a day or two the burned stuff comes off by itself."

"There'll be no soaking tonight," says Jasmine. "You go ahead and finish scrubbing that. You dry." She hands Jonah a white dish towel that is already soaking wet.

Jonah shrugs his shoulders at me — the universal gesture for *Oh well, I tried.*

Cody is back again with a clear bottle full of golden liquid.

"That's what I'm talking about," Amos says, licking his lips. "Pass me one of those glasses, James."

It takes me a few seconds to realize he is speaking to me. There is a brief moment when everyone in the room is silent. Then I grab the biggest glass I see and give it to Amos.

"Fill it up," Amos orders Cody.

"If he fills it up you'll be asking me to drive you to Montreal for you-know-what, just like you used to before you got married," Samuel Shackleton says.

"Don't get him started," Jasmine says.

"Why, what'd you guys used to do in Montreal?" Cody asks.

"Cody!" It's Jasmine again. "God, all of you are hopeless." She walks out of the kitchen.

"Where you going?" Samuel Shackleton yells after her.

"To pee! You mind?" she answers from down the hall.

"Cody, go get your fiddle while she's peeing," Samuel Shackleton says.

Cody stands up immediately. Apparently he thinks that's a great idea.

I hand the frying pan to Jonah.

"Don't worry," Jonah says. "We really won't stay too long. I won't let them."

"It is all right," I say.

Cody is taking the fiddle out of a black case when Jasmine enters the kitchen again.

"I give up," she says. "Go ahead and go in the living room."

"Will you play the piano with me?" Cody asks.

"No way."

Jonah hands the pan to Jasmine for inspection. "Have you ever seen this pan so clean?" he asks her.

She holds it up to the light and traces her finger around the inside and outside. "Not bad," she says.

"So where's the Spam?" Samuel Shackleton asks her as he and Amos walk out of the kitchen.

"Very funny," she says as she follows.

When Jonah and I are alone in the kitchen, he says to me, "When we were kids our two families used to go camping together. We'd take about a hundred cans of Spam in case we didn't catch any fish, which we usually didn't. Jasmine and I, we decided one time to break off all the tiny tabs that came with the cans to open them. Then when we got up to the lake, everyone was mad at us because they had to use can openers to open the Spam, and can openers don't work too well on Spam cans."

I realize that I have never seen a can of Spam.

"I think we're done here," Jonah says. He spreads the dish towel on the counter so that it will dry. "Is that your dog outside?"

"Namu," I say. I don't know where to put my hands.

"Great dog. He just kind of inspires respect, doesn't he? He doesn't really care whether you pet him or not. He lets you if you want to but he's happy either way."

"Gomer is a calm dog also," I say.

"Now he is. He's got no choice, he's about fifteen years old."

"Namu is nine. Do you have a dog?"

"About half a dozen at any given time. Cody there is always trying to breed something or other, only what doesn't get bought stays with us."

We are facing the group in front of us. Amos and Samuel Shackleton are sunk in the big living room sofa. Cody is trying to drink beer and tune his violin at the same time. Jasmine has sat on the chair that is the farthest away from the piano. She is motioning us to come in.

"Do you want a beer?" Jonah asks.

"I do not drink alcohol," I respond. I attach a smile to the response so that my statement does not appear rude.

"Wow. You scrub pans to near perfection and you don't drink. No wonder Jasmine is taken with you."

I am not sure whether this is intended as a joke or not. "Excuse me," I say, "I need to go fix Namu's bed. He is sleeping in the barn with Gomer."

"I'll go with you," Jonah says quickly.

"Where are you guys going?" I hear Jasmine ask.

Jonah yells, "We'll be right back. We're going to see Namu."

"Jonah. . ." I hear Jasmine's voice trail off as we step outside.

When the door closes, Jonah says, "She's afraid we're going to have a heart-to-heart."

"A 'heart-to-heart'?"

"A man-to-man. Two men talking straight and honest to each other."

I see Namu head towards the barn. I follow him. "Do you want to have a heart-to-heart?" I ask.

"To tell you the truth, I kind of do. Although she's threatened me with all kinds of tortures if I do."

It occurs to me that lately, heart-to-hearts are the only type of conversations I seem to be having. The last conversation with Wendell, when he poked my chest, falls, I think, under Jonah's definition of a heart-to-heart, although I do not think what I had with Wendell was a conversation.

In the barn Namu heads to the pile of blankets where Gomer is lying. He sniffs Gomer and then comes back to me as if wanting to see where I'm going to sleep before deciding on a place for himself.

"I am going to sleep inside the house," I inform Namu. Just as I turn to point at the house, I feel something push me in the middle of my shoulder blades. It is a push that for all its force I recognize as a simple nudge. I look around and see Kickaz smiling at me. I know a horse's smile from working with the ponies at Paterson. The ponies also liked to play practical jokes and then their eyes would sparkle.

I tap Kickaz lightly on the nose, which is what I always did with the ponies at Paterson. Kickaz responds by shaking his head and then lowering it and asking for another tap. Instead I pull both of his ears in jest.

"I never saw Kickaz be friendly to anyone other than old Amos," Jonah says. There is surprise in his voice. He tries to touch Kickaz's face as well, but Kickaz shakes his head away from his touch. "That's amazing."

I find a place for Namu to sleep. "There," I tell him. Just outside of Kickaz's stall there is a flattened-out cardboard box and two empty burlap sacks. I unfurl the sacks and Namu sits on top of them.

Now I look at Jonah. "How do you start a heart-to-heart?"

"I guess there's two ways to do it," Jonah says, walking out of the barn. "We can circle around slowly getting to know each other a little bit, or we can straight away say what's in our minds.

You have a preference?"

"No."

"OK. Uhh. I'm gonna compromise and just circle a little bit, if it's OK with you. While I'm circling I may be able to find the words for the heart-to-heart because I'm not sure I have them yet. Is that all right with you?"

"You love Jasmine."

Jonah gasps, "Wooo. Uhh. Ahh. That's a heart-to-heart, all right." He shuffles his feet. "Are you asking me or telling me?"

"Asking. Sometimes it is hard for me to turn a statement into a question."

"Are you asking whether Jasmine and I are boyfriend and girlfriend?"

"No, that was not my question. But you can tell me that if you prefer."

The flap in the back of Amos's truck is down and we sit there. Jonah takes out a cigarette and lights it, but this time I refrain from saying that smoking is bad.

"With regard to your question, the answer is no, I'm not her boyfriend or ever have been. Not for lack of trying on my part. I was seven when she was born and we grew up together. We live three miles down the road."

Someone in the house opens a window. The sound of the violin reaches us and for a moment I imagine a silk ribbon waving in the breeze.

"One of those things where you think that with time the person will . . . maybe not love you, that would be too much to ask, but see how good you are for them and take you that way. I think that after James died she went to Boston in part to get away from everything that reminded her of him, including me. You always do this to people?"

"Do what?"

"Get them to empty their guts out just like that."

"We do not have much time. We should talk about what is important."

"Well, that's pretty much the story."

"You would marry Jasmine if she let you."

"Yes. But I don't think that's going to happen. Jasmine needs someone smart like her . . . someone like you."

"Me, smart?" I laugh. "If you knew how much of what people say or do I fail to understand, you would not call me smart. I stop myself from asking what something means because otherwise no one would talk to me. I'm not smart. I have been trained. It is training and concentration. Years of learning how to communicate."

Jonah flicks the cigarette away. "Did she show you her studio?"

"Her studio?"

"The one's she's building on top of the hill."

"Where the hole is."

"We just finished digging the foundation. We'll be putting in the sewer pipes connecting to the septic tank next. Cody and I help her on weekends. She figures old Amos there will need some looking after in a few years, so she'll come live here, but she and Amos need their space, so she's building a house-*slash*-studio up on the hill. One of the rooms will be soundproof so she can eventually put some recording equipment in there. She's got the whole thing planned. Wood stoves in every room, practically."

"That's what she is saving her money for," I say.

"That and for taking care of Amos. She saves all she gets, living in that little cave the way she does."

"You know where she lives."

"She's told me about it. Not much she doesn't tell me. That's kind of what I wanted to have a heart-to-heart with you about, before you went for the *real* heart." Jonah touches his chest and coughs.

"You are worried about Jasmine."

"She says you are a good person. Are you? It's just that she's like a sister to me. I want to make sure she is not hurt."

I do not have the slightest idea of how I could possibly hurt Jasmine. Maybe he knows about Wendell's request. But how could he? Then I remember the memo and the risk she took by giving it to me. Whether he knows about these things or not, his question is relevant. "No," I say. "I will not hurt her."

"Good. That's what I wanted to know." Then Jonah looks at me deeply. "Can I ask you a question?"

"Yes."

"Are you attracted to Jasmine?"

"Attracted." I am at a loss as to what to say. I like being with Jasmine. I like the comfort and the ease and the not worrying about how I sound or look when I am with her. I like hearing what she says and how she responds to my questions. I like what I see through her, what she leads me to discover, and what her presence opens up for me. I like talking music with her and I like being here with her. I am *pulled* towards her in a way that resembles the pull of the IM. Is this the kind of attraction Jonah is asking about? "I do not understand what you mean when you use that word. Can you be more specific?"

Jonah hesitates. "Do you have sexual desire for her?" He looks away. I interpret this gesture as embarrassment, as if the question he is asking is not something he should be concerned about. I do not know, in fact, if it was proper for him to ask me that or if it is proper for me to try to answer it, but I decide to do so anyway, as best I can, not knowing exactly what I will say.

"As far as I have been able to determine, sexual desire is a kind of energy or attention directed at someone's body or even at parts of a body. It consists of imagining doing sexual acts with the body of a person or with a part of a person's body. But I do not imagine doing anything with Jasmine other than what I am doing at the time. That seems to be sufficient. I like spending time with her. I like it when we talk about music or when I ask about the meanings of words. She makes me laugh and makes me think about things I never thought about."

"Boy, you really break things down, don't you?"

"Some say it is an illness."

"We should all be so ill."

"The part of her body that I like the most is her eyes. When I look into them, I feel like staying there as much as possible. Is that force sexual, as far as you know?"

Jonah shrugs his shoulders. The shrug, as far as I can tell, means that he has no way of knowing the answer to my question. It is a question that only Marcelo can answer.

I am confused all of a sudden. Confused that Jonah could think that Jasmine and Marcelo could be more than friends. It has never occurred to me and I cannot believe that Jasmine could be interested in me that way. Perhaps the comfort I feel around Jasmine is also sexual in a way I don't understand. Maybe attraction for another person is like the IM, where body and mind cannot be separated.

Jonah looks in the direction of the open window and I hear the sound of the piano. The notes come slowly, one after another, each carrying a slightly different tone of sadness. We listen in silence, then Jonah speaks. "When Jasmine's mother was dying, they put up a bed there in the living room, and that's the song she wanted Jasmine to play to her at the end."

"*Gymnopédies*," I say.

"Pardon?"

"The music is called *Gymnopédies*, by a composer named Satie."

"Really? That's one touching piece of music. I wouldn't mind hearing that when I'm dying."

"The stars seem so close to the earth here."

"You like it here?" Jonah asks.

"Very much."

"There's not many places left where you can still make an honest living off the land. Amos can do it 'cause the farm is bought and paid for. He was nearly fifty when he got married. Jasmine's mother was a waitress downtown where Amos and Father used to go on Friday nights to have a few. She and Amos had this bantering going back and forth for years. Everyone knew they liked each other. One day Amos said something flirty to Lila, and she just turned around and told him that if he wasn't intending to ever get serious then she'd appreciate it if he left and never came back. They got married the following week. She was nearing forty. The doctor told her it would kill her to have kids but she went ahead and had two. After she died, Jasmine became a little mother for the whole family real quick."

The piano stops playing, and a few seconds later we see Jasmine come out the back door. She looks around before she spots us sitting in the back of the pickup truck.

"What are you guys doing? I don't like this. What have you two been talking about?"

"We were having a heart-to-heart," I tell her.

Jasmine glares at Jonah.

"It's OK, it's OK, don't look at me like that," says Jonah, jumping off the flap of the truck. Then he whispers to her loud enough for me to hear, "I think you finally met your match." He moves away before Jasmine can punch him in the shoulder. Jonah announces, "I'm gonna get me one last beer and I'll make sure those guys aren't getting too comfortable. One more beer and we're out of here, I promise."

Jonah enters the house and closes the kitchen door behind him.

Jasmine says, "You like it here. I can tell."

"Yes. Here you can still make an honest living."

"You got that from Jonah."

"Here a person would not have to pretend or lie."

"Not as much, maybe. That's not to say that it doesn't happen anyway."

"You are saving your money to take care of Amos in a few years and to build your house-*slash*-studio."

"Jonah talks way too much. In a few years I'll have saved enough to pay for Amos's medical bills and my health insurance, and maybe I'll have enough to finish the studio and a little extra to fix this place up. We need to get six more cows and a new steel tank to hold the milk until the truck comes to get it. They already told Amos they were going to stop buying his milk unless he got one. Then we have to cement the bottom of the cows' stalls. New regulations. Actually old regulations, but somehow Amos has gotten away with it. Knowing him, he's probably bribing someone. You got the milk and cheese from twenty cows, the honey, Kickaz's stud services, maple syrup we harvest from the trees on the hill, firewood – and I can give piano lessons and get a part-time job as a music teacher in a school. That should give us enough to get by."

"And your music?"

"It's part of the plan. It's at the centre of it all. Everything else supports it."

"When you went to Boston you always planned on coming back."

"Of course. My plan was, is, to make as much money as possible and then come back. Besides, after James died, Amos was impossible to be around at times. At the beginning of dementia and Alzheimer's, there's a lot of hostility, paranoia. I needed to give us some space. He's better now. If he takes his pills."

She looks up at the sky and studies a dot of light crossing the darkness. I follow the light as well. "Maybe I don't know any better, but I always knew this was where I belonged. It's not that life will be easier here. It's just that here's where I belong, that's all." She waits for me to speak. I am thinking about the places where I felt I belonged and how, maybe, these places are no longer there for me.

Cody's voice brings me back. "Jasmine, you better get in here! They're getting into it!"

We go back to the house. Amos is sitting on the sofa, blowing rapid puffs of smoke out his pipe. He is addressing Samuel Shackleton, sunk beside him on the sofa. Some of his words are slurred.

"Maybe old Eleanor wasn't hot like she used to be, but she was lukewarm enough for fucking. It's that bull of yours who's got no more yeast in his dough. Pecker's flabby as yours."

"Dad!" Jasmine cries.

Cody finishes putting the violin in the case and goes over to the rocking chair and sits down. He seems ready to enjoy himself. Jonah brings in two chairs from the kitchen, one for me and one for him. Jasmine is already seated on the piano stool.

When everyone has finished taking their seats, Samuel responds. "Shit! Old Bruno still hardens up like a telephone pole with every other cow that's put in front of him. Just 'cause the oven's warm don't mean it's hot enough to cook the rolls. That cow of yours is just plain too old and ugly. Besides, she's Bruno's momma."

"Look here," Amos says, "an animal is not made so as to be able to turn down the opportunity to get it on, unless his equipment is not working. An animal ain't like a person. If the female animal can conceive, the male animal will jump the female, willy-nilly. Now take you, for example. You gonna go home tonight warmed up by that cheap Scotch of yours, and you gonna look at Jane asleep there with her curlers, maybe snoring a little, and you're gonna say, 'Naaah, I don't think so', and you'll turn around and go into the bathroom and dig out one of those old magazines you got hidden in the towel drawer, and you'll try to handle things as best you can. But an animal is not put off by age or ugliness. If she still can, he will."

"Oh-*kaay*, time to go home." Jasmine claps and stands up but no one stands up with her. She sits down again. "Samuel, you're our guest, so in accordance with long-established custom, you get the last word. Say your last word and then you all have to scat."

Samuel Shackleton downs the last drop of Scotch in his glass slowly. Then he speaks. "All's I can say is that there comes a time in every bull's life when he decides to stop being a motherfucker. Wished the same principle applied to menfolk as well." He sits on the sofa staring at Amos. Then when he can't hold it any more, his laughter bursts out, together with everyone else's.

Amos sticks his pipe further down his mouth. I can tell that he is not happy with the long-established custom of letting the guest have the last word.

The Shackletons file by, each shaking my hand. When it is Jonah's turn, he says to me, "Good heart-to-heart tonight."

Chapter 24

At five forty-five the following morning, Jasmine comes out of the house. I am in the front yard, surrounded by the plastic animals, lifting weights. I stop long enough to see her rub her eyes. Either she is rubbing off remaining sleep or she cannot believe that someone would be up so early doing what I'm doing. I stop and put the ten-pound dumb-bells on the ground.

"What are you doing?" she asks, yawning. "How long have you been out here? What time is it? And where did you get those?" She is looking at the dumb-bells. They are round and coated with blue plastic.

"Which of the four previous questions would Jasmine like me to answer?"

"Don't tell me that you brought those dumb-bells in your backpack."

"Yes." I don't understand what is so strange about this.

"No wonder I nearly broke my back when I was getting your backpack down from the Jeep." Namu walks over and sits in front of Jasmine, waiting for her to notice him. "Your owner is one crazy boy, Namu. I gotta get some coffee." She turns around and goes back in the house.

After breakfast we load up Kickaz. Jasmine wants to take supplies to Amos's shack so that, come winter, Amos doesn't have to do it. She puts a blanket on Kickaz's back and then places an aluminium frame on top of the blanket. On various parts of the frame she places Amos's supplies, as well as the tent and sleeping bags and other stuff we'll need for our trip.

Amos seems unusually lucid this morning. He does not confuse me with James. He recognizes me as Jasmine's friend, although a couple of times he calls me "Marshmallow". Jasmine says that the reason he is so subdued is that the "meds" have kicked in.

By seven we are on our way. We ascend the knoll where Jasmine is going to build her house-*slash*-studio, go down the other side, and then go up over the forested mountain that Jasmine calls a hill. Here there is a trail that we follow, and from the trail I see paths to clusters of trees. "Maple trees," Jasmine tells me. "There's about fifty of them on this hill that we tap for syrup. The syrup you had this morning for your pancakes comes from one of those trees." Namu stops and cocks his ears. Jasmine stops as well. And I stop after her.

"Listen. Can you hear them?" Jasmine asks.

I hear popping sounds.

"People out hunting. It's illegal to hunt in August but they still do it."

"What do they hunt?" I ask.

"White-tailed deer."

"With guns."

"Yup."

"Has Jasmine ever hunted?"

"Yup."

"And killed a deer with a gun?"

"Yes."

It is a way of seeing Jasmine that I did not have before. I wonder how many new ways of seeing Jasmine there will be during this trip.

"Sometimes the meat from venison lasts us all winter." I understand that this is her way of explaining why she hunts.

We walk for more than an hour. She is leading Kickaz and I am holding on to the aluminium frame. "Look."

There, hidden in the middle of the hill, are a dozen or so thin and tall white trees. The green leaves on the top rustle with a breeze that is not felt on the ground but must exist up there. "Birches. Aren't they pretty? They're my favourite. I don't know why. Those white trunks in the middle of a brown-and-green forest. And in the fall, their leaves make a tinkling sound."

"This is where Jasmine . . . where *you* get *your* ideas for *your* music."

"There are so many sounds. The wind makes different sounds depending on the different trees it travels through. There are sounds that the earth makes. And wait until you get to the water. Then there are animals too. And they all come together sometimes."

I hear the popping sound again. "And guns," I say.

"Yeah, and guns. I guess I should include the sound of those as well."

The memory of Wendell poking my chest comes to mind all of a sudden. Here's another unexpected experience — this pleasure I feel when I imagine how I am going to tell Wendell that I will not ask Jasmine to go on a boat ride. What do I call that?

"That's a red-tailed hawk." We have reached the top of the mountain. Above us, a hawk circles and rises, dips and tilts without a single movement of his wings. "He's looking for a rabbit. There's tons of them in the valley below."

"Are we climbing that mountain too?"

"Hill," Jasmine corrects me.

Hidden Lake, she explains, is not only hidden, it is also secret. There are no roads to the lake, so people have to hike to it. Until recently, only a few old-timers like Amos knew about it.

We are halfway down the second mountain when we suddenly see the lake. We stop as if stunned by sudden brightness. From the side of the mountains I can see the full circumference. Here and there around the sides I see the fishing shacks. They are small wooden structures, and I don't know how any person can lie down and sleep inside of them.

"See that one painted blue with the white stars all over? That one is Amos's."

"How do they sleep?"

"The shacks just barely fit a cot. In the winter they drag the shacks to the middle of the frozen lake, make a hole in the ice, and fish and carry on like teenagers."

"But the cold."

"See this?" She touches a pouch inside the harness. "This is coal for the stove that warms Amos at night. In the daytime he toughs it out. Every time I come over I bring some supplies. Can you imagine making the trip we just made in the winter? Amos gets someone to take care of the animals, puts his snowshoes on and off he goes. A couple of years ago there was a civil war over generators. The younger fishermen wanted to bring over generators so that they could watch TV and have all the comforts of home. But the generators are so noisy and smelly. This quiet would be gone. You should have seen them. I had to stop Amos from bringing his shotgun out here."

"And then?"

"So far those in favour of modern comforts have relented, out of respect and maybe a little fear of the old-timers. But when the old-timers go, the generators will come on the back of snowmobiles."

We get to Amos's shack and unload supplies. There are bags of rice and cans of pork and beans and coal for the small iron stove that is connected to a black chimney pipe sticking out of the roof.

Then Jasmine unfolds the tent. We pick a spot not far from the edge of the lake with the front of the tent facing the water. It is a tent shaped like a triangle, big enough in the middle for a person to stand up. As we are putting it up, I look around for another tent. I realize for the first time that Jasmine and I will be sleeping side by side. I have never slept with anyone else except Yolanda, when we went to Spain, and then we each had a single bed in a hotel room. This is different somehow. It makes me nervous. "Pull up the pole on your end," she yells at me. My nervousness makes me think of Adam and Eve and how they realized they were naked after they ate the apple.

"What are you thinking about? Snap out of it. After we finish getting the camp ready, I'm going to get the canoe out in the lake and go fishing. What would you like to do?"

"Marcelo came to Vermont to ponder, remember."

"Well, here you are. You can stay here or come with me in the canoe. Either way you'll have lots of silence."

"Jasmine will not talk."

"You'll be facing forward and I'll be in the back fishing. You won't even know I'm there."

We paddle, or rather, Jasmine paddles close to the shore, where the shade of the trees reaches the water. Then Jasmine directs the canoe straight into a fallen tree. "Duck," she says. I put down my head quickly and we slide through a space so narrow that only a canoe as slim as ours can fit through, and we are in what seems like an even more secluded lake surrounded on all sides by bushes of red, yellow and white flowers. When we reach the centre of the cove, I hear a splash and the canoe stops. I turn my head around and Jasmine whispers, "The anchor." Then she places her index finger to her lips.

I lower myself to the floor of the canoe and listen. I listen to the periodic swoosh of Jasmine's fishing line. I listen to splashes in the water. I hear the buzz of insects, the wind ripple through the trees, lake waves, and now and then the high-pitched sound of a large bird, a sound of pain.

How did Ixtel become real for me? The world is full of Ixtels who I can help without hurting my father. Why this one? How was it *her* suffering that touched me? Father. I feel connected to her through my father's actions. I feel an obligation to right my father's wrong. But why? Shouldn't my father's welfare come first? His welfare is my welfare. How does one weigh love for a parent against the urge to help someone in need?

I feel like what is right should be done no matter what. This lack of doubt makes me feel inhuman. But it is not a question of my head for once. I hear the right note. I recognize the wrong note. Maybe the right action is a lake like this one, green and quiet and deep.

It is dusk now. Jasmine has divided the one fish she caught into two pieces and dropped the pieces into a plate of flour. She is now cooking them in a skillet she got from Amos's shack. I am thinking about time and how quickly the hours of the day passed.

"Did you know that when we were out there on the canoe, you sat still for almost two hours? I mean, you didn't even twitch. I couldn't see your eyes from where I was, but for a while there I thought you had fallen asleep sitting upright."

"No. I wasn't asleep."

"What goes through your brain when you're still like that? Were you thinking about what you were going to do when you got back?"

"Jasmine was still as well. She didn't speak to me."

"I was throwing my line every which way, trying to catch the one and only fish in the whole lake. For a while I sat on the floor of the canoe with my back against the seat and closed my eyes."

The fish is cooked. She puts my half on a tin plate and scoops corn from a can she opened before. "Dinner," she says. "Otherwise it would have been pork and beans."

"Does Jasmine . . . do you want to say a prayer?" I ask.

"OK." She puts her plate on her knees. I do as well and close my eyes. "Thank You for this place. Thank You for the fish." I open my eyes and see her begin eating. "What? Why do you look so surprised?"

"Your prayers are shorter than mine."

"OK." She closes her eyes. "Thank You for the company." She opens them again. "There. That covers it, don't you think? Eat. You have to eat trout while it's hot, otherwise it doesn't taste as good."

After a few bites, she says: "So you never answered my question. Out there on the lake, when you were still for so long, what was happening?"

"For the longest time I replayed in my mind all that had happened since I found the picture of Ixtel. These images of what happened were like the notes of music. Some sounded good, some not. I like the sound that was made when we tracked and found Jerry García. It all seemed as if we were meant to help Ixtel. That's what I thought for the longest time, and then I thought about my internal music and I looked for it."

"What's that — your internal music?"

"Ever since I was six years old, maybe before that but that's the first time I remember it, I could hear music, only it wasn't really hearing and it wasn't really music, it was *like* it. Does Jasmine feel emotions when she hears certain music?"

"Yes."

"Imagine just feeling the emotions caused by the music without the sound of the music, but you know the music is there. Only the emotions that you feel are always good — like longing and belonging all at once. I call it music because that is the best word for it. I used it to hear it whenever I wanted. I just had to search for it and I found it, only it was more like waiting than searching. But now it is harder to find it. It is almost all gone, I would say. I was hoping it would come at least while I was here."

"And?"

I shake my head to indicate that there was no IM. Then I say, "I found the memory of the music I used to hear, and then even this went away and I listened to all the sounds the lake makes. And also the sound of Jasmine trying to fish."

She puts her plate down. Her fish is getting cold. But so is mine. It is hard to talk about the IM and eat at the same time. Maybe it is also hard for Jasmine to listen to me talk about the IM and eat at the same time. "I can only imagine how beautiful that music must have been. You must have wanted to listen to it all the time."

"When Marcelo was little, it was hard to leave it. Fortunately I could only hear it if I went looking for it. But it was easy to find."

We are quiet, looking at our half-eaten fish. Jasmine picks up her plate and then puts it down again. "You want to know what I think?"

"Yes."

"I think that whatever it is you were doing out there on the lake, searching for the music or trying to remember it, as you say, is all most of us ever hope to do. This ability you had before, that was out of this world. A special gift, I don't know. What if it was impossible for you to have it and be a regular person? You don't hear the music any more, but now you can be flesh and blood like . . . me, for instance. Now you'll have to pay attention and listen, see if you hear anything. Does that make any sense at all? I'm a little out of my element here."

We sit with the fire crackling in front of us. Jasmine's words play slowly in my mind as if they themselves were the notes of a musical piece. She stands up slowly, picks up our dishes, and takes them to the lake.

When she comes back she looks up at the night. "It looks clear and it doesn't feel that cold. We could sleep out here. That way you can look at the stars. Wow! Did you see that? That was the most humongous falling star I ever saw. It went from one end of the sky to the other."

She is removing rocks and sticks from an area in front of our tent. Then she takes out the sleeping bags. She unrolls hers. My heart starts pounding. The area in front of the tent is small. There is no place to put my sleeping bag other than next to hers. She is patting her sleeping bag. She is unzipping it. I am standing paralysed, my head like lead.

"Are you going to sleep like Kickaz, standing up?" Jasmine is talking to me, I realize.

I grasp at a few words that pass by. "Where. Sleeping bag."

"That's probably the best spot." She points at the ground next to her bag. I kneel down and begin to unroll my sleeping bag in the spot she indicated.

"I need to go to the bathroom." I am standing up again. Jasmine is lying down on top of her sleeping bag, her arms behind her head, looking at the stars.

She hands me the flashlight next to her. "You know what to do, right?"

I am so nervous I only see the humour of her statement when

I am trying to find an adequate place.

"Don't go too far," I hear her yell. "It's swampy back there."

"It is only number one," I yell back.

"Thank you for that," she calls.

When I get back I see Namu on top of my sleeping bag. Jasmine has her eyes closed. Is it possible that she fell asleep so quick? I go back into the tent for my backpack. Am I supposed to put on the pyjamas I brought? Jasmine is wearing shorts and a T-shirt and by all indications she plans to wear those to sleep. I leave the pyjamas in my backpack.

"What now?" Jasmine asks.

"I need to find the wipes to wash my hands."

"Goodnight, Namu," I hear her say. "Take care of your silly owner."

I take as long as I can wiping my hands. Now it seems funny to me that I got so nervous at the thought of sleeping next to Jasmine. What is happening? Yesterday, Jonah asked me if I was sexually attracted to Jasmine and that notion seemed shocking to me. And now there is this. I touch my abdomen where I feel a tingling. That's what "butterflies in the stomach" feel like. These butterflies were let loose by what? The first one or two came out when Jasmine talked about the IM and how I could be flesh and blood like her, for instance, and then thousands fluttered when she pointed at the spot where we will sleep together. They are not unpleasant, these butterflies. Their tiny wings are pulling me out, tickling me with the anticipation of lying next to Jasmine.

I move Namu so that he is at my feet. Part of him is on my sleeping bag and part of him on Jasmine's. I take off my boots and slip into the bag fully dressed. I am looking up at the night sky.

The stars seem like tiny pricks on a dark ceiling through which you can see the brightness that exists on the other side. I lie with my eyes open, listening to Jasmine's even breath. Then I hear her voice.

"Yesterday when you were talking to Jonah, you said that you and he were having a heart-to-heart. What did you mean? You don't have to tell me if you don't want to."

"We talked about love."

"Oh God."

"He loves you."

"I'm going to kill him."

"But he doesn't think you will ever love him."

"I do love him. Just not that way. He's like an older brother."

"What does it mean to love someone 'that way'? That is what Marcelo doesn't understand."

"The love thing is difficult to figure, isn't it?" she says. "You're not the only one who has trouble with it."

"Jasmine also?"

"Sometimes . . ." she hesitates, "sometimes people do hurtful things to themselves or others in the name of what they think is love. They make mistakes galore because of it."

"Galore." I like that word.

"It's easy to make mistakes. I mean, it's just so easy to get lost. You can know what it is you have to do in life and where it is you have to do it, and then, *bam*, someone comes along and you get sidetracked and end up heading the wrong way or in the wrong place." She is quiet, as if her words reminded her of something.

"Is that love?"

"I don't know. How can it be if you end up unhappy?"

"It is possible that I am not able to love."

I hear her turn on her side to look at me. "How can you even say that? Look at what you felt when you saw the picture of Ixtel and your impulse to help her. That's love."

"But I do not love her 'that way', as Jasmine calls it. To love someone 'that way', with the desire that someone like Wendell feels, does not seem possible for me."

"Thank God for that. Wendell belongs in the lowest rung of the human species, which is a couple of rungs below most animals."

"And all the signs a person makes to indicate when a person likes you 'that way'. I do not know any of those."

"You'll figure all that out."

"Like now. I don't know if the fact that we are sleeping next to each other means we are going to have sexual intercourse. How does a person find out when to have sex with another? Assuming Jasmine wanted to have sex? How would that work?"

Jasmine is laughing. "I don't know. Knowing you, we would probably talk about it and then make a list. Or maybe we skip all that and I just jump your bones."

"Remember the first day in the office, you told Marcelo to stay away from Martha because she might jump my bones."

"And did she?"

"Jasmine, I thought of another question."

"Oh, no."

"If Jasmine and Jonah were camping together, would they sleep next to each other?"

"Mmm. I kind of see where you're going with this. I guess I'd have to say no. We wouldn't sleep like this." She reaches over and hits me in the chest with her forearm.

"Then why with Marcelo?"

"I don't know. Do you always ask so many questions? It just seems OK, that's all." She sits up.

"Maybe Jasmine doesn't see Marcelo as a man."

"Nope. That's not it. Not it at all."

She opens her sleeping bag and tucks herself in. The conversation is over. Then she pulls herself out, turns on her side and looks at me. The conversation is not over. She has more to say.

"I'm glad you came. I wanted you to see this place." She seems to have trouble speaking.

"You wanted Marcelo to think about the memo and the consequences of doing something with it."

"Not just that. I wanted you to have an image of this place in your mind because you need to know that it exists. People think a place like this is perfect. Living a simple life close to the land and all that. It isn't. There are mean people and alcoholics and medical bills to pay and depressed people galore. But some of us feel OK here, you know, despite all that. It is a simpler life than the law firm. More silence, I guess.

"Anyway, I wanted you to see it. You'll always be welcome here. You can come and stay for a few days or for . . . for as long as you like. Amos likes you, I can tell. And you're not much of a bother to me." She looks at me for a brief second and then closes her eyes.

I stay up listening to her fall asleep, feeling how it is not to be alone.

Chapter 25

I am sitting in the park in front of the law firm playing in my mind the scenes from our camping trip. Every once in a while, I catch myself laughing out loud. Whenever our family went on a trip we would, at the end of the day, ask each other our favourite thing for that day. "Marcelo, Marcelo, what do you say? What was your favourite thing today?" This is the song we would sing to each other.

So I sit here, seeing all that happened, not leaving out any details. *"Marcelo, what was your favourite thing?"* I ask myself. *"It is so hard to pick one. Do I have to?"* Another part of me responds. *"Yes, you must."* I stop the dialogue because I know very well, without a doubt, that my most favourite thing was being next to Jasmine under a million stars.

This is what I'm thinking about when I notice Wendell sitting next to me. He appeared out of nowhere, it seems. Wendell takes out a cigarette, lights it and inhales deeply.

"Smoking is bad for you," I tell him.

"I know it," Wendell answers. He takes a few more puffs before flicking the cigarette away. "How's it going with Jasmine?" he asks.

I feel my heart speed up. This is the time for me to tell him. There will be no pleasure in doing it. I take a deep breath and say, trying my best to look at him, "I will not ask Jasmine to come on a boat ride with you." I say it. It is out. I glance at Wendell's face and see him grimace.

"Oh? Well, that's a big surprise. Actually, I was asking how it was going between *you* and Jasmine?"

"It is not like what you think. Between Jasmine and me. We are friends. Like you and I were once."

"Pssh." Wendell makes a sound like air being let out of a tyre. "I understand you went on a camping trip with her. How was that? Did you poke her?"

"I have to go back to work," I say, starting to get up.

"Sit." Wendell's voice has anger. Then softer, "I want to give you something."

I glance at Wendell's hands but they are empty.

"It's the gift of truth."

I sit down again. I am confused. I wait for Wendell to begin, but Wendell is absorbed in looking at a pigeon that is edging closer to a potato chip near his foot. Wendell moves his foot back, clearing the way for the pigeon to approach. When the pigeon hops closer to the chip, Wendell kicks him, and the pigeon goes catapulting in the air. The dazed pigeon takes a few wobbly steps and then flies away. I look at Wendell, stunned. It is the first time I have ever seen anyone hurt an animal.

Wendell sits straight and turns his body to face me. "Are you brave enough to handle the truth, the whole truth and nothing but the truth?"

"Yes," I say nervously.

"Remember that conversation we had at the club? You know, I told you about your father and my father and the bond?"

"Yes."

"And we talked about this balance of power that we had between our families."

"Yes."

"Remember I told you that there were ways, easy ways to disturb the equilibrium. A mistake could be made by one of the partners and then the other partner would have more power?"

"You said that."

"What I see happening here is that the balance of power has been disturbed. You disturbed it. The balance existed in the first place only because I befriended you. And what do you do? I took you for this innocent moron while all along you want Jasmine. I cannot believe this. I cannot believe Jasmine prefers. . ."

I remember the conversation I had with my father on the first train ride to work. *He wanted to show everyone that my son was. . .*

"It is not true I wanted Jasmine all along." I hear my words but they don't sound convincing.

"I want to give you this." He hands me a folded piece of paper. "No, don't open it now, as much as I would like to have the pleasure of watching you read it. As part of the discovery I had to do, I had to go through some files that the attorneys kept in their offices. I found that in one of your father's personal files along with some other stuff. When I saw it, I said to myself, 'What should I do with this? If I show it to my father, the balance of power might be tipped.' Then you came along and I said, 'I don't want to hurt the kid. He's so naïve.'

"But now I think it's time. You broke the bond. Therefore you're ready for the gift of truth. That's yours to do with as you please."

Wendell leaves. I unfold the piece of paper and recognize Jasmine's handwriting.

Dear Mr Sandoval:

I know you want me to call you Arturo but in this letter I want to call you Mr Sandoval. I don't know what happened last Friday at the Christmas party. I should not have had those margaritas. I never drink hard liquor. Most of all when you came to me and asked me to meet you in your office because you had a present you wanted to give me, I should have said no. "Thank you, but that's probably not a good idea." I want to say that I honestly thought you had a present but the truth is that I kind of knew what was going to happen and I still went. Part of me was afraid to say no to my boss, but saying no to anyone is not a problem for me.

I have no idea how it happened. I say to myself that I was lonely and needed to be close to someone. My brother died a few months ago. I am homesick. But these are all excuses. It should never have happened. It was wrong. I don't think it is right for me to work here any more, so if it's OK I would like to stay just long enough for me to find another job. Otherwise, please consider this my two weeks' notice.

Jasmine

I read the letter one more time. And then a third time. Then I read it again until the letter's meaning finally penetrates my resistance to believe. I look at each sentence for its significance, for what each sentence says about my father and . . . about Jasmine. I see him asking her if she can come upstairs to pick up the present. I see him drawing her with the same deceit that Wendell wanted to draw her to his boat. Then they are in his office. What happened? Arturo and Jasmine had sexual intercourse in his office. Isn't that the only interpretation of the letter? How can there be any other interpretation? I see him using her. Or maybe there was love on his part? But how can there be love when you lie, when you take advantage of someone who has been drinking alcohol or who is lonely? How can there be love when you have promised to love Aurora?

I am standing. I don't know when it was that I stood up or if I have been talking to myself out loud. My impulse at this moment is to take the Vidromek memo to Jerry. "Here, Jerry. My father has what is coming to him." But I sit down again. As much as I am full of anger and disappointment, there is a part of me that wants to wait. When I came home from the camping trip, I knew my reasons for giving the memo to Jerry. If I give him the memo now, it will be out of revenge. I don't want to act out of revenge. There is something that is not right about that.

Then there is this other emotion that I'm feeling. I don't have a name for it. It centres around Jasmine. *Saying no to anyone is not a problem for me*. It hurts to know that she didn't say no. It hurts to think that there may have been love for him, despite the alcohol and despite the loneliness. It hurts to think that there may still be love for him. Is this what jealousy feels like? I remember lying next to Jasmine, listening to her breathe as she fell asleep, my first-ever butterflies of attraction dancing in my abdomen, and the memory saddens me, as if all that I felt then was for a different person, someone I made up. The real Jasmine is the one who could not say no to my father.

Chapter 26

"What is happening inside that head of yours?" Aurora asks me on the way to Temple Emanuel.

"Why?"

"I don't know. You have not said a single word since you came home from work yesterday. You refused to come down to dinner. You were up at four walking Namu. You wouldn't go to work today. I had to practically drag you out of that tree house to come with me to see Hesch. I know it's not the camping trip because you were happy when you returned. Did something happen with your father yesterday at work? Why are you so quiet?"

"Marcelo is always quiet."

"Yes. But it's a different kind of quiet now. You remind me of. . ."

"Joseph. Just before he died." I finish her thought.

"How did you know?"

"I know."

"Joseph's quiet was not a bad quiet, I don't think."

"He was waiting."

"Waiting for what?"

"The music."

We drive in silence for a few minutes.

"Is there anything you want to tell me?" Aurora asks me.

The IM has stopped. It will never come back. It was a temporary product of my brain, just like my special interest. I am lost. I have no way of knowing what to do about Ixtel, about my father, about Jasmine. I cannot tell any of this to Aurora. Instead, I say to her, "Aurora is acting too much like a mother."

"You haven't seen Hesch since I don't know when. You need to spend a little time around someone on your own wavelength."

"Aurora is on the same wavelength," I say.

"No. Your religious interests are way beyond me. Besides, you need to talk about them."

"Aurora's religion is like the morning dew. No one knows where it comes from. It is just there."

"Nonsense. I am not religious, morning dew or otherwise. The law firm turned you into a poet now?"

"It's from the Bible."

"What book and verse?"

"What?"

"That line about the dew on the flower, whereabouts in the Bible is it?"

"I don't remember."

"You're forgetting Bible references now? I knew something was wrong with you. I can't tell you how glad I am to have insisted that you talk to Hesch. I don't know why you resisted so much. You always liked going to see her."

It is true, I think. Talking to the rabbi was one of my favourite activities. But now I am afraid.

Aurora drops me off at the rear parking lot of Temple Emanuel. I am climbing up the steps to the back entrance when I hear the rabbi's voice.

"I'm back here!"

She's at the far end of the parking lot holding a green garbage bag in her hand. I walk towards her, carrying the book by Abraham Joshua Heschel that she lent me.

"Look at this," she says when I am close enough to hear her normal voice. She holds up an empty can of Bud Light for me to see. "The cops tell me that kids come back here at night to drink and make out. Can you believe it? A Temple parking lot of all places! Is there nothing sacred any more?" With her oversized, green-fluorescent sunglasses, she looks like one of the Amazon frogs that Yolanda once kept in her terrarium. She beams me a smile. "How is my young *mensch*?"

"I brought back your book." I hand the book to her. I notice a beer can half-buried in the leaves and bend over to pick it up.

"Thank you." She grabs the book first and places it on one of two tattered lawn chairs. Then she takes the can carefully from me with yellow rubber-gloved fingers. "It can't be any of our kids. No God-fearing Jewish kid would drink this stuff. If I find a bottle of vodka, then I worry." She tightens the bag and points to the tattered lawn chairs. "Let's sit outside. It's beeeautiful out here!"

It is the middle of August. The leaves on the oak trees are full-size and dark green. Rabbi Heschel waits for me to sit down and angles the chair so that she is not facing me directly. Then she takes a deep breath and folds her hands in her lap.

I remember some visits with the rabbi where no more than a

hello and a goodbye were spoken. That's one of the things I enjoyed about her. I didn't have to think of anything to say when I was with her. Now the silence is uncomfortable.

I do not know how much time passes before she speaks. "How's the remembering?"

This is a question I don't want to answer. I decide to counter it with another question. "Does Aurora believe in God?"

"Have you ever asked her?"

"Once," I reply. "She answered with a question, like the rabbi likes to do. She said, 'What difference would it make whether I do or not?'"

"And what do you think she meant by that?" she asks.

"You tell me what you think."

She sighs. I see her hands tighten around the chair's armrests. "Aurora believes in God in her own way." She speaks so quietly I can barely hear her.

"I know why Aurora does not like to talk about religion."

"Tell me then."

"There was a little girl at St Elizabeth's once who died because her parents refused to consent to a blood transfusion. Their religion prohibited it."

"Yes. I remember."

"Aurora was very angry."

"And sad."

"The parents of that little girl believed they were following God's commands."

"Their religion told them that, yes."

"Were they wrong? The parents? I know Aurora thinks they were wrong. What does the rabbi think?"

Rabbi Heschel takes off her sunglasses and dangles them by the side of the chair. "I think we, and I mean all of us, every single one of us who's in the religion business, have messed things up royally."

"It is not possible to know what God wants us to do."

"Let's just say that because we are human, there is an element of uncertainty in interpreting His will."

"People kill other people and they think God asked them to do it."

"That is correct."

We both look up towards the sound of a robin's double whistle: *pheee-pheeeu. Pheee-pheeeu. Pheee-pheeeu.* I can see the robin's ochre chest puff up with inhaled breath before the sound is made.

"I don't remember any more," I tell her. It feels good to get the words out.

Rabbi Heschel is unfazed, as if it were natural to one day suddenly stop praying or remembering. She waits for a while before speaking again. "The day after Lucy died — the little girl whose parents refused her a blood transfusion — Aurora got up in the morning and went to work. She had tried very hard to get the hospital to fight the parents' decision. A judge ultimately ruled in favour of the hospital, but by then it was too late."

"Yes."

Rabbi Heschel laughs a short, sad laugh. Then she says, "Do you think that God cares one whit whether Aurora believes in Him? She doesn't need to believe in God or even remember Him to do His work. Her belief is in her deeds, which is OK."

"God is with her like the morning dew."

"Thoughts about Him are not what He wants. He wants deeds. But that doesn't mean she thinks that's the only way for everyone. I'm her best friend and my head spins with God-talk day and night. I believe that the Holy One, Blessed be He, helps us to know His will through the words of His holy men and women and through the events of history, because He knows we need all the help we can get. And we need to remember the holy words and the events in history as much as we can because it's in our nature to forget. That's part of my tradition. And look, Aurora brings you here to talk God stuff with me, although I think she does that just to make sure I stay humble, which is what good friends do."

"Do you know where in the Bible it says that God comes to us like morning dew?"

"There's nothing that says the Holy One comes to us like morning dew," she says with absolute certainty. "Somewhere in there, there is something about His *favour* coming to us like morning dew."

"I am not able to remember where."

"It's a line from a poem of one of your mystics. Good old Metchild. You should know, you're the one that introduced me to her."

"God's love descends on us like dew on a flower." I suddenly remember those words. "But Metchild was only repeating an image found in the Hebrew Bible."

"Love, favour, God, it's still a beautiful image no matter what. No wonder one of our people invented it." She moves her eyebrows up and down rapidly — a gesture meant to imitate Groucho Marx, a favourite comedian of the rabbi.

"I am not interested in the Bible any more," I say.

"And the other holy books?"

"Also."

"Why?"

I reflect before answering. "Johnny is a kid at Paterson. He and I entered Paterson at the same time. Johnny's special interest is baseball. He is obsessed by baseball facts and statistics. 'In what game did Babe Ruth hit his four hundredth home run and who was the pitcher?' Johnny will tell you. I always thought it was a silly special interest. What good does it do to know that?" I stop.

"And you think that reading the Bible and your other books is just like Johnny's special interest."

"It is exactly the same. He can tell you when Babe Ruth hit a home run and I can tell you about Ruth the Moabite."

"I have to disagree. It seems to me you read the Bible for a different reason than Johnny studies his baseball books. You're not simply memorizing, you're searching, listening, responding even. The story of Ruth the Moabite taught you something about how to live. The Bible is alive for you in a way that baseball statistics are not for Johnny. The Bible and your holy books are reminders of what you want to remember. That's how you used to pray, yes? You memorized the words from your holy books and then remembered them, and in doing so brought to life the mystery and the reality behind the words."

"Johnny remembers also. He is the happiest when he is remembering his baseball. There is no difference."

I hear her sigh again. The robin is now in the middle of the parking lot hopping frantically here and there.

"Something happened at the law firm."

"Yes."

"You discovered something about the world we live in, some complication that pulls you in different directions."

I nod.

"You are at a loss as to what to do. You lost the bearings you used to rely on."

I nod.

Rabbi Heschel stretches her feet, lifts her face upwards and closes her eyes to the sunlight. "Have I ever told you how I ended up as a rabbi?"

"No."

"My Hebrew brain squirmed over the decision." I turn in time to see her grin. "Was it the Holy One that was calling me, or was it me just wanting to thumb my nose at the males, including those in my closest family, who believed the Lord's business was not a woman's business? My father wanted me to be a lawyer, of all things."

I try to picture Rabbi Heschel with her neon-green glasses sitting behind Stephen Holmes's immaculate glass desk. The image causes me to chuckle to myself.

"What? You don't think I'd make a good lawyer?"

"No. The brain of the rabbi is too powerful."

"That's exactly what I thought. I could be a lawyer, but then that wide green pasture in my brain would lie fallow. What a waste that would be, huh? I had to find a job that utilized my overpowering intellectual capabilities." She lifts the green garbage bag and rattles the empty beer cans inside.

I smile.

She continues, "I think your brain is like mine. I never knew for sure that going to seminary was what God wanted me to do. 'Sure,' I used to complain, 'to Moses you appear as a burning bush, but to me you come as a burning haemorrhoid.' I knew that going to seminary was what the Lord wanted only *afterward*, when the burning — not *stopped* — but at least got bearable."

"Burning." I know exactly what she's talking about.

"God's love descends on some like dew on a flower, blessed be He, but sometimes we trudge along our comfortable lives and *bam*, He descends on us like a splash of gasoline . . . and then He strikes a match. Why do I think that you have been soaking in gasoline all these years and He just set you on fire?"

Ixtel was the match, I say to myself.

She waits for me to respond. Then after a while she says, "How I found out what God wanted me to do is that the urge to do it got too painful to ignore. I ended up going to seminary just so I could finally get some sleep."

"The urge. Urge."

"Great word, isn't it? Sounds like when a piece of gefilte fish gets stuck in your throat and you try to dislodge it by coughing and gagging. Uurrrch. Uuurguh." She imitates a person choking.

"'Urgency' and 'urgent' are related to urge," I say.

"So is 'reg-*urge*-itate,'" she jokes.

"The urge the rabbi had . . . has . . . still has . . . is a longing, 'like a hart longs for flowing streams'."

Rabbi Heschel's eyes soften. She turns her face away from me and focuses on the steady working of a woodpecker. "I needed to hear that," she says, still not looking at me.

"You're welcome."

She sits up, her back flush against the back of the patio chair. "Only our longing for Him, the big longing, the one with a capital L, sometimes gets confused with a hundred little longings, some of them OK, some of them not. For most of us the big longing lies buried under a mountain of silliness and selfishness."

I think of Jasmine, Arturo, Oak Ridge High.

The rabbi continues, "He's urging you to do something that may be painful, isn't He?"

I shake my head yes.

"I don't know what I would do if I thought God was asking me to do something with painful consequences, something that required courage and sacrifice. Not that He doesn't, it's just that I'm afraid. Actions that require courage are all He asks these days. I know He needs me to do something with more shock value, like what the prophets used to do, to wake people up from their comfortable stupor. I'd preach to them naked like Hosea, but look at me. You think anyone would even look? 'Wake up, wake up!' I'd say, jumping around in my birthday suit. 'You're worried about upgrading your Mercedes or about whether so-and-so is sitting closer to the Tabernacle, and all along God is dying for your help. It's urgent! He's urging you. The urges that you feel are to do His work — you're getting the signals all mixed up. You think He's asking you to be a big success in whatever it is you're ambitious about, and that's not what He wants from you at all.'"

Then she stops talking and makes a concerted effort to calm herself. She resumes, her tone more subdued, more intimate. "If I told you that God speaks to us through our urges so long as these are safe and proper and totally civilized and don't hurt anyone, what would I be saying? If I told you longing is OK as long as it is within the bounds of what our world considers normal, I would be going counter to my whole tradition. My people *discovered* divine urges, for goodness' sake. Not namby-pamby urges either. It was loincloth-tearing, harlot-marrying, sacrificing, succumbing and surrendering kinds of urges. Not without bickering and haggling, I'll grant you, but ultimately urges of the worst kind, the kind that demanded everything."

Then she opens her eyes wide and I see her pupils darken as she speaks. "Do I think that the people who let children die or who blow themselves up for the sake of God are wrong? Yes, I do. They start out right and turn wrong. They begin holy and end up evil. Is the desire to do justice the same kind of inner fire that makes people deny transfusions to their dying child or blow themselves up or seek revenge? What can I tell you? I have to say that in essence it is. It is the same sap that comes from the ground, travels up the roots and then clambers up the trunk until it reaches the branches. Then it chooses. If the sap goes up one branch it is good and it bears fruit. Good, beautiful, nourishing fruit. And if it goes up another branch it is evil and there is no fruit except maybe a dried-up useless fig. But the sap, the sap is the same, only the fruits are different."

I feel her studying me as if she was trying to read my thoughts. "Your fire. The fire you're in. You have to make sure it goes up the right branch. It's up to you."

"The fire hurts."

"It does. There's no getting around it."

"And there is anger and revenge in the fire. The fire wants to hurt those who are deceitful and those who inflict suffering."

"Yes. But His urges are always towards life and more life and forgiveness and more forgiveness. And what comes from Him are like these juicy pomegranates I saw in Israel; they are plain on the outside, but inside they are loaded with light-giving rubies that are sweet and precious, and quench and fill. Like those outwardly simple but incredibly rich words of Micah: 'What does the Lord require of you but to do justice, and to love kindness, and to walk humbly with your God?'"

How is it possible to be kind to Arturo after his deceit, his own lack of kindness? And Jasmine? I tell myself that there is nothing to forgive her for and yet the feeling of being wounded by her exists. It seems to resist forgiveness.

But I can do justice for Ixtel.

We see Aurora's car pull into the parking lot. Rabbi Heschel places her hand on my arm. "Marcelo, before you go, let *me* play the part of the rabbi for a change and say this: it is a messy business, this trying to figure out what His will is. It is messy and painful and certainly never clear. But deep at the bottom of our conflicting desires and confusions there is the sense of what is right and what is wrong. What else can we do but trust and hope in this sense? What else can we do but *trust* that He is at the source of what we feel and *hope* He is at the end of what we want to do? Trust the sense you have that you are travelling the right direction because, when it comes down to it, that and the ability to tell the difference between a dried-up fig and a pomegranate is all you have."

We are both looking at Aurora. She steps out of the car, waves at us, takes a few steps towards us and then stops. Now she is attempting to remove strands of sticky gum from the bottom of her white-soled shoes.

"What if doing God's will hurts the people we love?"

"Ooof!" She takes a deep breath and there is a look of strength on her face, as if, beneath her goofy demeanour, there is someone who can elicit fear when necessary. "Look at me." I look at her. She says, "Trust in Him. He will know how to use whatever hurt results for His own ends. Is there more you want to tell me?"

"No," I say.

"How will you know what to do?"

"The rabbi helped me. And. . ."

"And?"

I remember the conversation Jasmine and I had in the cafeteria. "The right note sounds right and the wrong note sounds wrong."

"Ha!" she says. "Look." She opens the book by Abraham Joshua Heschel, flips through the pages, and reads. "Our effort is but a counterpoint in the music of His will."

"What if we don't hear the music?" I say.

"That's what faith is, isn't it? Following the music when we don't hear it."

She squeezes my arm and smiles at me. Then Rabbi Heschel nods at Aurora that we are finally done.

Chapter 27

The second trip to Jerry García's office is easier than the first.
Now I know which way is east and which is west. It is early morning but already there are people waiting for him. I find a chair
and sit down by myself. I didn't tell anyone at the law firm where
I was going. I was out yesterday. They will assume I am out again
today.

When he opens the door to let a young woman out, Jerry García
sees me. He says something in Spanish to an elderly man and
then he asks me in.

"Would you like to sit down?"

"No." I take my backpack off.

"Marcelo." He makes a motion for me to stop looking in the
backpack. "You found something that will help Ixtel."

"Yes."

"And you have thought through all the consequences."

"I have."

"You're sure about this. I'm not forcing you to do anything.
This is something you decided to do on your own. You can walk

out of this office right now without any problems or hurt feelings. You understand?"

"I understand." I look straight at him. "I found a memo from the head of quality control to the president of Vidromek, telling him that the windshields were defective."

"I know."

"You know?"

"I knew a memo with the results of the tests had to be there. It is standard procedure for the test results to be sent to the president by the head of quality control. But when other law firms asked for the memo, the answer came back that it was lost."

"I have it here."

"Don't give me anything. I want to be able to say that you never gave me anything. Just give me a clue. Something that will let them know I know of the memo's existence. You said it was a memo from the head of quality control to the president of Vidromek. What is the date of the memo?"

I read: "June 21, 2005."

"OK."

I put the memo in the backpack and get ready to leave.

"What's going to happen to you?"

"I will go to a public school for my senior year. No more Paterson. No more training the ponies."

"That will be hard."

"Yes. It can be done. What will happen to Arturo?"

"Why? Would you like something to happen to him? You're not doing this because you're angry with him or something?"

"No. I am sure that is not why I am doing this."

"Not that I care. I mean, you can have whatever reasons you want. Listen, I'm going to try to work this out so that the least possible harm comes to you and your father. But I make no guarantees. It depends on your father, on whether he wants to play ball with me or not. If he wants to play hardball then I'll do the same. But I gotta tell you, I would like to cream the living daylights out of Stephen Holmes and his a-hole son, what's his name?"

"Wendell." I remember the telephone conversation with Yolanda on my first day of work, ages ago, it seems.

"Little shits. I'll try to control myself. Hey, I just thought of something. I have to go see the Sisters later this week — I have to get them to sign some legal papers. Would you like to come?"

"I don't know."

"Two hours. That's all it'll take. I'll call you at the law firm just in case you can go." He offers me his hand and I take it.

Outside of Jerry García's office, I take a long breath. The memory of Hidden Lake comes to me, its waters green and quiet and deep.

Chapter 28

I am gathering files from Wendell's office. Juliet wants me to find them and then copy them. I came in late, after the first mail run, and successfully avoided seeing Jasmine.

Wendell stands in front of me. His face is fiery red.

"Ever screwed anyone, Gump?"

It is none of Wendell's business, but I go ahead and answer him anyway. "No."

"Well, you screwed us royally. By us I mean all of us at Sandoval and Holmes, you included."

I do not respond.

"This guy Jerry García calls my father this morning and says he wants a June 21, 2005, document from the head of quality control to the president of Vidromek. Now how would he know about that memo?"

I can see Jerry García and Stephen Holmes talking to each other, each in their respective offices — Stephen Holmes thinking that Jerry García is no one to be concerned about and then suddenly snapping to attention. Then I imagine Jerry García in those law school poker games and everyone thinking he's a dummy until he lays down his cards. I don't answer.

"I'll tell you how he knows." Out of his back pocket he takes out a piece of paper. He opens it in front of me and I recognize it as the Vidromek memo. "Guess where I found this? When this guy García called, I knew it had to be you. All I had to do was look in your backpack and there it was."

I realize I left my backpack in Robert Steely's office where I have been sitting. "That is private."

"You want to know what is private? This memo is private. Where did you get it?"

"I found it in the Vidromek files when you gave me the first assignment," I lie. But I enjoy watching Wendell look scared. He thinks it is his fault the memo ended up in the general files. As much as I don't know what to feel about Jasmine, I am glad that Wendell does not suspect her.

"This guy Jerry García is a lightweight. My father will swat him away with a little money. What we worry about is the big law firms once they find out we have settled with someone. They'll know we are vulnerable and they will hit us full force."

"It was not right to hide the memo."

"What the hell do you know? Huh? Look at this." He points to the second name in the memo: *Lic. Jorge Baltazar*. "The 'Lic' stands for *Licenciado*, the Spanish word for lawyer. On my father's advice, all correspondence and memos to the president of the company go through this guy — probably some kid who files papers all day, but a lawyer nevertheless. All the memos to the president had to be addressed to him as well. You know why he did that?"

I shake my head no.

"No, I didn't think so. That's why, when someone like you is given *directions* for an assignment, you are supposed to *follow* them. The system with the lawyer was set up so that the documents could be protected by attorney-client privilege. Do you know what that is?"

Again I shake my head no.

"A document protected by the attorney-client privilege does not have to be shown to the other side when they ask for it in litigation. The law allows this in order to let an attorney and his client communicate freely. Now let me spell it out for you. This memo did not have to be given to Jerry García or anyone else. The rules of civil procedure allowed us to keep it. Yeah, maybe there was a copy of it in the general files. But I had another copy in a file of all documents that we were not giving out because they were protected by the attorney-client privilege."

For a few moments I think that perhaps I made a mistake in going to see Jerry García. I try to grasp on to anything Wendell said so I can respond. "But . . . you say . . . this privilege is to protect the communication between an attorney and his client . . . but . . . here there was no communication. . . The attorney did not communicate anything. The memo was from the engineer to the president of the company." Then I see a ray of clarity. "The arrangement Stephen Holmes created was a way to evade the rule."

"You are one misguided retard," Wendell says.

Is it possible that this is the Wendell that I wanted as a friend? Was all this inside of him all this time? I feel his hatred towards me. I think that Wendell has so much to lose, maybe more than I do. Maybe he will lose his car and the boat and even the women.

"What world do you live in? You are an idiot. An imbecile."

I smile.

"What's so funny?"

"I think it is funny that in your anger you are treating me like a normal person. There is nothing that you are not telling me that you would not tell someone who was normal by your definition."

Wendell grabs the skin on the back of his neck and pulls it. "Oh, hell. What do I care? I got three more weeks left of this crap and then I'm out. Your father wants to talk to you."

I stand up.

"Did you think about the bond when you found the memo?"

"Yes."

"But you went ahead and gave it to Jerry García? Why? Why did you do it?"

"I found the picture of the girl that Jerry García is the lawyer for. Her name is Ixtel."

"The girl." I can see Wendell remembering the picture of Ixtel in his mind and perhaps throwing the picture in the trash. For a moment I believe that he wants to agree with me that what I did was right. But he is not able. "Well, you did what you did," he says, exhaling. "Now you have to pay the bill."

"Pay the bill."

"The bill. We are all going to pay the bill for what you did. How big the bill will be remains to be seen. They're all in there trying to figure out how to keep the bill as small as possible, but there will be a bill. But I'm thinking, what will be *your* bill? Oh, sure, you won't get to go to your school for the retarded like you wanted, but . . . I don't know, that doesn't strike me as enough, compared to what the rest of us might lose. So I thought that maybe I should send your mother a copy of that little note from Jasmine. What do you think?"

I know he is waiting for me to show fear. And it is there, the fear. I fear Aurora's hurt if she sees the letter. But it is not hard for me to hide my fear, and so I walk away without any expression on my face.

I go to Arturo's office. He continues looking at the papers on his desk as I stand in front of him.

After what seems like a long time, he looks up. "I just got off the phone with Jerry García," he says.

"Yes."

"He's agreed to disappear."

I start to open and close my hands but then I stop myself.

"Of course" — Arturo is sitting straight on his leather chair, his eyes unblinking, fixed on me — "he now wants seventy-five thousand dollars. 'We all have to live,' as he says. Do you know what you have done?" His voice begins to tremble.

"Yes."

"When he first called Stephen, García didn't say anything about you. He just asked for the June 21, 2005 memo. Wendell figured out it was you."

"You knew the memo existed."

"I know everything that happens in this law firm. Stephen and I do not keep secrets from each other."

I hear reproach in my father's voice. Unlike Stephen Holmes, his own son does keep secrets from him. Then again, Arturo also has secrets. I look around his office and imagine Arturo and Jasmine that night of the Christmas party and wonder where they had sexual intercourse and how. Something that feels very heavy descends and settles in me, settles everywhere in the room. I reach inside my pocket and touch Jasmine's letter. I want to take it out and throw it at Arturo, but I stop.

"Do you have anything to say?" he is asking.

"No," I say.

"I know you think we were doing something wrong in keeping that memo from García. I'm sorry about the girl. But we were doing what the law allowed us to do. We were representing our client zealously, using all reasonable arguments in support of its case. There is a reasonable argument that a document, once it is reviewed by counsel, comes under the protection of the attorney-client privilege. We are entitled to use that argument on our client's behalf. And the memo itself does not prove liability. The engineer that wrote it could have been wrong, or maybe he had a gripe against his boss and wanted to get even, or it could be that the windshields are not being properly installed and the people that do the installation are at fault and not Vidromek. You . . . you . . . you just took it upon yourself to decide what was right and what was wrong. Who the hell gave you authority to do that?" He stops. "Why didn't you come talk to me?"

"What would Arturo have done?"

"We would have talked about it. I would have told you how the law works. Maybe we could have made a personal donation to this place where the girl lives. Didn't you trust me?"

I don't know what to say. Why didn't I come to him when I found the picture of Ixtel? I felt doubts inside of me. "If I had come to you, would you have given Jerry García what he asked?"

"No. Absolutely not. That would be admitting that Vidromek was responsible."

"But you were willing to give the man at the fitness club what *he* asked. You said to him that you would convince Vidromek to pay in return for a little bonus. Why is he different than Jerry García? Why are his clients different than Ixtel? What is the little bonus that makes such a difference?"

I see on his face the look of momentary shock. It is as if my father suddenly discovered that I had a brain. "Dammit, Marcelo! The world is not all black and white. There are rules you know nothing about. Rules I need to follow in order to survive. Those are the rules of this game I play, the system I live by! The system that puts food on the table and lets you live in a damn tree house and go to a special private school." He raises his voice and stands up all at the same time. "And those are the rules you were supposed to live by this summer. You did not! You were given an assignment and did not follow it. Do you know what you did?"

"I know," I say. "I knew what could happen to all of us. Marcelo did not succeed in following the rules of the real world. He knows. He will spend the next year at Oak Ridge High. He knows. He knows. He knew that would happen before he talked to Jerry García. He thought it all through. All that would happen. And still he did it. And still he would do it again."

And now he is silent. I see his hands open and shut, the way mine do when I cannot find words for what I want to say. I wait and wait and then he says, "You know what? There's only a few weeks left in the summer. Why don't we end this summer job at the end of the week. Use the next two days to finish up what you're doing. Then you can use the rest of the summer to get ready for Oak Ridge. Get the books you'll be using. Get some help to bring you up to speed."

He sits back on his chair and bends his head to look at the document in front of him.

I turn around and take two steps towards the door. I stop. I feel Jasmine's letter folded in my shirt pocket. I remember Rabbi Heschel's words. *Trust in Him. He will know how to use whatever hurt results for His own ends.* And so I turn around, walk towards the edge of his desk and extend my hand with Jasmine's letter to him.

"What is it?" he asks before taking it.

"Wendell gave me this. He called it the 'gift of truth'. I think you should have it."

He takes it from my hand. I wait for him to begin reading it before I leave.

Chapter 29

We get off the interstate when we see the signs for Lawrence. As we wind our way through the streets, I begin to see more and more signs in Spanish — storefronts, restaurants. The beat of Latin music fills the air. The people's skins are brown and black. We stop in front of a three-storey green building. All the windows are open and from the top floor, I see a white curtain float out into the street like a flag.

"Here we are," Jerry says. "That's the place."

We get out of the car and walk to the door. Now I have this sense of embarrassment. What will I say to Ixtel? Why am I here? Through the screen door I hear someone crying. Jerry García rings the bell and a few moments later, the door opens.

"Gerónimo!" a woman's voice says. "Come in, come in."

It is a large woman with wiry white hair who immediately reminds me of a darker and bulkier version of Rabbi Heschel.

"And this is Marcelo?"

"I brought some things," Jerry tells her as he heads back to his car.

"I bring you lemonade." The woman grabs my hand and pulls me inside. Before I know what is happening, she embraces me and holds me tight against her soft, large body. "Thank you for all you done," I hear her say. "My name is Sister Juana. I speak in bad English to you, OK?"

"Yes," I manage to say. I am out of breath from the embrace. She takes me down the hall in the direction of the crying.

"Let's go in here," Sister Juana says. We turn into a doorway opposite the room where the crying is coming from. The room we enter is half-full of metal folding chairs. At one end of the room, a television set has been moved to the side and there is a table covered with a white tablecloth embroidered with blue, orange, pink and green flowers. A cross stands in the middle of the table and a candle in a red glass next to it. "On Sunday we say Mass here," she says.

"You are a priest," I say. Immediately I realize that there are no women priests.

"No, not priest. *Díos mío*, no!" She laughs. "Padre Antonio comes on Sundays to say Mass. Sit, please."

Just as she sits down, we hear the sound of glass breaking. She stands up and says, "I be back. Here, I turn on the fan for you." She goes over to a tall, rusty fan in the corner and clicks a button. She waits until she hears the blades begin to rattle and then she leaves the room. Her plastic sandals make a smacking sound as she walks.

Out in the hallway, I hear Jerry and Sister Juana speak. Then he leans in the doorway to speak to me.

"I'll be back in twenty minutes. The sister just gave me a list of errands." He waves a piece of paper and disappears.

I am alone for a few moments when a girl walks in, sees me and freezes. She looks like a smaller version of Ixtel, only this girl's face has not been hurt. Her hair is tied in a ponytail and it falls over the front of her shoulder. "Ay! You scared me!" she gasps.

"*Hola*," I say.

"I speak English," she responds.

"Oh. My name is Marcelo," I say.

"I'm María," she says brightly. Now I see the full resemblance to Ixtel. "You're looking for Ixtel?"

"Yes," I answer.

"She's upstairs. I'll get her." Then she asks, "Do you know how to fix the TV?" She is pointing at the television set with a coat hanger sticking from the top.

"No."

"It is the stupid antenna," she goes on, not paying attention to me.

We hear an angry scream from the room across the hall. María sticks her fingers in her ears and grimaces. "Is Ixtel your sister?" I ask when she unplugs her ears.

"Not real, real sister. She is everyone's sister."

"Do you live here?" I am nervous and am speaking out my thoughts as they first appear.

She looks at me. "You ask crazy questions. I'll go tell Ixtel her boyfriend is here." I think she's kidding. She walks out of the room, lightly and quickly, like someone who is happy.

In a few minutes, I will see Ixtel, I think. I can't remember any of the things I practised saying to her. I go up to the wooden crucifix and touch it. The Christ that hangs on it is made of bronze and his head does not slump on his chest the way it usually does.

"Come outside, is hot in here." Sister Juana is in the doorway, wiping her hands on a white apron.

We walk through a hallway lit by a single light bulb dangling from the ceiling and out a screen door in the back of the house. We are in a garden. I see small trees heavy with pears and taller trees with pink and lavender flowers. Almost every inch of the yard, except for the stone paths that cut vertically and horizontally, is filled with roses of different colours. Sister Juana holds my arm as she leads me to a small fountain in the middle of the garden where there is a stone bench. I see the leaves of trees move at the same time that I feel a breeze cool my face. The garden is surrounded on all sides by the walls of buildings, and I wonder how it is that a breeze has managed to enter and flow.

We sit side by side on the bench. Sister Juana is breathing deeply as if to make sure that the scent of roses reaches the bottom of her lungs. On the opposite side of the garden from where we entered it, there is another door. I do not fully understand the nature of this place that seems in part a jail and in part a church. Perhaps I should enquire about it, but there is something about asking questions just then that seems inappropriate.

After another deep breath, Sister Juana speaks. "This house once was from rich family. When last daughter die, she leave it to us. Is a big house. Now some nights we have forty girls. In rich family there only four live here. Father, mother and two daughters. And maybe five servants." She laughs. "Imagine."

"Forty girls," I say to myself out loud.

"Me, Ixtel, Sister Camila and Sister Guadalupe, and María

you just met, we are, how you say, permanent. There are so many, many more girls out there and we have this only." She glances at the walls as if noticing for the first time how small the house is. She goes on, "We not force the girls to come, they must want to come here. Some come for a few days only and then go out for more drugs, more abuse. Some like Ixtel do not have homes."

"Are the girls happy here?" I don't know why this question pops up in my mind.

"Happy?" It's like she never heard the word before. "This is safe place where they can be safe for a while. That is all we can do."

I feel Ixtel's presence a second before the screen door opens. "Ah, there is our Ixtel," Sister Juana says. She struggles to stand up.

I see Ixtel walk quickly towards me like I am someone she hasn't seen in a long time. She is wearing khaki slacks and a white button-down short-sleeved shirt. As she draws nearer, I recognize the delicate features on one side of her face: the eyebrows, the eyes, the forehead, all as in her picture, but also different. I try to determine what is different about her. Her face is calmer. The eyes that pierced through me in the picture are softer.

"I go now," Sister Juana says when Ixtel stops in front of us.

We watch Juana hobble away, pausing once to lift up a drooping rose. When we see her disappear into the house, Ixtel sits on the bench and waits for me. I feel a sudden fear that I may have lost the ability to speak.

"You're Marcelo," she says, reminding me of who I am.

"Marcelo," I repeat.

"It's OK, you can look at me, I don't mind."

I don't know why she says this at first and then I understand. "I always have trouble looking people in the eye. Not just Ixtel."

"You've seen me before anyway. In the picture."

"Yes."

There is a pause. It seems like so much has happened since I first saw her picture.

"Did Jerry tell you that the surgery has been scheduled?"

"No."

"No? He must have wanted me to tell you. First the reconstructive surgery, and then when that heals, the cosmetic part to make me look like a movie star." She smiles with one side of her mouth. She is sitting on my left so that I see the good side of her face when I look at her.

"Ixtel is already beautiful," I say. This time it is hard to keep my eyes on her.

"You ever have anyone do something so good for you that you feel bad because there is no way to thank them? You say the words 'thank you', but they don't seem enough. That's how I feel. But anyway, I'll say it. Thank you."

I don't know what to say. If "thank you" is not enough, then neither is "you're welcome", but I say it anyway. "You're welcome."

I inhale deeply. The fragrance of the roses reminds me of Abba. She grew roses in our backyard. I bend down to look closely at a rose that is a colour I have never seen before. It is not one colour but various shades of white and pink and even violet on the rim of the petals. The drops of dew remind me of Aurora.

"The roses are full of dew." It is the only thing I can think of saying.

"Sister Juana is the rose expert. She mixes and matches roses trying to invent a new colour. She tries to get us to help her but no one wants to. Even with gloves on, we get all scratched up with thorns."

"My grandmother liked roses. She planted them all over our yard. Once, when I was a small child, she asked if I wanted to see something special. She got this thing from the kitchen that looked like a giant eyedropper. I forget the name of the utensil."

"A baster. The big eyedropper thing is called a baster."

"A baster? I did not know."

"Trust me, I know about basters. Cooking is something we do a lot here."

"Abba, that's what we called my grandmother, filled the baster with water and sugar and made me sit in the middle of the roses. She told me that if I held the baster very still in front me, squeezing it just enough for a drop to form at its end, a hummingbird would come and feed from it."

"And did one?"

"Yes. After a while a hummingbird came. It was amazing to see one so close. Its wings were moving so fast they seemed to be still."

"That's neat. You were like St Francis over there." She points to a cement statue of St Francis hidden in the rosebushes. The stone bird that sits on his shoulder does not have a head.

There must be a proper response I can make to that statement, but instead I ask: "Are you happy here?"

She looks at the roses and then at the walls enclosing the garden. "This is a good place. I didn't think so when I first came. After the car accident I was very bad. I was fourteen and I was on the street on my own. Even with this face I could sell myself easy. Maybe they thought it was good to make it with a freak. And there were drugs. There's so many ways to hurt yourself if you want to. Finally, Social Services brought me here. I hated it."

"How long have you lived here?"

"Almost a year. When I turned sixteen, I could have left. But I stayed. Look at this." She points to the walls that surround the garden. "It's kinda like being sent to rehab and then staying for good. Now I feel like this is where I belong. I must be crazy. And the people who come here are no angels — that's for sure. They're all like me when I first got here. 'Get me the hell out of here. I need my fix.'"

"But how did you change? What happened? What made you different?"

We both turn to look at each other at the same time. I can feel her wondering why I want to know. Maybe she can see that I'm not asking just out of curiosity or to make small talk. I'm asking because I want to find what she found.

"Little by little, I don't know, what was eating me up went away."

"But how did it go away? What did you do?"

"Like, at the beginning, I felt sorry for myself, I guess. Not like, you know, pity or anything. But then one day I stopped being so angry. 'You're just a little girl,' I said to myself. 'It's not your fault your parents died. It's OK you messed up. It's OK to be angry about your face and hate everyone. You're just a little girl. I forgive you, little girl, for all the bad things you did.' Like that. It's crazy, isn't it? To have one part of your self be nice to another part. Like the nice part of my face saying nice things to the ugly part. After a while, the nice part and the ugly part stopped hating each other. There was peace inside of me, like the different parts disappeared and there was only one me. After that, I saw how the other girls were like me, and I started doing the same thing with them. I saw their ugly parts — and around here that's not too hard, believe me — and I tried to be nice to their ugly parts."

Then it comes to me. It cannot be that this is the first time I realized this, but it is. *We all have ugly parts*. I think of the time in the cafeteria when Jasmine asked me what the girl in the picture was asking me. How do we live with all the suffering? We see our ugly parts, and then we are able to forgive, love kindness, walk humbly.

"We all have ugly parts," I say to myself, forgetting for a moment that Ixtel is sitting next to me.

She gives a short laugh that sounds like a cough because of the shape of her mouth. "You say that as if you never knew it."

"I never knew it like I do now."

"Do you have any? Ugly parts, I mean," she asks, looking at me intently.

I feel what must be shame at the fact that I have to think very hard before I find an answer. "Is not seeing any ugly parts in myself an ugly part? Is not wanting to forgive someone's ugly parts an ugly part in oneself?"

"Yeah. I didn't understand a word you said, but yeah."

She laughs her laugh that sounds like a cough again and I rock back and forth on the bench, the way I do when I finally understand something that was obscured.

"What will you do after the surgery?" I ask.

"The same as now. I missed a year of high school while I was being crazy. I need to catch up."

"Do you want to go to college?"

"Man, that's so far ahead. I gotta make sure I stay clean, finish high school, help the sisters. Besides, I never was that smart to begin with, and the drugs sure didn't help."

We hear Jerry García's voice through the screen door and we both stand at the same time. "It was good to meet you," I say. I turn to face her and stretch out my hand, but she doesn't take it.

"Would it be OK if I gave you a kiss?" she asks.

Without thinking about it, I lower my head the way I do for Aurora, and she kisses me on the forehead.

"It's half a kiss," she says, "but it's all I got."

Chapter 30

Aurora picks me up at the train station. She doesn't ask why I'm coming home earlier than usual. She knows that I've been fired. She thinks my silence is sadness at the fact that I will not be going to Paterson. But I wouldn't call what I feel sadness. It is more like resolve.

When we get home and she turns off the car, she asks me if I want to talk about it.

"Not right now," I say.

"I would like to hear about what happened from you."

"Arturo is right. It is better for me to go to Oak Ridge High." I can feel her eyes scanning me. "It is all right," I say. "Maybe I can work with the ponies on the weekends."

"You're not upset?"

"No."

"We can talk to your father."

"Oak Ridge High will be better. I will not like it as much as Paterson, but it will be better."

"Why the change?"

"Aurora was right when she told me that working at the law firm would help me be strong. Remember? Gentle and strong, like Aurora. Oak Ridge will help me as well."

"Help you for what?"

"Aurora already knows. That has not changed."

Aurora wants to ask me more questions, I can tell, but I open the car door and hug Namu, who is waiting for me to greet him. This is a sign to her that I want to be alone. Aurora touches the top of my head and goes in the house. Then Namu and I go for a walk and when we get home, there is a note from Aurora under the tree house.

> *Dinner is on top of the stove. Whenever you want to talk, I'm here.*
>
> *Love you,*
>
> *Mom*

From the window of the tree house, I can see her moving about in the kitchen, perhaps making my lunch for my last day of work. I look at her and there is a wrenching, as if my heart were a sponge full of love being squeezed. Tomorrow she will get up in the morning and put on that silly uniform with the green smiley faces and she will go to comfort as best she can her dying children.

Why the change? I thought about her question as Namu and I walked on the horse trails behind our house and I think about it now as I sit at my desk. For all the pain I saw at Paterson, it is nothing compared to the pain that people inflict upon each other in the real world. All I can think of now is that it is not right for me to be unaware of that pain, including the pain that I inflict on others. Only how is it possible to live without being either numb to it or overwhelmed by it?

I see the light in the kitchen go off and I picture Aurora making her way up the stairs. I think that maybe I will move back to my room in the house. I never thought of Aurora as being lonely, but why wouldn't she be? What is it like to have a son who is perfectly content living on his own, without any need or desire to communicate; a daughter who is away; a husband who works all the time? What will happen if Wendell sends a copy of Jasmine's letter to Aurora? I don't know. We will all have to figure it out together.

Faithful. Faith-full. Full-of-faith. If the letter comes, will it help Arturo and Aurora remain faithful to each other if I am full of faith? My father. Are your ugly parts any uglier than mine?

There is so much to be done. Plans. Preparations. Oak Ridge High will be hard. As good as Paterson was, I know we lagged behind students in public schools in certain subjects. Public school students study in order to pass standardized tests. We studied what needed to be learned. I will need to learn the way they learn and this means working twice as hard as a regular student. It will mean contact with kids with whom I don't have much in common. But it can be done. I will do it. Going to Oak Ridge High will help me.

Help you for what? Aurora asked. I missed an opportunity to tell her that it would help me to be like her. That the way she is strong and gentle on behalf of children will be my way as well. The road seems so long. Another year of high school, then college, then a degree in nursing and then work — doing what I can to lessen the hurt in the world. But where? There has to be a place where I belong.

I think of Vermont. The stars there seemed closer to the earth. I go to my desk and click on my laptop. There is some research I need to do.

Chapter 31

The first thing I see when I enter Robert Steely's office is an envelope with my name on it. I recognize the handwriting. It is Arturo's. I sit down and hold it in my hands. There's a part of me that doesn't want to open it. I want to get through the day with the same resolve I had yesterday. I put the envelope down. Then I pick it up and open it with a letter opener I find in the top drawer of the desk. I read:

Marcelo,

I feel it is necessary to respond to the note you gave me yesterday. First of all, don't misunderstand this letter. I still think that giving the Vidromek memo to Jerry García was ill-advised. I'm treating Jasmine's note as a separate matter.

There are certain boundaries that need to be maintained between an employer and an employee, between an older man and a young woman, between a man and a woman who is under the influence of alcohol, between a married man and another woman. A year ago at the Christmas party I crossed all those boundaries. I wish I could tell you that I recognized this error as soon as it occurred, but the fact of the matter is that I always considered the events of that evening a minor transgression. It was only yesterday, when I read Jasmine's note the way you would read it, that I recognized the extent of my lack of judgement.

I hope you understand the nature and the reason for this letter.

Your Father

I am still holding the letter in my hands when I hear Jasmine say, "I heard you got fired."

She is standing in the doorway of the office, her arms crossed.

I fold Arturo's letter. "I got fired," I repeat.

"Were you going to tell me or were you going to leave without saying anything? If I hadn't gone to get your father to sign a cheque, I wouldn't have known. Why didn't you say anything to me? And where have you been hiding? Ever since we got back from the camping trip I've hardly seen you." It never occurred to me that she would be upset, but she is.

"What did my father say to you?"

"He told me what you did. And that's another thing. Why didn't you share with me what you were going to do?"

"Maybe you would have told my father."

"Is that what you think? Are you forgetting who gave you the memo?"

I don't know why I said that. I am confused as to how to speak to Jasmine.

"So you are off to Oak Ridge High?"

"I have three weeks. I will use the time to prepare for next year."

"You gonna be OK?"

I shrug my shoulders. This means, *I'll survive*. Then I ask, "Is Arturo upset?"

She raises her eyebrows as if to say, *You have no idea*. "They're all scrambling around trying to figure out how to rescue the Vidromek litigation from disaster. It's good to see Holmesy walk around like he has stomach cramps and there's no bathroom in sight. I think your dad is enjoying the fact that his son is responsible for Holmesy's misery."

"Maybe the law firm will close and everyone will lose their jobs."

"No, they'll figure something out. It suddenly dawned on them that the best strategy is to have Vidromek spend the extra money to make safer windshields."

"I have the CDs you lent me," I say. I can hear a strand of coldness in my voice.

I see her cocking her head trying to figure out if something is wrong. So I say it. "I know about you and my father . . . at the Christmas party. Wendell found your note in my father's files. He gave it to me. Wendell said it was the gift of truth."

"Oh God," she says. She pulls out a chair and falls into it. "The gift of truth." She places both her hands on the side of the chair as if she could fall off at any second. In the brief second that I glimpse her face, I see the colour drain from it. I know immediately that my words have hurt her.

"Is there something in particular you want to know about that?" Her tone is reserved, subdued. The warmth she first brought into the room has been pulled back.

Last night I decided not to speak of this, never to say anything to her. I decided it was not for me to judge her. How did it happen that my resolution buckled? What else simmers down there unnoticed?

"My father. . ." I start to say but have no idea how to finish the sentence.

"Is a man," Jasmine says. "He hired me, we worked together. I had a crush. He could tell, I guess. Men like your father can tell. Then there was the Christmas party. I had been in Boston only a couple of months. I had a few drinks. Your father came by and told me he had a small present for me. That it was in his office. I knew I shouldn't go. He said things that flattered me, that made me feel less lonely. We kissed. The next day I wrote him that note. Sounds like I'm trying to make excuses. I don't mean to. I know I don't owe you an explanation, but that's what happened."

"You kissed."

"When I realized what was happening, what was about to happen, I ran out."

"You kissed? You ran out? He used force to kiss you?"

"Not really. Is it force when half of you says no and half of you says yes? I could have stopped it. I shouldn't have let it happen."

"But you were my age."

"I was eighteen. I was old enough to consent."

"It was wrong of him."

"It was wrong, period. He knows it. I know it. The subject has never been brought up again. He came to me after he got the note and asked me to stay. I agreed but on condition that the matter be forgotten, as if it never happened, and our dealings with each other would always be professional. He agreed. He has kept his promise. Enough said."

"I hurt you just now," I say.

"Yeah," she says. "I don't know why, but you did. Not so much that you mentioned it, but that you know. Still, the truth is best. 'The gift of truth,' as Wendell says." But she doesn't sound as if she truly believes that.

"Do you love him?" It is what I most want to know, I realize, the real reason I blurted out what I blurted out.

"No. Of course I don't. What I did was insane. Temporary insanity. I had a childish crush. The thing about crushes is that afterward you see how silly they were."

"My mother never found out," I say.

"I doubt very much he would tell her. I would have seen it on her face when I picked you up." She covers her face briefly with her two hands. "If I could redo that Christmas party to the point where your father and I are having a conversation by the bar and he asked me to go to his office, I would say 'Thanks, but no thanks.'" She stands up. "Well, I think I'm going to go back to my little mailroom and try to finish out this day."

"Is Belinda a better worker than Marcelo?" I ask.

"Yes," she answers quickly. "Faster, anyway."

"That is good. In the real world, fast is better."

"In the real world," she says.

There is a pause and I think: *I don't want to say goodbye*. She pauses as well. Is it that she doesn't want to say goodbye either? Is she waiting for me to speak first? As she turns to leave, I say, "I saw Ixtel yesterday. Jerry García took me."

She hesitates a moment before speaking. "How was she?"

"The reconstructive surgery has been scheduled. After that is the cosmetic surgery so she can look like a movie star, she says."

"She's a beautiful girl."

She waits for me to speak. I talk fast, afraid that she will walk away. "She lives with the Sisters of Mercy permanently. We talked about how she had found a place where she belongs. It reminded me of the time you told me how your house in Vermont was the place where *you* belonged."

"May I?" She points at the chair.

"Yes." She doesn't know how happy it makes me to see her sit down.

"I was just thinking about the time you asked me how we can live with so much suffering. Remember?"

"Yes, I remember."

"I thought a lot about it. I don't have an answer. But your question reminded me about composing a piece of music. I start off with a feeling and this feeling leads me to find notes and a tempo that match the feeling, and then I expand and respond to the initial notes. After a long, long time and much work I end up with something that I can't take any further. The thing is, when I reach that point, I feel terribly frustrated because the end product never fully reflects the feeling that I started out with and is for sure never as beautiful as I wanted it to be. At the end I have to accept that this is all I can do. I'm no Keith Jarrett and never will be. I'm Jasmine. So I let the piece go, hoping that the music will make someone feel what I felt." She laughs a short, nervous laugh, and then before I can say anything, she says, "You must be wondering what all this has to do with Ixtel?"

"No. Vermont is where you belong."

She shakes her head yes. "You made me wonder whether my house-*slash*-studio was just a place to hide. I thought about it constantly after you asked me that question and after you started trying to help Ixtel. I realized that if I was going to live there, it needed to be a place where I could make the best of my special interest, as you call it." She pauses and takes a deep breath.

"Did you mean what you said when you told me I could go to Vermont whenever I wished?"

"Do I look like the kind of person who would say something like that and not mean it?"

"After I graduate from Oak Ridge, that is what I want to do. I can help Amos with the farm chores. Namu can come also."

"Do you see me somewhere in that picture or is it just you, Amos and Namu?"

I smile. "I see you also."

"Amos would work your bones off."

"I can do all that." Then I look at her. "You are crying," I say, amazed.

She continues without seeming to respond to me, "You've seen so much this summer. Good and bad. It's only natural to want to exclude the bad."

"No." I know what she's going to say.

"Let me finish. What I want to tell you is that there are no places to hide, not anywhere."

"That is not why I want to go to Vermont. There is a college forty-two miles from your house that offers a degree in nursing with various specializations. Physical therapy is one of them. After college and after I am a licensed nurse, I could get some Haflinger ponies and provide hippotherapy to autistic and disabled kids. Amos can help me breed and take care of the horses. It is not possible to have this be a full-time job, so I will also be a nurse like Aurora, working with children. Vermont will be the place where I can follow my special interests." Then I remember the quote from Abraham Joshua Heschel that Rabbi Heschel read to me. "Vermont will be the place where Marcelo plays his counterpoint," I say.

"Plays his counterpoint?" She grabs the box with her CDs, stands up and looks to the heavens as if asking for God's help.

"God will help you," I say, trying to be funny. I stand up as well.

She doesn't laugh as I expected her to. She stops and says seriously, "You checked all this out, the college, the physical therapy degree? The nursing? You really thought about it?"

"Yes."

"When?"

"Last night."

"All of last night?" She pretends to be amazed. I don't know whether the gesture means she thinks this kind of decision needs more time or maybe she likes the fact that I was checking out ways to be close to her.

"No. Yes. Not just last night but also before that. Last night was when I first thought about Vermont. But the ponies and the kids and the nursing, I thought about before." I decide that she wants me to go on, that she is enjoying hearing about my plans. "It will be five years before I can be a nurse. I plan to work with the children at the medical centre you took Amos to. I won't have to wait until I get a degree to do that. I can start right away as a volunteer. And with the ponies, I'll get a job at Paterson this year working weekends, to get experience. Then in Vermont, I will start with one pony. Then we'll get more and eventually we will need an indoor track because of the winter. I made a list. Would you like to see it?"

"Mmm." I see unmistakable happiness illuminate her face. When she speaks, this is what she says. "You will always be welcome there, regardless of why you come. But if it's to be your home, you need to make sure you come for the right reason."

"It has to be the right note," I say.

"Yes. In the overall piece."

"But how do I know the next note is the right one?"

"The right note sounds right," she says, laughing.

Then she looks at me in a new way. It is a serious and tender look I've never seen before, and I want to rest my eyes in hers for as long as I can. Then she walks to where I stand, and she kisses me softly on my cheek.

And when she steps out, I hear or I remember, I can't tell which, the most beautiful of melodies.

author's note

Thirty-four years ago, during my junior year at Spring Hill College in Mobile, Alabama, I got a job working weekends for the Department of Mental Health. From Friday evening to Sunday evening I lived in a halfway home for the "mentally handicapped" (the term used then) while the regular staff person rested. During my senior year, I moved full-time into a newly founded home that was part of L'Arche — a faith-based community where persons with developmental disabilities and "normal" persons lived together and learned from each other with as few barriers between them as possible.

In those days, autism as a diagnosis was reserved for those persons in the very low-functioning end of the spectrum. And even in those cases, likely as not, the diagnosis would be of a known mental illness rather than autism. Looking back, however, I know that some of the young men and women I lived with were persons who fell within the autism spectrum, including Asperger's syndrome. This book in a small way acknowledges the gifts of these young people and in particular the gift of love I received from them.

I want to dedicate this book to my nephew Nicholas, who I

know will one day read this book with pride in his ability to overcome the negative aspects of autism. I want to thank Ann and Jack Syverson for their support; Faye Bender, my agent, for her unwavering faith through the many years it took to bring this book to life; and Cheryl Klein, my editor, for her dazzling vision, solid direction and in-the-trenches hard work. She is a co-creator. And finally, I thank my wife, Jill Syverson-Stork, for her insight, her patience, her contagious hope.

Look out for...

Pancho is going to murder his sister's killer and seal his own fate. But then he meets D.Q., a boy who's dying of cancer. Can D.Q. show Pancho that there are some things, some people, worth living for?

"Exceptional"
Sunday Telegraph